The Terror on Broadway

Was Faceless—

but not nameless. It crept through the crowded streets, the theaters, the strip-joints, seeking out the warm young bodies of girls—not as normal men do, but with the cold steel of a knife. He signed his murders, "Waldo."

Bart Hardin, editor of *The Broadway Times,* knew just about all there was to know about his beat—the dope-pushers, the hustlers, the gamblers, the horse players. He even knew who the killer was—

But he had to catch "Waldo" with his knife in his hand, catch him in his moment of ecstasy—just before his knife did its work.

TERROR ON BROADWAY

by

DAVID ALEXANDER

And down the long and silent street,
The dawn, with silver-sandalled feet,
Crept like a frightened girl.
        Oscar Wilde "The Harlot's House"

WILDSIDE PRESS

Terror on Broadway

Published by Wildside Press LLC
www.wildsidepress.com

To the old-timers on the staff of *The New York Morning Telegraph* who knew Broadway when it was the Big Street instead of a freak show.

1 Bart Hardin sat at an ancient roll-top desk with overstuffed pigeonholes in his office at the *Broadway Times.*

His right hand held a fat pencil with thick black lead poised over a sheet of copy paper. At the top of the copy paper he scribbled a slug-line: "8-cols—p 1—48 pt." He thought a minute and wrote the banner line:

WALDO WARNS HE'LL MURDER AGAIN TONIGHT

Hardin's pale eyes gazed reflectively at the cracked plaster of the soot-smudged ceiling. His eyes moved downward, rested upon a yellowing proof sheet tacked to the wall above the roll-top desk. A composing-room wit of another era had set the sign that hung above the desk in 72-point type:

THE NEW YORK TIMES PRINTS ALL THE NEWS THAT'S FIT TO PRINT; THE BROADWAY TIMES PRINTS ALL THE REST

The slogan was amusing, but oversimplified, Bart reflected. The news he handled was fit enough to print in a paper of the *Broadway Times'* limited interests. The *Broadway Times* dealt exclusively with news of show business and the turf. It was a Broadway paper and the Big Street concerned itself mainly with the Fast Dollar. The fastest dollars of all were made and lost in theaters and night clubs and at the horse parks.

Hardin returned to the black-penciled headline. He counted off the units in the head rapidly, tapping each letter and space with the fat pencil. About four units too long. He scratched out the word "Murder" and inserted the word "Kill" above it. He wrote a drop-head and a jump-head on separate sheets of copy paper. He attached the heads to a story of Waldo's murders he had just banged out with two fingers on a beat-up Underwood that jumped three spaces every time you hit the letter N.

Hardin picked up the photostat of Waldo's letter that the photographer, Pete Cruise, had just laid on the desk. He had sent Orville Cartwright, the copy boy, to deliver the original of the letter to Lieutenant Romano of Homicide, at Manhattan West on Twentieth Street. Pete had brought the photostat down in folded blotting paper. The print was still wet. Bart Hardin read Waldo's letter:

EDITOR
The Broadway Times
Sir:
Allow me to introduce myself.

I am a murderer.

My name? I am best known to the press, the public and the police as "Waldo."

I am the murderer of Alice Kenyon, Bertha Del Rey, Margaret Stringer and Geraldine McLennan. You may recall that I left little calling cards on each of my victims. The cards read "Compliments of Waldo."

There will be another little card—and another victim very soon now. I will strike again on Wednesday evening between the hours of eight and midnight. My work, duly signed, will be found somewhere in the Times Square district. Once again my victim will be a woman steeped in sin.

I give the press, the public and the police fair warning through this letter to your esteemed journal.

Respectfully,
"Waldo"

Bart thought it would point up the Waldo story if he had Pete Cruise make a positive of the photostat and send the letter through for a two-column page-one cut. But the story was exclusive now and it might not remain that way if a lot of engravers got a look at the letter. Besides, running a cut of Waldo's letter would mean killing the two-column cut of the tall and luscious young actress, Miss Arlene Lash, who was opening in a new play on Friday. Miss Lash was not only highly decorative; she happened to be the latest protégée of Mr. Maddox Slade, owner and publisher of the *Broadway Times* and the principal "angel" of her new show, *A Borrowed House.*

Pete Cruise, the photographer, was an old-timer and he could be trusted. Orville Cartwright might possibly have broken the seal on the letter he took down to Romano and might have read Waldo's sinister message, but Hardin doubted that he had. Orville, whose size and muscularity had earned him the nickname of "Li'l Abner," was a very serious and ethical young man. Engravers in an outside shop would be a different matter, though. They'd have friends on other New

2

York dailies and even though Waldo's latest kill was ten months old the psycho murderer was still very hot news on the Big Street and in the big town, too.

To make assurance doubly sure, Hardin picked up the phone and asked for the photographer. "Pete? Anybody see that letter or print but you?"

"You think I got assistants, maybe? Who could see it?" Pete asked.

"Okay. Keep it in the bottom drawer for now."

"Photographers don't talk to nobody but themselves," Pete assured him.

Hardin tossed the story and the heads he had written onto the top deck of a wire basket. He opened his mouth to bellow "Copy! Copy boy!"

Then Hardin changed his mind and shut his mouth.

This thing was going to take a little thinking. If the letter he had received earlier in the day by special-delivery mail was legit it was the hottest news beat around until somebody got careless with an H-bomb. Waldo, the invisible madman, had struck terror to the Street the year before when he had committed a series of murders and mutilations upon showgirls. Broadway's teeth hadn't chattered so loudly since the explosive gang wars of the Twenties. The panicky cuties and chorines and hookers and hoofers and hatchicks had all come down with a sudden case of the old-time religion and the Broadway wolf pack found its game had gone to cover. Some of the more nervous babes had even been driven to packing their nylons in their make-up kits and taking off for home and Mother. Then Waldo had faded back into the limbo from which he had so terrifyingly emerged and the main stem resumed its usual rowdy routine. If Waldo was really back again, it was big news. But this letter had the earmarks of a crank. It mentioned the Geraldine McLennan murder, and the cops hadn't credited Waldo with that chill. They thought Geraldine had been murdered by a character who doubled in brass as her common-law husband and pimp. Anyway, the character had disappeared right after the kill, Bart recalled.

Hardin took the copy out of the wire basket, picked up the photostat of Waldo's letter, opened a drawer of the desk and hid them beneath a freshly laundered shirt wrapped in cellophane, a greasy deck of cards, a pair of green dice with red spots and a half-filled bottle of Irish whisky. He locked the drawer.

He had plenty of time. His deadline was more than three hours away.

Bart Hardin leaned back in his creaking swivel chair, lit a cigarette and yawned. He was five feet eleven and weighed 170, but there was a spare look to him, a kind of rugged angularity. He was in his early thirties. His hair was pale gold and seemed almost white in contrast with his skin which was a light copper color that must have derived from some inner pigmentation rather than the sun. Hardin lived on Broadway and seldom saw the sun. Sometimes he tried to remember whether his skin had been pale or dark before he became a marine in the Second World War. Maybe the sun of the Solomons had burned him permanently. Or maybe he'd got snowburn when he captained a company of gyrenes in Korea. Hardin's nose had been broken when he was a punk throwing haymakers in the Golden Gloves and it had never set quite right. The S-shaped curve in the bridge of the nose gave a harlequin look to a face that might otherwise have seemed too grimly aggressive because of the firm jaw and chin and the strange, hard eyes. The eyes were Hardin's most remarkable feature. They were a peculiar shade of gray that glinted with warm flecks of bronzish brown in a certain light.

On Hardin's piled and littered desk there was a leather-framed photograph of an elderly man with a strong and handsome face. It was a picture of Bart's father who had come back from World War I to edit the *Broadway Times* until he died while his son was fighting in Korea. Bart had worked under his father during the interval between War II and the "constabulary action" against the North Koreans. He had returned to find that Maddox Slade had held his father's job open for him.

The office was little more than a cubbyhole for a man who had such a high-sounding title as "managing editor." It was not an office at all, but a space in the corner of the city room partitioned off by beaverboard that ran halfway to the ceiling on two sides. All available space on the two walls and the two partitions was covered by dusty photographs of chorus girls wearing bras and G-strings, horses wearing saddles and jockeys wearing silks. Bart's restless eyes fixed on the photograph of a girl who somehow managed to seem more naked than the others, though she wore the same brief panties and bras. It's just that she's got more to spill over, Hardin told himself. He liked women who looked like women and weren't at pains to flatten out the pleasant curves and bulges that nature gave them. His mouth twisted in a wry grin. The photograph was of Miss Angelle Brann who displayed her charms at Mr. Hymie Keppel's Salome Club on a bawdy block of cement between Fifth and Sixth on Fifty-second Street. Miss Brann had informed him the previous evening that she had purchased a girdle and was going on a diet. He was against it. Miss Brann was quite all right just as she was. Damn fine, in fact. She was a realist, and he admired realistic women.

Hardin reflected that he had nothing much to do that night

4

except to wait for Waldo to drop another corpse in some dark alley. He contemplated calling Miss Brann. He'd seen her the night before, but she wore well. First he'd have to look on the other side of the partition and make sure that portly Cole Denham, the *Broadway Times'* drama critic, wasn't at his desk. He knew that the fiftyish Mr. Denham had a proprietary interest in Miss Brann, although he was a highly respectable citizen with a home in Far Hills and a rich and ailing wife.

Denham was not at his desk, and Bart rang Angelle Brann's number. Angelle's voice was huskily affected.

"Yeah-uss?"

"Hi, sugar. Remember me?"

"Is that you, you blond beast?" Her voice was higher pitched, more natural.

"How about picking you up at the club after the late show?" Bart asked.

"Again?" Miss Brann pretended shock. "You're a glutton. But I'm not going to the club tonight."

"No? Hymie Keppel get mad when you said no and fire you?"

"Uh-uh. I never say no. It's a nasty word. Just taking the night off. Got things to do."

"Such as?"

"Oh, cleaning the apartment. Touching up my hair. Taking a nice, long, sudsy bath. Relaxing, kinda."

"Sounds domestic. Maybe I'll drop over. I could wash your back."

"You'd tickle. Not tonight. I've got a kind of appointment. Business."

"Monkey business?"

"Uh-uh. *Money* business."

"Okay, sugar. Tomorrow, maybe."

"Maybe. Oh, Bart?" She drawled out his name.

"Yeah?"

"You find something of mine in your apartment this morning?"

"You forget your panties again?"

Miss Brann's throaty chuckle sounded. "Uh-uh. Wasn't wearing any."

"What'd you leave?"

"Something you don't like. You'll find it. 'Bye now, you blond beast."

"Tomorrow?" asked Bart.

There was a short silence. Then Angelle said, "Bart?"

"Yeah, sugar."

"Good-bye, that's all."

"Don't sound so damn final," said Bart. But Miss Brann had broken the connection.

5

Hardin glanced at the stainless steel watch on his wrist. Nearly four. Tea-time at the Sligo Slasher's bar. Bart's father had been born in Kentucky and one of his maxims was that no gentleman took a drink before noon. Bart had extended the self-imposed deadline until four o'clock. He didn't eat his first meal much before midday and he disliked booze for breakfast. He loved the smoky taste of Irish and he drank a lot of it, but he thought that so long as he held off the first one till four he'd never become one of the bleary-eyed, quivering has-beens who make up a large part of Broadway's permanent population.

A galley-boy with a four-cornered paper hat made from yesterday's edition, a filthy apron and a face Comanche-painted by printer's ink came in and tossed a sheaf of proofs on Bart's desk. As usual, the galley-boy lingered to admire the luscious ladies on the editor's walls.

Bart glanced over the top proof of the "Big Street" column which had run on page one of the *Broadway Times* for nearly fifty years. It was by-lined "Boulevardier" and was actually a co-operative product of everyone on the staff who had a gossip item to contribute. Bart frowned at the lead, which was a bum joke about Jane Russell in Three-D. He noted that Cole Denham had worked in another plug for a foreign ballet troupe. He found his own contribution, a puff item, near the bottom of the galley: "Angelle Brann, the prettiest pretty in Hymie Keppel's line at the Salome Club, says she's planning a diet. Don't do it, sugar. Broadway has too few angels with curves." It was small enough payment for the favors of the previous evening, he thought.

Hardin hoisted his lean length from the swivel chair. He rolled down his shirt sleeves, buttoned the cuffs. He fastened the collar of his shirt and pulled up the black knit tie. Then he began to button the embroidered, flowered vest that hung loosely from his square shoulders. The vest was quite a production. It was a steamboat gambler's vest. Fancy vests were Hardin's sole concession to sartorial elegance. His suits were dark and plain. His shirts were white. His ties were black. But he owned eleven vests that were floral and gaudy. Fancy vests were his trademark on the Broadway of the Fifties just as dark shirts and white ties had been Mark Hellinger's trademark on the Broadway of the Twenties and Thirties. Bart's latest acquisition, which he was wearing now, was a dove-gray number with yellow tulips. Hardin took his dark jacket from a coat rack and donned it. He took bills and change from his pants pockets. He folded the dollar bills carefully and put them in the right-hand pocket of the jacket. He dropped the change into the left-hand coat pocket. This was a customary preparation for the panhandlers he would meet between the office and the Sligo Slasher's tea shoppe. Hardin referred to his coat pockets as "The Chiseler's Bank and Trust Company."

The phone on the ledge of the roll-top desk rang. Bart picked it up, said, "Hardin speaking." A vague, croaking voice said something indistinguishable. Then coughing exploded in the earpiece. Finally the caller regained control of his vocal cords, said, "Bart, this is Fritz Graham. Remember me?"

"Yeah," said Bart. "Yeah, sure." Graham was one of the has-beens of Broadway who was making his last stand in the Sligo Slasher's bar. He'd been a feature writer on the old *Morning World* years before. Then he'd drunk himself into jobs doing publicity for burlesque houses in New Jersey. Now he did nothing but drink and bum money for drink.

"Bart, you still buy Sunday copy on space rates?"

"Sometimes."

"What column rate you pay, Bart?"

"Depends on the story," Hardin answered.

Graham's alcoholic cough exploded again. "Bart," he said, "I got one hell of a story. You know that ex-cop Mark Clements that drinks with me at the Slasher's?"

Bart sighed. Clements was a worse drunk than Graham, even. The two were out of money and were trying to cook up a pipe yarn to chisel a stake from him. Before Bart could answer, Graham pressed on urgently.

"It's a hell of a story, Bart. It's about the Geraldine McLennan murder a couple of months ago. You remember it? Old-time showgirl? Listen, Bart. Clements knows who killed her."

Hardin's eyes narrowed and his mouth went tight. It was too much of a coincidence, Clements and Graham inventing such a story right after Waldo's letter mentioning Geraldine McLennan had arrived.

Bart kept his voice level when he spoke into the mouthpiece. "It didn't happen a couple of months ago," he said. "It happened about ten months ago." Drunks like Graham, he knew, always lost track of time. "Clements was right in the next room, and he had a badge and a gun then," Bart continued, "but he couldn't catch the murderer."

Graham said, "Listen, Bart, I'll give you this much on the phone. The cops held out on that one. Clements says Waldo killed Geraldine McLennan."

2   Lieutenant Romano laid the typewritten sheet aside, stared off into space. Then he picked the letter up again and reread it. He put it down, examined the envelope. Romano's rough-hewn, swarthy face took on a weird patina in the light of the green-shaded desk lamp. Crystal pebbles of sweat glistened at his temples. It was a mild spring day in New York but the little office at Homicide, Manhattan West, was airless. Romano looked up at the large, square young detective named Grierson who stood beside the desk. Grierson's broad face was as calmly expressionless as granite. Romano said, "How'd it get here?"

Grierson raised his hand a couple of inches above his own six feet, said, "A young character who looked like the Empire State Building with muscles brought it. Eager beaver with pretty red hair. He was hell-bent on delivering it in person. Said your friend, Bart Hardin, who edits that Broadway and horse-race paper, had a message for you. I had to hurt his feelings to keep him off you."

Romano nodded. "I know the kid. Kind of a glorified copy boy at the *Broadway Times.* They call him 'Li'l Abner.' "

Grierson said, "He's bigger, even, but he's kind of sissy."

"What was Bart's message?" Romano asked.

"He said you could keep the note for processing. He made a photostat before he sent it over. Said it was handled with care so fingerprints, if any, wouldn't smear."

Romano said, "There's not much time. Today's Wednesday. The letter was mailed special delivery around nine last night, but Hardin wouldn't have got it till around noon because he doesn't go to work till then. The *Broadway Times* comes out around eight, when the late results from Western tracks are in. That's the time Waldo's note says he's due to start his prowl. I don't want that letter printed."

"What's the difference if it's printed?" Grierson asked. "It's just a crank note anyway."

"It's not a crank note," declared Romano. He picked up the piece of paper gingerly between his thumb and forefinger. "This letter is from Waldo himself."

Grierson said, "What makes you think that? When Waldo was slicing up his victims a year or so ago we got crank letters in nearly every mail. Dozens of psychos even came in and confessed."

Romano said, "You worked on the Waldo kills. Did you read this letter?"

"Yeah, I read it. I say it's crank stuff."

Romano shook his head and the tiny sweat pebbles slid down his dark face. "You read it with your eyes. You didn't read it with your head."

Grierson raised his left eyebrow up to his hatbrim, which was about as much change of expression as he permitted himself. He said, "I read a letter from some screwball who says he committed a bunch of Jack-the-Ripper chills that happened a year or more ago. It's been ten-eleven months at least since the last one. My hunch is the real Waldo is either dead or in the booby hatch picking butterflies out of his hair. Waldo never wrote letters to the editor when he was doing his carving. Why should he start now?"

"Jack the Ripper started writing letters to the paper after his third or fourth kill," Romano answered. "Maybe it's a psycho pattern."

Grierson said, "Why'd he write to the *Broadway Times* instead of the New York *Times* or the *Herald Trib?* Only chorus girls and horse players read the *Broadway Times.* That rag's not interested in murder. It's interested in hot babes on Broadway and hot horses at Belmont."

"The *Broadway Times* was interested in Waldo's murders," Romano asserted, "because they were all committed on Broadway and all the victims were what you call Broadway babes. Bart Hardin's a friend of mine. So was his old man who edited the *Times* way back yonder in the days of Irene Castle. But Bart Hardin crucified me in print last year when the victims with little calling cards pinned to 'em started piling up in the alleys outside theaters and night clubs and we couldn't find a trace of Waldo."

"Waldo's last victim wasn't any Broadway babe," protested Grierson. "Geraldine McLennan was an old bag."

"Now you're getting hot, honey boy," the lieutenant said. "Geraldine McLennan was over forty. Also she was a hop-head and probably a prostitute. But Ziegfeld glorified her once." Romano tapped his finger lightly against the piece of paper on the battered desk. He said, "This letter mentions Geraldine McLennan as one of Waldo's victims. That's why only Waldo himself could have written it."

Detective Grierson's expressive eyebrow flicked upward again like a tilted question mark. "By God!" he exclaimed. "By God, you're right, Lieutenant."

"Came the dawn, baby doll?" asked Romano. "We got a break, if you can call it that, in the McLennan squeal. Every paper in New York was howling for blood. After the mutilated bodies of three young showgirls had been found smack in the middle of Broadway they wanted to fire me and Inspector Sansone and the police commissioner and maybe even the mayor. Right when they were howling the loudest this fourth murder happens along. This one wasn't in Waldo's usual pattern. It didn't happen in a blind alley beside a stage door. It happened in a room of a cheap hotel on Forty-seventh Street. Waldo was in a hurry, so there wasn't any fancy work. The victim's throat was cut and that was all. Waldo didn't even have time to pin his rubber-stamped calling card to her clothing. He simply shoved it down the neck of her dress and we found it stuck in her underwear when the ghouls at the morgue were stripping the body. The McLennan dame was middle-aged instead of young, like the other three. She'd been a showgirl once, but she was a long time forgotten. She had a boy friend, who was maybe also her pimp, and he disappeared conveniently and never has been found. There was nothing to connect the McLennan squeal up to Waldo except the little card. No reason to give out any information about *that*. The papers and the public were hysterical enough. So only the people at the morgue and a few cops and the killer knew that Waldo chilled Geraldine McLennan."

Grierson said, "So Waldo's loose again!"

"Don't sound so happy, honey boy," Romano answered. "Nobody's going off the eight-to-four from here tonight. That means you, sixteen hours straight through till midnight and maybe more if we find a body. I'm going to see there's double the number of harness bulls that're usually in Times Square, too, if I can. I want Waldo, and it means my job sure if I don't get him this time." He sighed. "To think, we almost had him last time. There was a cop in the room right next door to the murder scene."

"If you can call Mark Clements a cop. He was fired off the force for lushing six months ago."

"He was a good cop till the booze got him," the lieutenant declared. "Cops get a lot of aggravation. They got to do something to take their minds off things. Raise tropical fish or beat their wives or hit the booze."

Detective Grierson allowed a brief grin to supplement the eloquence of the eyebrow.

"What do *you* do?" he asked.

"I think about my pension," the lieutenant answered.

Grierson said, "It's funny Clements being right there in the next room. I always thought his story was kind of phony."

"Nothing funny or phony about it," Romano declared. "He was always sleeping off his binges in those two-dollar pads in the Forties. When he heard the scream, he was half-fogged. Rushed out into the hall in his pants and undershirt with a gun in his mitt. Thought the scream came from down the corridor and took a wrong turn. By the time he found the right room, there was a body and nothing else in it except the furniture. Waldo must have gone down the steps, or maybe up them, and taken the elevator with a lot of other people at a different floor."

Romano glanced at his watch, rose. "Going on four," he said. "You might as well come along with me and have a drink. You're not going off duty, honey boy. I got to make arrangements about the four-to-midnight and see about some extra harness bulls. Then I got to see Bart Hardin about killing this story."

"You going up to the *Broadway Times?*"

"Uh-uh. Hardin won't be there. He drops over to the Sligo Slasher's, across from Madison Square Garden, every afternoon about this time for a spot of tea."

"Tea?" asked Grierson.

"Irish whisky. It's the same color, about."

"I could use a shot," said the bulky young detective.

"So could I," replied the lieutenant. "But I shouldn't take it. Medics gave me a checkup the other day. Say I got to cut down the salt and the liquor. Blood pressure. First I get blood pressure, then I get Waldo."

The swarthy police officer lifted the envelope and the letter from the desk. His thick, big-knuckled fingers handled the papers with remarkable delicacy. He seemed to hold them only by the nails of his thumb and forefinger. He dropped Waldo's missive into an official-looking brown envelope. He sealed the brown envelope and scribbled on it with a pencil, said, "I'll drop these off for processing, but I lay six, two and even all we get is a report of smeared prints and standard typewriter paper anybody can buy, plus the make of the machine that wrote it."

"The machine hit a high A," said Grierson.

"You got bright eyes, honey boy. Some day they'll make you commissioner."

"You really think this letter's legit, don't you?" said Grierson. "Don't you figure one of the guys at the morgue or a cop or maybe Clements could've leaked about the McLennan squeal to some crackpot?"

Romano took a battered gray felt from a hat rack, stuck it on the back of his head. Grierson held the door open.

"Could've," replied Romano, passing through the door. "But I doubt it. Waldo's getting more like Jack the Ripper every day. Now he's writing letters to the papers. Next he'll be sending his victims' livers and kidneys to us."

"What?"

Romano nodded. "That's what Jack the Ripper did. Mailed

assorted anatomical parts of his victims to Scotland Yard and the vigilante committees that were after him."

"Nice things to open up in the morning mail if you've got a hangover," Grierson commented.

3 Bart suppressed an exclamation. So the letter he'd sent Romano hadn't been from some crank who'd put one murder too many in his story!

He spoke into the phone, said to Fritz Graham, "Where you now? The Slasher's?"

"Yeah," said Graham. "Clements is with me."

"I was on my way over there anyway," Bart said. "See you in a few minutes."

Hardin cradled the phone and stood for a moment tapping his fingers against the desk. Bluish light from the fluorescent tube in the ceiling reflected on him and made the bright bronze flecks dance in his gray eyes.

Bart had planned to go to his apartment above Bromberg's Flea Circus and Fun Arcade on Forty-second Street before he went to the Sligo Slasher's. Old Bones, the ancient bulldog that had belonged to his dad, had to be fed and walked. But he could send Orville Cartwright down to do the chore. Orville and Old Bones were pals.

Bart walked out of his cubbyhole office into the city room. The city room was vast. The *Broadway Times* was located on the west side of Eighth Avenue, between Fiftieth and Fifty-first, in premises that had been a firehouse in the nineteenth century. Engines and horses had been quartered in the city room in those days. A brass pole still led up to the composing room which had been the firemen's quarters. Drunken reporters and printers and exuberant galley-boys sometimes slid down the brass pole just for kicks. Pops Taylor's horseshoe copy desk circled around the pole, with Pops in the slot. Pops was the turf editor. The copy-cutter's desk was directly above in the composing room. It was a convenient set-up. Editors and printers could shout at each other through the hole in the ceiling, affording a wireless office intercom system.

Cole Denham, the drama critic, was now at his desk, just outside Bart's door. The critic's desk was very neat in comparison to Bart's. Except for a signed photograph of Ethel Barrymore it was barren of ornament. A copy of *Variety* and a handout from the Theatre Guild were placed directly in the center of the desk. Denham himself was a neat little man in well-draped blue serge and a white shirt with a deep actorish collar. He had a shock of hair the color of soiled snow. The flesh of his face was the same unhealthy shade. His eyelids were heavy and puffed and he had a perpetually sleepy look that was deceptive.

Bart said, "No opening tonight, huh?"

Denham shook his soiled-snow locks. "One last Monday," he answered. "A turkey that won't fly through Saturday. One Friday. Another gobbler, probably, despite Arlene Lash's protuberant charms. I'm reduced to going back to the 1920's for a Sunday piece. Comparing the slick, fast-paced, unadorned *Little Show* revues favorably with the modern musicals that are overmounted and garishly pretentious and that follow a ridiculously complicated plot line."

"My old man took me to see a *Little Show* when I was about ten," Bart said. "I'll never forget that 'Moaning Low' number with Libby Holman and Clifton Webb."

Denham nodded. "I recall it well," he said. "A bit on the erotic side, perhaps, but highly effective. Webb's eccentric dance was superb and Holman's husky voice was eminently adapted to the number."

Cole Denham was a prim little man who could lash out viciously when he thought he detected signs of vulgarity, bawdiness or suggestiveness in the theater. He was pedantic, but Bart respected him. He was a sound critic whose standards were high, despite the fact he had married into his job many years before when he had wed the daughter of Jules Lesser, who owned the paper then. Bart's father and Denham had been among the few editorial employees who had survived the shake-up when Maddox Slade bought the paper. If Denham had married a salary, he had more than earned it. His wife had taken to her bed soon after their wedding night and had remained there for more than twenty years suffering from a complicated neurosis.

Bart crossed the big room to the horseshoe copy desk where old Pops Taylor, the turf editor, presided. Pops' bald dome was fringed by white, his eyes were merry, his nose was pink and rabbity, his jowls were pendulous and his paunch belonged to Santa Claus. Pops had only recently heard about the younger set's jive talk and it fascinated him. He looked at Bart's vest, said, "Man, dig those tulips! They're gone, man, gone! Why don't you give me your old vests so I can put my pot in a flower garden, boy?"

"You get the fifth at Jamaica yet, Pops?" Bart asked.

Pops reached for a flimsy that had just come from the leased wire operator, said, "A horse named Royal Purple win it. A sawbuck to an ace and your money back."

"Sonuvabitch!" The way Bart spat out the exclamation it

13

was a contraction of three words. "I bet that pig last week when he was favorite and he winds up at the eighth pole."

"All horse players die broke, son," said Pops wisely.

Bart looked around the city room for Orville Cartwright and didn't see him. If Orville was anywhere around, you could see him. His red hair was like a danger signal flown from a tower. In his spare time, Orville filed clippings in the morgue, which the precise Mr. Denham insisted upon calling "the library." The morgue was located off a long corridor. Bart cupped his hands to his mouth and bellowed, "Copy! Copy boy!"

He was answered by a rifle shot.

The old firehouse was infested by rats which loved to gnaw the yellowing files in the morgue. Orville often blasted away at them with a twenty-two rifle. When Orville wasn't shooting rats or filing clippings or running copy to the composing room he was reading paper-backed "sex psychology" books. The vastly overgrown seventeen-year-old pretended a scholarly interest in abnormal patterns of sex behavior. Old Pops Taylor jumped a foot when the shot rang out. "Damn!" he said. "Can't Mr. Slade afford a soundproof rat trap for this joint?"

Bart grinned. "You just want to take all the fun out of a young boy's life, Pops," he said.

Orville appeared suddenly, the rifle still in his hand. He was six feet two in his socks and his shoulders were massive. The face between the lurid red hair and the weight-lifter's body was startling. It was almost effeminately pretty. "You call me, Mr. Hardin?" he asked. Orville was very respectful and Bart had to confess he liked it.

"You get the rat?" Bart asked.

"Splashed him all over the wall," said Orville happily.

Pops Taylor made a sick-stomach face and clutched his paunch.

Bart tossed Orville a key from his ring. "Go down to my flat and feed and walk the dog, will you?" he said. "There's a can of dog food in the kitchen."

Orville caught the key in a big paw. "Glad to, Mr. Hardin," he said. "And might I ask a favor? My girl friend, Helen Larsen, is a dramatic student and she's in a play at a church Friday night and they want me to help with the props and sets and things. They want me to set up the stage. Could I leave a little early that day?"

"Sure, take off," said Bart. "But be sure you lock up the rats first so they won't bother Pops here."

"The rats don't bother me," said the old man. "It's the shooting. Like reading copy on Yucca Flat."

"I'm sorry, sir," Orville apologized contritely.

"Don't mind Pops," said Bart. "He was shell-shocked at the Battle of Gettysburg."

Bart left the city room. He passed the phone desk, presided over by a big girl named Bertha who affected sweaters and conical uplift brassières. Her heavy breasts were not made for such contrivances and formed a meaty circular frame around the cups. Bertha batted her mascaraed lashes at Hardin in a manner meant to imitate Miss Marilyn Monroe in a film she'd seen the night before.

Hardin said, "That sweater's going to choke you some day, sugar. Be back in about an hour or so. Gotta see a man about a butcher."

4 The first one was waiting just outside the door.

He was an old man with rheumy eyes who had made pathetically ridiculous attempts to give his frayed clothing a dashing look. The brim of his stained gray hat was snapped down rakishly on one side. Spats half-hid his cracked shoes and a wilted flower was in his buttonhole. As soon as Bart stepped out of the doorway of the *Broadway Times,* the old man hurried up to him. Bart fumbled in the right-hand pocket and wadded two dollar bills together. This was a special case. The broken-down old actor, James Lennox, had been friendly with his father.

The old man extended a shaky, eager hand, said, "Bart, my boy! I've been standing here debating if I should interrupt a busy man and drop in to see you. Wanted to assure you I'm writing out that story I told you about for the *Broadway Times*. The anecdote about Richard Mansfield."

Bart took the outstretched hand and pressed crumpled bills into it. "Fine," he said. "An anecdote about Richard Mansfield is stop-press news any day."

Tears floated in the old man's eyes when he felt the money in his hand. "God bless you, Bart," he said. "This isn't charity. It's just an advance against those memoirs of the theater I'm going to give you. You're the last gentleman on Broadway since your father's death, Bart."

"Uh-uh," said Bart. "I'm not a gentleman. I'm just a sucker. The gentlemen are with the dodo birds."

Bart crossed Fiftieth Street. The marquee of Madison Square Garden advertised that the welterweight champ was going to meet an old stumbling block who Bart knew was

15

suffering from a double hernia and a fatty heart. Outside the Garden stood an immense and ancient Negro with a scarred and battered face. The Negro tipped his cap and said, " 'Day to you, Mist' Bart." Bart dropped change from the left pocket into the Negro's hand, said "Howzit going, Tom?" The Negro said, "Thank you kindly, Mist' Bart. You the onliest one on Broadway remembers Tom Trigg went the limit once with ole Sam Langford."

Bart said, "I never saw you fight, Tom. My daddy said that you were good."

"I was mighty good," Tom answered. "But ole Sam Langford, he was better."

Hardin hadn't even got past the Garden when old Bessie came bustling up. The disheveled creature with a basket of fading flowers upon her arm was a Broadway character reputed to have been an actress once. Without preliminaries, she stood on tiptoe and thrust a wired cornflower into Bart's buttonhole. He would throw it away as soon as he turned a corner, but he jingled change into the cup beside the flowers in Bessie's basket. Bessie said, "Thank you, sport. You ain't a pretty boy but you're the kind of guy old Bessie went for when she was young."

Hardin wondered why the hell he did it. It wasn't charity. It wasn't even a cheap impulse to make himself a big shot. It was just a compulsion he seemed unable to resist, handing out money to the bums and chiselers. The two bucks would buy old Lennox a flop and a meal to eke out another day of his miserable life that had really ended twenty years ago. Tom Trigg would buy cheap gin with his change and for a glowing moment feel the old power surge back into his flabby muscles. Old Bessie doubtless had a mattress stuffed with bankbooks. Bart made two-fifty every week but between the Irish and the girls and the chiselers and the gambling and the fancy vests, he'd never had a bank account.

On the corner of Forty-ninth, just outside Mickey Walker's place, a tall girl with flashy clothes and a painted face was standing, her eyes darting up and down the street. She was a professional but Hardin knew she wasn't looking for a customer at this time of day. You could tell from her eyes she was mainlining it again and she was probably seeking the schmo who shoved the stuff.

Bart said, "How's business, Gert?"

Gert said, "Hi, handsome. Business is lousy. Too many amateurs. You gotta know shorthand and typing to get ahead in this racket nowadays."

Bart turned west on the south side of Forty-ninth.

On the side street, directly across from the Garden, was an

16

ancient tenement building. On the store front of the building was a pane of glass on which appeared the legend: "The Sligo Slasher's Bar." In the dead center of the window was a badly painted oil of a boxer in old-fashioned trunks that reached below his knees and a lettered card that read, "Tony Maclaren, the Sligo Slasher, Former Lightweight Champion of Ireland." About the central portrait were grouped photos of Jack Dempsey, Gene Tunney, Joe Louis, Benny Leonard and Sugar Ray Robinson. There was nothing in the record books to indicate that a Tony Maclaren had ever been lightweight champion of Ireland, the Sandwich Isles or any other place, but Maclaren had awarded himself the title back in the days when his gin-mill was a speakeasy in the same location.

There was sawdust on the floor, photos of fighters and race horses on the walls, a huge glass bowl filled with a mountain of hard-boiled eggs on the bar. In front of the glass bowl was a sign that read, "Free to Friends, a Nickel to Strangers." The sign was one of Maclaren's numerous compromises with the alcoholic beverage control laws that forbade free lunch, among other things. Since the ABC also insisted that drinking places must serve food, Maclaren had put up another sign reading "All Kinds Sandwiches." If a customer requested a sandwich he was informed that the Nedick's stand on the next corner served excellent hot dogs.

Maclaren himself was a short man whose broad shoulders and pugnacious face barely reached above his bar. He appeared to be constructed entirely of coiled springs and truculence. He wore a striped shirt, sleeve garters and a diamond horseshoe stickpin in his bright green tie.

At this time of day the bar was almost deserted. Maclaren's was no place for the cocktail hour. Maclaren distrusted bartenders and refused to hire them and he had never learned to make cocktails himself. If a customer ordered a martini he would be handed a straight shot of liquor on the house with the admonition, "This is a sporting man's bar and we don't serve sissy drinks. Even the ladies that drink here got to drink like gentlemen."

Maclaren was completing his afternoon telephone call to his two-hundred-pound wife whom he called his "Little Irish fairy" when Hardin entered the bar. "Wash yer feet and take yer nap!" Maclaren bellowed endearingly into the mouthpiece. He hung up the phone, shouted at Hardin, "Hello, ya Protestant bum, ye're late." Maclaren called only his best friends "Protestant bums." That even included a bishop of the Roman Catholic church for whom he had boundless admiration. Maclaren half-filled an old-fashioned glass from a bottle of Irish, dropped a lump of ice in it with a hand that was not quite clean and slid the glass down the bar to Hardin. He poured himself an even more generous portion without the ice, said "First one's on the house."

There were two other persons in the bar, at the far end of the mahogany. Mark Clements, the ex-cop, was thin and bloodless to the point of appearing tubercular. There were sallow semicircles between his dead eyes and his knobby cheekbones. The one-time reporter, Fritz Graham, had an immense belly, a shrimp-pink face and a shock of curly white hair. The two were fondling schooners of beer with trembling hands and sipping them as if the precious fluid had to last a long, long while. Bart nodded to them, put money on the bar, said, "Give the boys in the back room a shot of Irish to chase their brew."

Graham clutched his whisky with two shaky hands that were as small as a child's, drank from it, carried it up the bar until he was alongside Hardin. He said, "Thanks for the shot. We needed it. That story interest you?"

"Maybe," replied Bart. "If you can prove it."

"Clements can prove it." Graham told Hardin about the ghouls at the morgue finding Waldo's calling card on Geraldine McLennan's body.

Bart said, "That pimp boy friend of hers who disappeared could have printed the card with a dime-store rubber stamp."

Graham finished his whisky, burst into a phlegmy cough, said, "Maybe, but the cops didn't think so. The cops thought it was Waldo in person."

"Question is, when will Clements be sober enough to dictate and you be sober enough to write?" said Hardin.

"We're not drunk, we're hung," Graham answered. "With a few shots to steady us along . . ."

"Uh-uh," Bart shook his head. "Maybe you could hit a typewriter with your hat, but you couldn't hit the keys with your fingers. Tell you what. I'll send you over to the Karnak Baths to sweat it out and sleep it off. I'll send a typewriter and a chaperone along. I'll give the chaperone a bottle to taper you off, a teaspoon at a time. I'll give you a sawbuck apiece if you can even write the story. I'll double the ante if I can use it."

"It's a deal, Bart," said the pink-faced man.

Hardin said, "I got to find a chaperone. Tony, you see the Old Top Sarge today?"

"Sergeant Eddie O'Grady dropped in for a wee drop of sarsaparilla after he finished work last night," Maclaren replied.

"Work?" said Bart. "You mean the Old Sarge is working? He's been avoiding work even since they discharged him from the First World War with a Congressional Medal of Honor.

18

Thinks playing the horses is the only work dignified enough for a national hero."

"The Protestant bum's got himself a job befitting an Irish Catholic gentleman and a military hero," Maclaren replied. "He's lookout for Moe Selig's bookie joint."

"Well, I'm damned," said Hardin.

"Doubtless y'are," Maclaren answered, pouring Bart another shot of Irish.

Bart turned to Graham, said, "You and Clements have a couple of shots on my cuff. I'll be sending the Old Sarge over for you. I'm going to shove after I swallow this."

The pink-faced man returned to his place at the bar to tell the trembling Clements the good news about the stake they could earn. The door opened and a large, middle-aged man entered in company with a larger young man.

"Well, if it's not the boy editor," said Lieutenant Romano to Hardin. "Fancy meeting you here. You know Detective Grierson, don't you?"

Bart nodded, said, "Seen him around. You drinking on the job, Lieutenant? There's a horrible example why you shouldn't right down the bar."

Romano turned to Maclaren, said, "Bourbon twice. Water chaser." He spoke to Bart. "We're on the eight-to-four this week. It's half-past four."

"You're not hanging around to look at Waldo's latest corpse?" asked Bart.

"Hope you don't take that crank letter serious enough to print it," Romano said. "Thanks for sending it down, but we get that kind by the basketful."

"I'm printing it under an eight-column banner on page one," Bart replied.

"You're kidding!" exclaimed Romano. "A crank note like that? You'll make your sheet a laughingstock."

"What makes you think it's a crank note?" Hardin asked.

"We can smell 'em," Romano said disarmingly. "Take this one. Poor goof mentions the McLennan chill. Waldo wasn't in on that."

Bart said, "He was in on it. I'm running *that* story as a special feature Sunday, maybe."

Romano's swarthy face assumed astonishment. "Now what makes you think a thing like that?" he asked.

Grierson nodded toward the distant figure of Mark Clements. "I said he'd spill," he declared.

Romano's dark face set in grim lines. He said to Bart, "I'll level with you, honey boy. We found a little Waldo card in McLennan's clothes. Maybe it was Waldo, maybe it wasn't. No use to increase hysteria. We had enough headaches. No use you running the letter, either. You get on the street about eight. That means for four hours the town goes nuts and puts the cops under pressure. Doing it quiet, we got a chance. Nobody's off duty from my station. We'll be on Broadway tonight between eight and midnight, all of us. We'll pick up a lot of psychos. Maybe that way we can stop the kill. One in every hundred people you meet on Broadway is strictly psycho. Some of the nuts we'll pick up will swear they're Waldo. Always happens that way in a psycho kill. The way it is, if one of the bugs mentions the McLennan chill, he's it. You print the letter, and all of 'em can know McLennan was a Waldo victim, so there'll be no telling."

Romano signaled Maclaren who was chatting with Graham and Clements at the other end of the bar. When the glasses were refilled and the little man had danced away, Romano said, "Your old man wouldn't have printed it. But you're not your old man, of course. You're not a better editor, but you're tougher. There's something eating you inside. Maybe it's something left over from the fighting, I don't know. But it's there. You don't want to believe anything you hear. You got to take everything you see apart to find out if it's phony."

Romano drank his bourbon, chased it, said, "Maybe you figure I'm just thinking about my job and maybe I am. It'll look even worse if Waldo kills again and the cops had notice he was going to. I got a daughter going to Marymount College in the fall if her old man keeps his job."

Bart said, "I'm not tough. I'm the street's prize sucker. I've got the best exclusive in town, but I'll kill it. I'll almost kill it, anyway. I won't run the letter or the story. But I'm going to run a new lead on the 'Big Street' column, just a question asking if Waldo's loose on the town again."

"That's something, honey boy," Romano said. "That's a lot, in fact. Have another on the cops."

Hardin shook his head. "I got to shove," he said. "I got to hire a baby-sitter."

The tall girl with the flashy clothes and the painted face was still standing on the corner of Eighth Avenue. Her eyes were wilder now as they ceaselessly searched up and down the street.

Bart said, "What's the matter, Gert? The boy with the bindle kind of late?"

Gert said, "Don't gag about it. It ain't funny, not to me. I got the monkey on my back so bad I'm itching."

"Sorry I can't help you, sugar," Bart said.

Gert scratched her neck with a long, red fingernail, made a visible effort to control the torture of her craving. She said, "Hey, honey, you want to hear a laugh?"

"Laughs are nice these days," Bart said.

"You know that old pappy-guy over at your shop, the one that handles the race news?"

"Pops Taylor?"

"Yeah. He tried to pick me up the other night."

"No harm in that." Bart grinned. "Pops is a widower."

"I didn't go with him," said Gert. "I can handle myself all right with hoods and gunsels and prize-fight punks. But those old guys with the sweet, gentle faces, they're the ones who're really nasty."

Gert's eyes lit up suddenly. "Scram, quick, will you, honey?" she said. "The man is finally here."

Bart said, "Yeah, I better." Out of the corner of his eye he saw the ratty little dope-pusher. The dirty sonuvabitch had a broad grin on his ugly face. He was sauntering along, enjoying the torture of the helpless street-walker. Bart felt the sweat oozing in his armpits. His fists had clenched tight and his teeth were biting the inside of his lower lip. Why the hell should I care? he asked himself. "There's something eating you inside," Romano had said. Maybe every man had a fire inside that had to come smoking out sometime. Maybe the fire had come smoking out of Sergeant Eddie O'Grady that day in 1918 when he killed some incredible number of Krauts and won a Medal of Honor. Maybe the fire that smoked out of Waldo when he killed wasn't so very different, even if Waldo was a psycho. Maybe keeping the fire smoldering and slumbering and burning hot inside all the time was what made a man a psycho, even.

5   The sight of Bart Hardin always left Waldo with a vague sense of uneasiness. In his saner moments, Waldo merely envied Hardin. To Waldo, Hardin seemed so maddeningly *sure*. Each of his movements appeared too quick, decisive, purposeful. Waldo thought Hardin's clipped speech was his way of sneering contemptuously at those he despised.

When premonitions of the headaches throbbed in Waldo's temples, he thought of Hardin differently. He thought of the lean, copper-colored man entirely in relation to women. Hardin would be very sure in his attitude toward women, too, Waldo felt. Sure and slightly contemptuous. At such times Waldo appeared lost in reveries, torturing himself with thoughts of Hardin's hands on women's flesh. Oftener than not the women Hardin touched assumed a real identity in Waldo's mind. When he thought of Hardin in this way, Waldo hated the intense man with the strange gray eyes.

Waldo could know a woman only with his knife.

The city and its sounds were all around Waldo now, swirling, pressing, shrieking, thundering.

The city's people were on all sides of him, chattering, cursing, laughing, shouting.

But Waldo was withdrawing from the city and the city's sound and the city's crowding people. A muscle in his jaw quivered and jerked. Slowly his lids lowered and curtained glazing eyes. The waves in the sea of pain that had surged with stormy suddenness over the back of his skull and his neck and even his shoulders were subsiding. Now the ache was gentle like the ache of yearning.

Waldo's hand crawled slowly forward like a pale, tired tarantula, groping. Instinctively his hand sought the small bottle with the innocuous aspirin label that contained potent codeine tablets. But he had no need of the tablets now. The peace was coming. The engulfing numbness. Waldo was not unconscious. It might last for seconds or for minutes or for hours but at no stage of it would he be unconscious. The city's drumbeat sound would still assail his ears but no longer would it clamor frantically. It would be far away and soft like the murmur of the sea. The city's people would still be near and loud, but the sight and sound and smell of them would fade into a blurred and distant grayness until Waldo walked alone.

Some might stare at him as if he were drunk or doped or sick, but none would care.

Waldo knew quite well what came next.

He would withdraw, float into himself.

It was strange that the thing should come upon him now.

This one would be different from all the others, though it must appear the same. There had been no reason or no planning behind the others, nothing but the burning urge of the flames inside him and the lust of the cold, sharp blade. The first had been the most unexpected and the most overwhelming of them all. There had been no warning that time, or none that he could recognize. The young boy and the thick-thighed girl with the crazy eyes had wandered off from the others into the deep thicket of the wood and they had lain side by side upon the moldering leaves with the pungent perfume of the wood ferns and the sick-sweet smell of decaying vegetation in their nostrils and the fluttering music of the birds in their ears. Then her wet, devouring mouth was on the boy's and his hand was being guided urgently to the young breasts that suddenly were bare. It had come then, like a torrent. The pain and then the sweet, numb peace and finally the hot and awesome beauty of the flames. Instinctively his hand had found the many-bladed knife he carried for his woodcraft expeditions. The girl's scream had set up a feathery clamoring in the trees, for the birds had fled from the bright and fearful beauty of the flame-red blood.

It was months later when they found the body in the shallow grave, and none suspected the young boy, for it was never known that the boy and the thick-thighed girl were together on that afternoon. But the second time might well have ruined his life or ended it forever if he had not recognized the warning and fled from the woman before the flames grew too blindingly bright. The woman could never understand that he had run into the night like a sweating madman to save her life.

There had been warning before each of the other four, the Broadway murders that had struck terror to the Street. But each time the flames had burned with beauty too pure to be denied, and Waldo's knife had answered. Three of them had merely gasped, but the last one, the blowsy, ageing whore, had screamed just once and there had been no time to revel in the flowing flames of blood.

Waldo's hand closed over the knife, slowly, lovingly.

The flames that were the core of Waldo's being roared and sputtered, "Now! Now! Now!"

Waldo shook his dazed head, fighting against the awful urge. His lips formed silent words.

"No, wait!" Waldo's lips commanded. "Wait until tonight!"

6 Bart crossed Eighth Avenue and entered the cement lane to Broadway popularly known as "Jacobs Beach." It derived its name from a shifty, conniving and widely hated little man who had managed to set up one of the world's great monopolies by cornering the market in human brawn and making a modern slave block of the prize ring. Beside Mike Jacobs, such boxing promoters as Sunny Jim Coffroth and Tex Rickard had been naive amateurs. The block-long slab of paving stone that was the man's memorial was lined by theaters and cheap hotels and dingy business buildings and, incongruously, dead-center of it, there was a church. The church bore the name of one of the more undistinguished saints, but was more familiarly known as the Church of the Theater. Many chorus girls attended four o'clock Mass at the church after the Broadway night clubs closed, and it was a commentary on the times, Bart thought, that a special police detail had to surround the house of worship at such times to protect the girls from the sex offenders who lurked and waited in the shadows.

23

Jacobs Beach was mainly notable for its squirrel-faced citizens with florid ties, the "managers" who pimped for battered hulks whose brains had long ago been scrambled by flailing eight-ounce gloves.

Bart paused at a dusty store-front window with a sign that read "Cigars, Cigarettes and Tobacco." In the window were faded, fly-specked cards advertising cigarettes and pipe tobacco. Bart entered the store. There was a glass counter in the front which displayed dummy cigarette cartons. At the rear was a stout door. Beyond the door, Bart knew, was one of Broadway's fanciest horse rooms, with illegal leased wires, a battery of telephones, blackboards with race results.

Behind the prop glass counter in the front room sat a big, ageing man with the face of a mastiff and a Napoleonic forelock. Eddie O'Grady, the Old Top Sarge, had two great prides in a life that was singularly devoid of accomplishment otherwise. He claimed to have kept a promise to his dear old mother and never to have touched strong beverages. He frequented most of Broadway's favorite taverns and always drank sarsaparilla, which the tavernkeepers stocked especially for him. His second pride was the star-shaped piece of metal that hung from a pale-blue ribbon about his brown, great-veined neck in place of a tie. It was an eccentricity that could be tolerated in an old soldier who, had, single-handed, wiped out half a platoon of Germans in a French forest some thirty-five years before. For years now the Old Top Sarge had been losing his small disability pension and all the money he could bum on the horses. He was engrossed in studying the past-performance pages of the *Broadway Times*. He looked up quickly when Bart Hardin entered.

"Manager!" the Old Top Sarge exclaimed. He always addressed Hardin as "Manager" or "Captain." "You must have a hot one in a late race on the Coast."

Bart said, "I just dropped in for a pack of cigarettes."

"Hell, manager, don't buy 'em here. The Lucky Strikes we got still have them green packages they used before the war."

Bart said, "How's the job going?"

"Not bad, Captain. Way it figures, I lose just about enough on the horses to Moe Selig every week to even up what he pays me in salary. That way I got the pension for flops and eating."

"Convenient arrangement," Bart said, grinning. "Could you use an extra saw?"

"Could I use a sawbuck! Manager, there's a real, gone fuzzy in that fourth at Suffolk Downs tomorrow. You want I should give some jerk the treatment for you? The Sarge is getting old, but he didn't win this piece of tin for tossing rocks through Sunday School windows."

"Nothing strenuous," said Bart. "I want to hire you for a baby-sitter."

"What, Captain?"

"When you finish here, go over to the Slasher's and pick up a couple of drunks named Graham and Clements. Take 'em to the Karnak Baths and cool 'em out. There'll be a room for you. Later on there'll be a typewriter sent over. Graham'll know what to do with it."

Bart reached in the right-hand pocket, tossed dollar bills to Eddie O'Grady, said, "Take a bottle of cheap rye along. They don't care what they drink. Spoon feed it to 'em though. About an ounce an hour." He grinned, reached in the left-hand pocket, added a quarter to the currency, said, "And buy yourself a bottle of sarsaparilla."

Hardin left the bookie shop, headed east up Jacobs Beach. He turned right and suddenly became a tiny cell in the flowing amoeba of Broadway. He was in the very center of it now. This was the half-mile of the winding lane that had once been a cowpath and now was called the Crossroads of the World. It smelt of carbon monoxide and stale beer and doughnut grease and dime-store perfume and it was hot the year around with the heat of human bodies. It was shrill with the sound of traffic and the filtered thunder of loud-speakers and chattering human voices pitched insanely high. Once it had been the street of famous actors and lavish spenders and great restaurants. Now it was the street of sucker traps and legless beggars and joke shops and garish stands dispensing synthetic pineapple juice, the street where dark-faced little men with gold teeth and fetid breath paid cash to clutch the body of a taxi dancer for the time it takes a brassy orchestra to play five bars of music, the street where bored sailors waited for girls in bright-tiled ginmills and eager fairies waited for sailors. At the alley doors of theaters stage-door johnnies no longer lingered to thrust bouquets at Lillian Russell, but beside a picture palace young girls, whose plump bottoms strained their blue jeans, milled, eager to set up a strange, sexual squealing at the appearance of the stage-show star, a thin-necked young man with a prominent Adam's apple and a lank lock of hair. It was strange, Hardin thought, that this squealing vogue had begun during the greatest of the wars when the services had conscripted the prize physical specimens among the males. Perhaps the pubescent female had rebelled against war and had expressed her rebellion by acclaiming with little pig sounds the sickly singers with the sobbing voices who were then the apotheosis of the rejected and forgotten man.

Over the street, over it all, rising from its own exclusive triangle of cement, the building of the New York *Times* frowned down with contemptuous dignity like the weary guardian of a madhouse.

At Forty-seventh, Hardin entered the small lobby of the Karnak Baths which was decorated in a style he thought of as Broadway Egyptian. "Howzit, Soljer?" Bart said to a thick man with woolly eyebrows who stood behind the desk.

"Beefs, always beefs," the thick man answered glumly. "First the stinking cops claim I got a hideout for hoods. Now they say I got a call house for fags. Can I help it if fags like Turkish baths?"

"I'm sending over two drunks to sweat it out," said Bart. "Along with a chaperone, O'Grady, the Old Top Sarge. Got a room for three?"

"Only way I can get three cots in these rooms is put one across the door," Soljer answered.

"That's right where I want it. Charge the room and baths to me. There'll be a typewriter sent over later."

Soljer looked alarmed. Bart grinned, said, "Not the kind of typewriter hoods carry in violin cases. The kind that writes."

"What the hell for?" the thick man asked. But Hardin was already back on the teeming street, heading north. He returned to the *Broadway Times*. Denham was still at his desk, struggling with his Sunday feature that had to be set early. Observing the lizard lids of Denham's eyes, Bart thought, He always looks as if he's half-asleep. Hardin crossed to the horseshoe copy desk, said to Pops Taylor, "Set the lead on the Jamaica running story double-column and put it under the eight-column banner, Pops. Nothing hot from the Broadway side today."

"It's a lousy race," the old man said.

"Pipe an angle if you've got to, but banner-line it," Bart replied. "Got an aspirin, Pops? Walking on Broadway in the daytime always makes my head ache." Pops Taylor ate aspirin like candy when he had a hangover, which was frequently.

The old man fumbled in his drawer, jiggled a little bottle, said, "Just took the last. That damn rat-shooting busts my temples."

Bart walked down the dark corridor to the rat-infested cubicle that housed the paper's morgue. He paused discreetly outside the open door when he heard upraised voices. Orville was ferociously jabbing the wicked-looking blade of a Boy Scout knife into the scarred top of his desk. Beside him stood a tall and very lovely girl of about sixteen with blonde hair hanging to her shoulders. She was saying, "But I came over here especially to explain I can't keep our date tonight. We've got to have more rehearsing on that play for the church that we're presenting Friday."

26

"Okay, okay, you can't," Orville grumbled. "So I'll probably go to some night club and get drunk and pick up some floozie."

"Oh, Orville, you're impossible!" said the girl.

Bart grinned, tapped on the door's wainscoting with his knuckles, entered the little room. The youngster with the overactive pituitary glands scrambled to his feet, blushed.

"Miss Helen Larsen, may I present our managing editor, Mr. Hardin," Orville said, with elaborate formality. "Miss Larsen is a dramatic student," he added.

Bart said, "How you do, Miss Larsen," smiled at the girl. It wasn't a grin. It was a real smile. Miss Larsen was young and fresh and clean and something to smile at. The girl acknowledged the introduction, and took her leave, prettily flustered. Bart looked down the corridor into the city room, grinned as he saw Denham's lizard-hidden eyes following the motion of her retreating hips.

"You walk and feed the pooch?" Bart asked Orville.

The young man nodded his red head vigorously. "Yes, sir, Old Bones is well taken care of." He paused and a flush stole over his face. Bart knew that Orville was about to say something he considered very bold. "Mr. Hardin? I saw what was up on the mantelpiece. It's interesting that you should go in for fetishes. I've just been reading about them in one of these psychology books. Krafft-Ebing."

"What the hell's on the mantelpiece now?" Bart asked. "I've got a colored maid named Adele who cleans the dump. She's very moral. Puts empty Irish bottles and any other evidence of my misspent life on the mantelpiece to accuse me silently."

"There are a couple of empties, all right," said Orville. "And there's something else."

"What?"

Orville's face was as red as his hair now. "Well, sir, it's— it's kind of a lady's corset, sir."

Bart broke out laughing. So that was what Angelle Brann had left behind her this time! Her brand-new girdle. He said, "Don't let it throw you, Orville. It's a present for my dear old grandmother. Kid, you're in charge of office supplies. You got an extra typewriter around?"

Orville motioned toward a machine with a black cover. "Just that one, Mr. Hardin. The business office sent it in for repairs a week ago. I keep on calling, but the service people haven't picked it up."

"It work?" Bart asked.

"Nothing really wrong with it. The editorial wouldn't even have sent it for repairs, but you know how the business office is. It just hits a kind of high A."

"On your way home tonight, drop it off at the Karnak Baths," Bart said. "Tell the man it's for Eddie O'Grady."

Orville merely nodded. He was used to queer orders from Mr. Hardin.

Bart returned to his cubbyhole office, picked up the proof sheet of the "Big Street" column and the fat black pencil. He marked the lead item about Miss Jane Russell in Three-D "Kill." He scribbled a new lead at the top of the proof:

"Is Waldo back on the Big Street again?

"Broadway butterflies had better stay out of dark alleys tonight."

Suddenly Hardin's forehead creased into small interrogatory wrinkles. Orville had mentioned a typewriter that hit a high A. He'd seen copy written on a mill that hit a high A recently. Probably some memo from the business office about using too many pencils. Then he remembered the photostat of Waldo's letter in the locked drawer of his desk.

Hardin shrugged.

What the hell, a lot of old typewriters hit high letters, didn't they?

7   It was night and Waldo waited.

The hard glare of Broadway was an afterglow, a soft reflection, in the place where Waldo waited. He had chosen the place carefully. He must be very wary, for this one would be different from all the others.

The fingers in Waldo's pocket fluttered against the sheathed blade as if he needed constant reassurance it was there. The blade was clasped and harmless now. But it was there—cold, sharp, sure.

The flames had died a long time ago in Waldo. The hot, demanding urgency was gone, a sudden-passing wave that left him weak after it had swept away. He had fought the wave, as a dead-tired swimmer fights, longing all the while to submit to the sucking sea, to merge with it and sink slowly into dark, forbidden beauty. Waldo had resisted and he had triumphed, but he was weak now and it was not time for weakness.

The time had almost come.

He would be with her soon. He must have the strength to strike. His hand must be steady, certain. He could afford no mistake now. This was very different from the times when the flames had surged inside him and his eyes had been bedazzled by beauty that was pure and bright. Then the burning lust had been a power apart from Waldo that had carried him along, directed him, led him surely until the thing was done. The exultant power had gone with the sudden-passing wave. This time Waldo had only his own poor resources, his cunning and his knife, and he was afraid. This time it was planned, the time, the place, all of it. The police had been forewarned as part of Waldo's plan, and now they roamed the streets from Times Square to Columbus Circle, singly and in pairs, in uniforms and plain clothes, afoot and in prowl cars. But Waldo did not believe they would find him in this place.

Waldo's hand clutched the knife convulsively.

It was almost time.

Bart Hardin would never put his hands on *this* girl again.

In the afterglow of light-bathed Broadway, Waldo waited, as another familiar of the night called Jack the Ripper had waited in the dark byways of London's Whitechapel more than sixty-five years before.

8   No one observing Miss Angelle Brann, née Annie Branowski, would have believed that she was dressed for the part of an angel. She was not dressed at all unless frivolously feathered mules might be counted as apparel.

No one should have been observing Miss Brann, of course, for she was secluded behind locked doors in her small apartment in a brownstone house that was just off Broadway. She had even retreated farther to the fastness of her bathroom.

Miss Brann did not appear in the least angelic. She did not have the figure for it, if the flat, hermaphroditic torsos attributed to angels by popular religious art are a criterion. The terrain of Miss Brann's anatomy was decidedly hilly. Her five-foot-four body was firmly constructed. Her lips were an inch wider than ample and her breasts were perfectly round and very solid.

The task in which Miss Brann was engaged did not indicate that she was serving an apprenticeship for the Heavenly Choir, either.

Miss Brann was very busily dyeing her hair.

Under such circumstances it was not difficult to determine that Miss Brann must touch up her locks frequently if they were to remain the marigold shade which seemed attractive to the customers of Hymie Keppel's Salome Club. Miss Brann was a natural brunette. A rather dark brunette, in fact.

As Miss Brann's fingers distributed the dye evenly over her tresses she did not hum Mary Martin's famous song about washing that man right out of her hair. Miss Brann liked men. She found men necessary but by no means an evil. However, she was thinking shudderingly of a very evil man at the moment. Miss Brann was thinking of Waldo and his terrible knife.

The thought of Waldo had been haunting her all evening. It was one of the reasons she had double-checked the lock on her door and lowered the latticed shades of her windows. Miss Brann seemed nervous and intent but she did not seem mortally afraid. In her present state of complete nudity Miss Brann seemed soft and vulnerable, but slowly during the twenty-five years of her life she had built up a protective shell just as a mollusk gradually develops a calçareous shield for its fleshy body. Nature had built the shell for Miss Brann just as it builds the shell of the oyster and the clam to protect them from their natural surroundings. In her childhood Miss Brann had known dark poverty and a brutal, drunken father and a pain-wracked mother and a sister slightly older than herself who was a pious sadist. In her adolescence, when she was barely fifteen, she had run away from that to become the companion of a little perfumed gunman with dead eyes and a pipestem body and they had caught her and sent her to a reform school in her native Maryland. There she had associated with delinquent girls who were astonishingly precocious in the ways of wickedness. After her release from the institution there had followed the one soft and sweet interlude in a turbulent existence. She had met the young man she always thought of, even now that he was dead, as the Gentle Boy, and she had loved him madly and with complete selflessness. There was one thing they could never take away from her. He had loved her, too. He was studying at a college, studying things that little Annie Branowski could never understand, and he wrote poems to her and gave them to her timidly. They weren't proper poems because they didn't rhyme, but they were full of pretty words and even though she could never quite comprehend their meaning it made little Annie Branowski, who had grown up in the soot-stained steel town of Sparrows Point, kind of breathless to know she had inspired them. When the boy touched her, he didn't clutch and paw and sometimes hurt as the dead-eyed young hood had done. His slim hands caressed her young flesh as if it were as tender and easily bruised as the petals of a flower. They both knew the boy would have to serve his time in the Army when he was graduated but they planned to marry first. Then her older sister had found out about the Gentle Boy and she had told him of the young hood who carried a gun beneath his armpit and reeked of perfume, and of Annie's term in reform school. The boy's young illusions were shattered beyond repair and he joined the Army at once and they killed him a few weeks after he landed in Korea. Her sister Polly, whose moralistic pretensions were a cloak for vicious sadism, had killed the boy just as certainly as she had killed her mother.

The Gentle Boy and her pain-wracked mother were the only things on earth that Annie Branowski, who became Angelle Brann, had ever really loved. Often as a child she had thrown herself in front of her mother to shield the gasping woman from her drunken father's blows. She had stolen from her father's pocket when he lay drunk to buy the expensive pills that the doctor said her mother must have to keep her weak heart going. When she had moved into the furnished room with the perfumed little hood, she had taken all the money that he gave her and sent it home for her mother's medicine. She was in reform school when her mother died and later on she learned that her sister had intercepted the money she sent home and had not bought the pills at all but had donated most of it to a strange religious cult operated by a wild-eyed charlatan who demanded that his disciples scourge their flesh and surrender all their worldly goods to him. Her sister was no more than seventeen or eighteen at the time, but she became a murderess when she withheld the medicine and she became a double murderess when she destroyed the dream of the young boy and sent him to his death.

After the Gentle Boy had gone away to die, Annie Branowski became Angelle Brann and there was nothing more of softness in her life. But there was little of hurt, either, and there was a great deal of purely animal pleasure, for the protective shell was fully developed by then and warded off the slings and arrows of a life that many might consider rough and sordid. She had danced in a cellar club beneath a burlesque theater in Baltimore's tenderloin wearing nothing but a bangle that dangled from a string around her waist. She had accepted the hot and hungry eyes of the men at the tables as part of the work she did. She had accepted many of the men, too. If they were young and burly and good to look at she enjoyed their maleness and the urgent excitement she inspired in them. If they were ageing and often pathetically impotent, they paid in another and more usual coin, but now there was no need for the expensive medicine, she cared little for money and was never heartlessly greedy.

When she had come to New York and gone to work for Hymie Keppel at the Salome Club she had substituted relatively modest panties and bras for the G-string that she wore in Baltimore and she had met more interesting and sometimes wealthier men and made more money and lived a little better, but her life was really much the same as it had been since she first took the name of Angelle Brann. Except for one thing.

31

Lately she had been seeing a lot of the man she affectionately called the Blond Beast and he was different from the others. He wasn't the Gentle Boy, of course, but down there somewhere under his crust of toughness and cynicism, Miss Brann suspected there was a core of tenderness. Anyhow, she liked being with him in a certain way better than she'd liked being with any other man. Except the Gentle Boy, of course. She'd even appropriated a photograph of him from his funny apartment over the flea circus, a photograph of a young Marine in World War II combat clothes that he had sent his father from overseas. Miss Brann had borrowed a hammer from that creepy Joe Latti, the superintendent of her house, and hung the picture on her wall. She hadn't returned the hammer yet, she thought.

Miss Brann fluffed her wet-dyed hair with her fingers, observed herself in the bathroom mirror and seemed satisfied. She wrapped a towel around her still moist hair. The domestic, dustcap look of the towel made her nakedness seem suddenly lewd and brazen by contrast. Miss Brann added another domestic touch by donning a pair of pinkish-red rubber gloves. She caught a glimpse of herself in the full-length mirror on the bathroom door and chuckled. She wondered what the Salome's customers would think if she came out for a number clad like that, with a towel around her head, rubber gloves on her hands and her feet in nests of feathers. They'd probably like it, she concluded. Such unusual embellishments to nudity would whet their jaded appetites.

Miss Brann opened the bathroom closet and took out a tin pail and a metal box of lye, which, like the hammer, she had borrowed from the superintendent, Latti. She didn't like going to the super's apartment to borrow things, though. If Mrs. Latti wasn't around, the superintendent was likely to try to paw her. He was a creepy thing with dark, smoldering eyes and Angelle couldn't stand him. A real Waldo type, she told herself. He'd been a photographer once professionally and he still made pictures and developed them in a little dark room in the basement. He was always hinting he'd like to photograph Miss Brann without her clothes on, and once he'd left some nude photos spread out suggestively for her to see.

Miss Brann handled the box of lye gingerly, as if it were the explosive element of an atom bomb. She poured water from the faucet into the pail and dropped lye into the water. She recoiled violently when the corrosive powder hissed and sputtered, as if the fumes might scar her smooth, bare flesh. She obtained a long-handled brush and washed the toilet fixtures and tiled surfaces of the bathroom. Then she poured out the lye water, holding it far out from her, rinsed the bucket and mixed another lye solution. She did not use the fresh mixture, however. She obtained a pail of her own that was really a cooking utensil and mixed a more innocuous solution of hot water and detergent. She got another scrubbing brush and went into her bed-living room. She washed all washable surfaces of wood and metal furiously. She washed the kitchenette. After that she dusted and polished the furniture and bric-a-brac. The phone rang once. She did not answer it. Seldom has a completely naked lady been engaged in such homely domestic tasks. It was an hour and a half later when Miss Brann finished and her young body was perspiring freely with the exertion.

She returned to the bathroom and exchanged the draped towel for a rubber shower cap. She got into the tub and turned the warm shower on full blast. She creamed herself from neck to toes with scented lather.

When she had dried herself she took a small kit from the medicine cabinet and busied herself with manicure instruments. Still completely nude except for the dewed rubber cap and the feathered mules, she returned to the bed-living room. She looked at a little clock. Five to ten. Miss Brann seemed expectant now and much more nervous as the minutes ticked away.

At ten o'clock the bell of the front door rang. Miss Brann was very tense now. Her small upper teeth were biting her ripe lower lip. Without donning any garment she went to the door of the apartment and pressed a button that would release the lock three stories below. Miss Brann obtained a gold and red housecoat and slipped it on, but left it open, so that her lush body was fully revealed.

Suddenly, as if acting on an impulse, she crossed to a small desk, took out a leather-bound diary and opened it to the page bearing the current date. She took a ball-point pen in a trembling hand and scrawled on the page:

"10 P.M. Help! Waldo is coming!"

She laid the diary on the desk, crossed to the door. She unbolted the door and opened it a crack.

She stood beside the door, slowly buttoning the housecoat and listening to footsteps that steadily mounted the stairs.

9 At ten o'clock Bart Hardin left the Saddle and Whip Chophouse near Fiftieth and Broadway full of rare steak and good Irish whisky. The Saddle and Whip was the last distinguished restaurant in the Times Square area. All the other great cafés had moved farther and farther east or gone out of business entirely. The Saddle and Whip, which drew its diners mainly from the more prosperous figures of the sports and theatrical and newspaper worlds, had been well established when Bart's father first came to Broadway. It had weathered Prohibition, Depression, Repeal and war and still served man-sized steaks and man-sized drinks to those who could pay for them.

When he was replete with good food and good brown Irish, Bart was always pleasantly conscious of his body and its appetites. Right now he wanted an extra-special cigar, and he stopped in a tobacconist's where he knew the humidors were kept properly moist, and obtained a long panatela in a light tan wrapper for a dollar. He paused outside the shop to light up. He puffed on the cigar, relished the aromatic tickling in his throat and nostrils, gazed on the fluid swirl of the Mazda-flooded thoroughfare. If the letter wasn't a fake, Waldo was lurking somewhere near. But Waldo was a creature of the shadows and Broadway was a street without shadows. Broadway was a street of cold and merciless glare in which human frailties were revealed in ludicrous nakedness. The incandescent signs winked on and off like derisive eyes and the neon tubes twitched as violently as the pallid faces of the hopheads and mainliners who haunted the world's greatest midway.

A cigar wasn't all that Bart desired. When he was pleasantly stuffed with food and whisky he liked the warm comfort of a woman at his side. He would have especially liked the comfort of Angelle Brann at the moment. But Miss Brann would be busy. She would be conducting what she had termed "money business," whatever that meant in her young life. For the next fifteen minutes Bart wandered slowly up Broadway, pausing to glance in glittering windows at displays of black lace panties, knee-length sports coats with blade-sharp shoulders and hand-painted neckties. At ten-seventeen exactly, Hardin decided he would risk calling Miss Brann anyway. Maybe the black lace panties in the glittering window displays had had an effect on him, he thought.

He entered a long, narrow drug store that sold far more sodas and contraceptives than drugs, went to a phone booth, dialed Angelle's number. The phone rang a long time. No answer.

Knowing it was wishful thinking, Bart wondered if Angelle had changed her mind and gone to the Salome Club after all. He walked to Fifty-second Street, turned east, crossed Sixth Avenue, which a mayor with a flair for the dramatic had futilely renamed the Avenue of the Americas. The strip of pavement on Fifty-second between brawling Sixth Avenue and sedate Fifth Avenue was the gaudiest midway of them all. On the uptown side of the street just two of the old places were left. At Leon and Eddie's a couple from the Bronx could still have a mild fling for a twenty-dollar bill. At the Twenty-one Club, whose façade was decorated with hitching posts in the shape of jockeys wearing silks, those who were approved by the discerning arbiter of the velvet rope might dine and wine elegantly at from twenty to fifty dollars a cover, plus tax and tips. The site of Tony's famous speakeasy, where the great talents of the theater and writing worlds had assembled during Prohibition, now was a bar with the name of a flower and its clients were mainly homosexuals. With the rare exception of a sandwich shop or an antique store, most of the other houses were sucker traps standing shoulder to shoulder and bellowing dissonant music and barkers' appeals into the night. It was a crazy concert that flaunted one sure-fire appeal—flesh. Outside each of the dimly purple interiors was an enormously enlarged color photograph of a girl whose pink-tipped breasts billowed beneath a wispy veil, symbols of the lush abundance of female flesh within the dusky depths of the night club.

The red-uniformed doorman who was barker at the Salome Club had a voice that was from a sawmill and a face that belonged in the Chamber of Horrors at Mme. Tussaud's museum. He was intoning, "Fah-loor show on now, folks! See the EX-otic, undraped beauties of the Suh-LOW-mee Club. No cover, no minimum. See the EX-otic, undraped beauties. . . . Hiya, Mr. Hardin . . . Fah-loor show on now!"

Bart nodded, entered the Salome Club. He tossed a dollar to the busty girl at the hatcheck counter as he passed, grinned, said, "Guys without hats pay in advance." Skinny little Hymie Keppel thrust his sharp face out of the smoky shadows, said, "Hey, Hardin, where's that girl friend of yours tonight?"

Bart said, "Angelle? Didn't she call?"

"Uh-uh. Just didn't show. She's been acting kind of screwy lately, anyway."

Bart said, "Maybe she eloped with a maharajah."

Hymie said, "I see in that gossip column of yours tonight you think Waldo's loose on the street again. Hope Waldo didn't get her. By the way, thanks for plugging the trap along with plugging your sweetpea. The Irish is on the house tonight."

Bart said, "Uh-uh. Hardin always pays. That way he can say all the nasty things he wants to in his paper."

Hymie Keppel melted into the gloom again. The head waiter escorted Bart to a tiny ringside table in the darkened room. A waiter brought Irish on the rocks without an order. Amber Lane, who had just been promoted from the chorus line to a specialty, was doing a peel under a blue spot. There wasn't much left to peel except the talcum powder and that

35

meant the show was almost over. As Amber dropped the last lacy shred, the colored orchestra burst forth into a reasonable facsimile of oriental music and the entire chorus came hip-wriggling onto the dance floor wearing harem veils and diaphanous bloomers. The featured male and female singers appeared on the orchestra stand and rendered a chorus of the oldie, "Dardanella," as the wriggling hips reached a crescendo of bumps and grinds, then the plump posteriors of the girls glowed pinkly through transparent gauze as they retreated off the floor. Brighter light stabbed through the smoky twilight and the master of ceremonies' filtered twang resounded from the mike. "That concludes our floor show for now, folks, but don't go away. Dance to the music of Rollicking Rollie Bates and his New Orleans Revelers. The girls will be back soon. And remember, the bar is open and the waiters are here to serve you."

Bart was working on his second Irish when Amber Lane came to his table. She was a statuesque redhead and she was wearing a strapless chartreuse gown that seemed to derive its sole support from her swelling bosom. "Don't breathe too deep, sugar," Bart said, "or you're naked to the waist."

Amber shrugged and the prophecy almost came true. "So what?" she said. "If the boys at the next table get a close-up they can't complain about a padded check. Say, Bart, what the hell's eating that chick of yours?"

Bart said, "I can't claim proprietorship exactly, but if you mean Angelle, she was all right a little before four when I talked to her. Told me Hymie gave her the night off but I guess she lied. Girls do, sometimes."

"It's not only tonight," said Amber. "She's been acting nuts all week. I thing she's getting neurotic. Told me she was afraid of Waldo."

"When? Tonight after she read that lead on the 'Big Street' column?"

"Uh-uh. Let's see. Monday night. The night she drove the chef, Guido, crazy."

"How'd she drive Guido crazy?" Bart asked.

"She stole his pet knife out of the kitchen. It's a long, real thin one that he uses to shave the roasts down to tissue-paper slices for the suckers. He came storming into the dressing room and claimed he'd seen her in the kitchen and his knife was missing. Angelle said he was bughouse, that she'd just sneaked in to snitch a snack. But later on, I saw her, when she was getting dressed, and she was trying to sneak the knife out. It's got the club's name stamped right on the handle. I didn't tell Guido or Hymie, of course, but I asked her what the hell, and she said she was afraid of Waldo and was taking it home to defend herself. She was nuts all evening, you ask me. She don't get potted often, but she was kinda drunk. She went out between shows and she was late getting back. The girls were on for their first number when she blew in. Then she wouldn't stay for the last show. Claimed she had a headache. Hymie was biting the rug."

Bart replied, "I talked to her about four this afternoon and she was all right then. Said she had some kind of business engagement and had to tidy up the house. I called her apartment on the way over here and she didn't answer."

Amber was peering into the smoky gloom. The head waiter was escorting a man to their table, pointing them out. The man hadn't checked his hat. He still wore it on the back of his head. Amber said, "Looks like we're getting visitors. Know him?"

Bart looked in the direction she indicated, nodded, said, "He's a copper. Better pull that dress up, sugar, or he'll arrest you on a morals charge."

Amber said, "No jury would convict. I got good legs."

Lieutenant Romano took the battered gray felt from the back of his head when he reached the small table, said, "Hello, Hardin. I been on the prowl all night looking over the Broadway spots. I'm getting to be a rounder. They said at the Slasher's you might be here. I wanted to thank you for killing that item. What you ran can't hurt much. I'm beginning to think it was a gag after all. It's only about an hour to midnight now."

"Always glad to serve the cause of law and order," Bart answered. "I hope you're right about the gag. Miss Lane, Lieutenant Romano. Sit down, Lieutenant, and have a drink, if we can find a chair somewhere."

Amber rose, said, "Pleased, Lieutenant. I gotta go undress for the next grind, Bart. Hymie runs practically a continuous performance when he's got more than six customers in the house."

Romano took the girl's chair, said, "I shouldn't. I'm on duty and I got blood pressure, but they only give you half an ounce in these traps, anyway. Bourbon."

Bart ordered, said, "Nothing at all popped yet, huh?"

Romano shook his head. "Not yet, honey boy. We got so many prowl cars on the stem there's no room for taxis and the cops are crowding the pedestrians off the streets. There's men in every stage-door alley. Outside the clubs, too. One right outside this trap. We figure that if the letter did come from Waldo, he's a psycho and he'll do it just the way he said he would, in the Times Square district between eight and midnight. It's a couple of minutes to eleven now."

The drinks arrived. Romano swallowed his straight, said, "It's really got alcohol in it and it's a lot of booze for a sucker trap to serve."

"You're with the press," said Bart. "That gets you special treatment."

Romano rose. "I'll be going. Another hour to prowl. Bed'll be nice after sixteen hours straight duty."

Bart finished his Irish. "Mind if I tag along the last part?" he asked. "I got nothing much to do."

Romano said, "I don't mind, honey boy, unless that vest scares Waldo off."

On instructions from Mr. Keppel, the waiter refused to give Bart a check. Bart left twice the price of the drinks on the table for the waiter. Romano said, "The Street ain't had one like you since Diamond Jim Brady's liver give out on him."

In the foyer Bart said, "Can you wait just a minute? I want to make a call." Romano nodded, put the hat on the back of his head, stared with fatherly admiration at the busty hat-check girl. Bart went into a phone cubicle, pulled the three-cornered doors shut, dialed Angelle Brann's number.

The phone was answered at once by a shrill, hysterical woman's voice, a voice with a foreign accent: "Please! Please! Is this the police? Please, come! I called you, I told you, she's on the floor, dead at my feet. Please come!"

Bart's jaw became rigid. "Who's this?" he snapped.

"The superintendent's wife, Mrs. Latti. Mrs. Joseph Latti. I come up here and found her dead on the floor. Murdered! Oh, God, oh, please, won't you come, mister?"

"Who's dead on the floor?" Bart asked.

"Miss Brann, the tenant on the fourth floor front, is dead! Wait, please, I gotta hang up now. They're at the door. The cops are here. . . ."

There was a click and the connection was broken.

Romano looked at Bart's face as he left the booth, said, "What's the matter? What's the matter, honey boy?"

"Angelle's dead," said Bart.

Outside the Salome Club, Romano flagged a cruising police car. The lieutenant and Bart piled in.

"Where'd you say?" Romano asked.

"This same block on Forty-ninth. A converted brown-stone," Bart told the driver. The car screamed east, hurtled southward through a red light, spun west again, crashed to a stop beside two other prowl cars that had answered the woman's first alarm. A uniformed cop held the front door open. In the basement areaway a chattering group of people who had been drinking looked upward with frightened faces. Romano and Hardin raced headlong up three flights of curving stairs. On the fourth floor a door stood open. Inside the room police were questioning a middle-aged dark-haired woman. Other policemen knelt beside something on the floor.

On the floor was a body clad in a red and gold housecoat and a shower cap and frivolously feathered mules. A little card was pinned to the body. Beside the body lay a hammer. Close scrutiny revealed there was a small amount of blood on the hammer's head. A tin pail was overturned near the body. A very little of the contents of the pail had spilled upon the rug and was eating at the nap. Most of the contents of the pail had been thrown into the face of the body on the floor. The seared and scarred face of the body on the floor was recognizable only as the horrific figment of a nightmare.

Bart Hardin took one brief look, turned his back, walked out into the hall like a man who is suddenly and horribly sick. He was no longer in a brownstone flat off Broadway. He was back in the Solomons the day his outfit had come upon the first of the marines the Japs had tortured and mutilated before they killed them. He was fighting out of the Yalu gantlet and he saw the staring eyes of the kid marines who stumbled on black-frozen feet when the crossfire caught them.

Hardin's thumbs and fingers curled into tight fists. His hard body began to shake. He pressed his lips together to stop their spastic quivering.

From inside the room he could hear voices. The woman was saying, "We were having a party in the basement, it's our kid's birthday. My drunken bum husband passed out cold before our friends arrived. We ain't got a refrigerator makes ice cubes fast enough so I bought a hunk of ice for the drinks. We chopped it with a screwdriver, see? But we broke the screwdriver and there wasn't no way of chopping it, so I looked for the hammer and I remembered Miss Brann had borrowed it from Joe to hang a pitcher and I come up here and brought the key because I thought she'd be dancing at the club. I opened the door and I found her there on the floor. I started yelling but nobody heard me. I made myself look at the little card pinned to her. It said 'Waldo.' 'Compliments of Waldo,' it said. So I picked up the phone and I called the cops, that's all I know."

Bart could see into the room but he did not want to look at what was on the floor. He could see that Angelle Brann had used the hammer to hang the picture. It was a picture of Bart Hardin as a kid marine. Waldo had found the hammer useful, too.

A cop was saying, "Waldo's up to new tricks now. He's killing them inside the house instead of up an alley. He's using a hammer instead of a knife and he's throwing lye in their faces."

Suddenly Bart Hardin's glazed eyes saw the swarthy, sweating face of Lieutenant Romano. Fury surged inside him.

"God damn you!" he said, "God damn you, you said you could stop the kill if I didn't use the story. I'm going to nail you to the cross, copper. This kid was a friend of mine."

10 Hardin lurched down three flights of stairs, through the street door, past the chattering, tipsy group of Italians outside the superintendent's apartment. Instinct carried him back to the street where the million baleful eyes glared down. For an hour he walked, heedless of direction. People spoke to him with the false heartiness of those who seek publicity and could not understand why he barely nodded in return. He stopped in many bars and had quick drinks and left again and walked and walked. Several times he was within yards of Waldo, who also walked the street, but they passed each other unnoticed in the crowds. Hardin was in the Sligo Slasher's bar drinking Irish in double portions between twelve and one when the tabloid extras hit the street, with wood-block headlines as black as mourning crepe to herald the news that Waldo was on the loose again. Bart bought a paper and stared unseeingly at the story, drinking down the burning whisky in great gulps.

Just a few blocks away, Waldo read the story, too, in the flickering light of an electric sign. In his pocket, his fingers, like fluttering spider-legs, crawled over the cold knife. Tonight it had indeed been different from all the others, more different than he had dreamed it could be. The thing was done, of course, but not as he had planned it. He had not even used the knife!

Tony Maclaren was saying to Bart, "I know how you feel. You wanna smash." His gnarled old knuckles crashed down on the bar. "Things get me that way, too." His left ripped the air with an uppercut. "I'd like to tear the head off Waldo's shoulders with the punch that stopped Davey Brean, the Killarney Killer, on St. Patrick's Day in seventeen." Maclaren splashed whisky into Hardin's glass. "She was all right. I liked her the times you brought her here. A sport. A real Protestant bum. She come here by herself on Monday night, or rather Tuesday morning, about three. She was feeling low. Said she'd skipped the last show at the club. She and Mark Clements, the cop that got bounced off the force, were exchanging their troubles. Come to think of it, I believe they even mentioned

Waldo! Anyway, she took Clements home with her. There wasn't nothing wrong. She just found out he never eats when he's dead drunk and she took him home to cook some eggs for him."

"I didn't know she knew Clements," Hardin said.

Maclaren said, "He'd seen her here with you. They got to talking, crying on each other's shoulder, that was all. There wasn't nothing wrong. She felt sorry for the mugg. She was all right. Regular. A Protestant bum like you."

It was two o'clock when Hardin finally reached his apartment house on Forty-second Street. Once, half a century or more ago, it had been an apartment building that sheltered the persons of some of the greatest names in Broadway's lights. On Broadway it had been an Address with a capital A. Now its first two floors were devoted to Bromberg's Flea Circus and Fun Arcade. Even at this hour of night rifles exploded at clay pipes in the Fun Arcade on the street level and half-drunken sightseers gawped through magnifying lenses at the performing fleas on the floor above. Just below the windows of Hardin's third-floor apartment, red neon tubes belted the building entreating passers-by to "See The Performing Fleas, Educational and Entertaining."

Just a house or so away was the site of Joel Rinaldo's once famous restaurant. Now it was the location of a dingy shop that offered neckties with breasty mermaids painted on them, glass jewelry and parlor tricks that included a bladderlike device that emitted flatulent sounds when placed beneath the cushion of a chair. Close by was the New Amsterdam where Evelyn Nesbitt Thaw had once teetered on a velvet swing in the roof garden. Now it was a picture house and its current offering featured Balinese maidens with thrusting bosoms.

The street door to the living chambers above the arcade and flea circus was never locked. Inside the dusty entryway, Bart found an empty bottle, a memento of some wino who had sneaked inside to quaff the last of his sweet poison. Bart walked up two flights of creaking, uncarpeted stairs. In the hall outside the door of his flat someone was waiting. It was Eddie O'Grady, the Old Top Sarge.

Bart said, "I thought I gave you a baby-sitting job."

The Old Sarge shuffled uncomfortably. "I gotta confess, Captain," he said. "I didn't accomplish my mission. I got them rumdumbs a bath and a steam-sweat and I ladled 'em out a little booze and I took 'em upstairs, but that Clements kept begging for more like he was going into the rams. I put my cot across the door and figured they couldn't get out. But Clements must of crawled over me. I woke up about a hour ago because Graham was snoring so loud and Clements was gone. He just come back, so dead drunk he could hardly walk. I

41

went out and spent half a hour looking in all the bars around for him. Soljer said he didn't see him go out. I didn't find him so I went back and a few minutes later in he staggered. I give him another blam and put him to bed and when I was taking off his clothes I found something, so I come right over here. I read them tabs about Waldo when I was out looking for Clements."

"What did you find?" asked Hardin.

"Let's go inside, Manager, and I'll show you."

Bart unlocked the door, switched on a light. An obese, floppy-jowled and very ancient bulldog awakened from a nap beside the fireplace, growled once interrogatively, sniffed and made whimpering sounds of frantic welcome as he waddled toward Bart. The light that flared in the huge living room revealed an entirely different world from the tawdry microcosm that was modern Broadway. The elder Hardin had rented this apartment some twenty-five years before when he found himself a widower with a small boy, and Bart had grown up in these strange bachelor quarters at the Crossroads of the World. This had once been the apartment of Flo Matthews, an enormously talented and entirely giddy actress who was in her heyday at the turn of the twentieth century. The furnishings were old and scarred and massive and generally baroque and reflected the lavish though somewhat vulgar tastes of the glamorous woman who had occupied it half a century before. A great chandelier of amber glass hung from the ceiling. A fine, faded oriental rug covered the floor. Two great tasseled divans with curling arms were in the room. The gas-log fireplace was of solid black marble and two startlingly white sculptured figures supported the mantelpiece, like twin Atlases holding the world upon their backs. The fact that no fig leaves or other draperies veiled these marble males had been one of the numerous scandalous tidbits whispered about the unconventional Miss Matthews in the early century. Bart had named the figures Klaw and Erlanger after the famed theatrical producers of the time. The figures were exactly alike, but for some reason the dog, Old Bones had taken a great liking for Klaw, who played left end, and curled up beside him for his naps. He often expressed his disapproval of Erlanger by growling, barking and even snapping at him.

Several gold-framed oils of lush ladies in Turkish harems were relics that Miss Matthews had left upon the walls, but there were also reminders of Bart's father in the chamber, mainly in the form of autographed photographs of personages from the sports and theatrical worlds. Over the fireplace hung a painting of a raw-boned horse and a fat Shetland pony. The horse was Exterminator, the great route-running thoroughbred, and the fat pony Peanuts, the old gelding's constant companion in retirement. Bart's father had always said he judged a man or a horse by his ability to go the route. Exterminator had been nicknamed "Old Bones," and that was where the bulldog got his name.

The dog Old Bones was sniffing at Eddie O'Grady's ankles and expressing his approval with lazy wags of his stub tail. The old soldier with the mastiff face said, "He likes me. You know why? Because we look alike."

The Old Sarge sat down on one of the great sofas. Bart said, "What did you find on Clements and what's it got to do with Waldo?"

Eddie O'Grady opened his coat. Something wrapped in brown paper protruded far out of the inside pocket. He unwrapped it, handed it to Bart.

It was a long and thin and wicked-looking carving knife. Closer examination revealed that the handle was stamped with a name—"Salome Club." Hymie Keppel, Bart thought, was a fiercely possessive little man who liked to brand his belongings, his silver and napkins and cups and plates and kitchenware, and sometimes even the girls he employed. Bart said, "What about this?"

"He had it wrapped up in thick paper and stuck down inside his belt, Manager," the Old Sarge answered. "I found it on him when I was undressing him a few minutes ago."

"You know what time Clements sneaked out on you?"

The Old Sarge tugged at his Napoleonic forelock. "Captain, it could've been almost any time. I ain't much good on any job, I guess. We come upstairs from the steam room. Fritz Graham had a blam and corked off to sleep right away. Clements kept groaning and moaning and begging for booze so finally I give in and let him have another and after that he was quiet and I thought he'd gone to sleep. I was all tired out from betting the horses and keeping a lookout for cops and keeping them bums from drowning themselves in the pool at the baths, and I must've dozed right off myself. That would be early, some time between nine and ten, I guess."

"You only woke up an hour ago?"

"Yeah. When Graham started snoring. An electric sign was shining right into the room and it was plenty light. Clements wasn't there. He wasn't anywhere. His clothes were gone, too. So was the change from that money you give me for booze. I bought some real cheap stuff. He'd taken all the dough out of my pocket, even the pennies. I busted downstairs. Soljer, the manager, was in the office in back playing gin rummy with some character. You hit a little bell at the desk if you want him. He hadn't seen Clements. I went in and out of ginmills looking for him, but they hadn't seen him, either. I barged around about half an hour. Few minutes after I got back to the Karnak Clements showed up blotto. I undressed him again and found this thing. I'd seen a tab and I knew about the Waldo kill and I knew the girl was a hoofer at the Salome, so I thought I'd better come over here. You awful mad at the Old Sarge, Captain?"

Bart said, "I'm not mad at you. I got mad at another guy earlier tonight, but it did no good. He was doing the best he could, I guess, like you. All of us do the best we can. Trouble with the world is our best just isn't good enough."

He patted the creased jowls that Old Bones had thrust into his lap, said, "You know, of course, that Clements will probably be gone again when you get back."

The Old Sarge looked cunning as a mastiff that has just secreted a choice bone. "Not this time," he declared. "Bartender in one of the joints I went looking for Clements in is an old buddy of mine from the Fighting Sixty-ninth. He slipped me some knockout drops. Said they'll keep a guy to sleep for at least five hours. I put 'em in the nightcap I give Clements."

Bart said, "Maybe you can still earn the sawbuck, then. First, take Old Bones out for a walk. I'm bushed. Then go over to the Karnak and stand guard again. Wait a minute." He walked to the bathroom, returned with a small bottle, shook pills into O'Grady's hand. "Take these. They're benzedrine. They'll keep you awake. I use 'em for hangovers sometimes."

The Old Sarge said, "It must be that sarsaparilla that gets me so drowsy all the time." Happy to be back in good standing, he attached studded harness to the bulldog, led him out. Bart got a bottle of Irish from an ornate liquor cabinet that had once belonged to Flo Matthews and was filled with crystal glasses and decanters he never used. He got a plain water glass from the kitchen, obtained ice cubes from the interior of an ancient gas refrigerator that would probably asphyxiate him some day. He seated himself in a chair by the open window of the living room. The neon tubes of the flea circus' sign glowed on his somber face like reflected hellfire. When the Old Sarge and the dog returned, Bart said, "Get back to the Karnak. Don't let Clements out before morning, even if you have to slug him. I'll be over early. I want to talk to him." He picked the knife up from a small table, said, "I'll keep this. Remember, now, keep him on ice till I come over. Escort him to the bathroom. Don't let him out of your sight. Don't foul up this time, Sergeant. You may have a killer on your hands."

"I'll stay awake on duty, sir," the Old Sarge promised earnestly. "I'll take all them pills you give me and I'll sit on tacks if I feel sleepy."

Old Bones growled menacingly at Erlanger to keep him in

his place, and deserted his pal Klaw to come and sleep at Hardin's feet.

For the first time Bart noted what was on the mantelpiece. Two empty Irish bottles and the brand-new girdle that Angelle Brann had bought. The satiny elastic had been bought to encircle her warm, sweet-scented flesh that had been so abundantly alive and eager. Now Angelle Brann lay cold and dead, her pretty face eaten by lye, the victim of some mad monstrosity who hid himself among the faceless people of a teeming street. Bart looked away from the mantelpiece because he did not wish to see the thing that reminded him so poignantly of the girl who had lived so hard and died so violently. What had Orville called the girdle? A fetish.

Bart sat drinking whisky and staring unseeingly out the window, his hard face fiery in the neon blaze. He was still sitting there when the timid daybreak stole into Times Square like a child who enters a strange, unearthly place.

The pale shafts of dawn, as nimble as the fingers of a thief, were plucking out the shining jewels that were the lights of Broadway when Bart Hardin fell asleep at last.

11 On Thursday the pall of fear hung like a black fog over Broadway.

Broadway is afraid of Death.

On Broadway the brightest lights on earth are massed to drive away the night, for night is remindful of Death's dark, hovering wings.

When a show dies on Broadway, vans like great hearses steal up in the dead-still middle of the night to cart away the props and flats to a graveyard called a storehouse and soon the theater marquee twinkles with the names of living shows and living actors.

Broadway shrieks and roars and screams to show the bellows-power of its living, breathing lungs.

Broadway abjures sleep, for sleep is only Death on the installment plan.

Broadway flaunts naked flesh, for flesh is warm and trembles with the breath of life.

Old actresses on Broadway spend the pitiful sums they need for food and lodging to obtain paint for their faces, dye for their hair, massages for their sagging muscles.

Old actors bronze their skins to the coppery caricature of glowing youth beneath the artificial suns of barber shops.

When one of Broadway's "darlings" or "sweethearts" or "right guys" dies, the street holds a long, obscene and maudlin wake, but the drunkenness and lewdness and braying mourning are not respect for the dead or awe of the unknowable; they are mad and drunken *défis* hurled by the living at the awful specter that they fear.

All the billions of watts in all the millions of lamps could not banish from Broadway the fearful shadow of Waldo who walked unseen in the blazing night.

Men had no need for terror. Waldo struck only at young women. But all of Broadway was pale with fear beneath its paint and barber's suntan, for Broadway feared Death itself and Waldo, who walked the Street, was Death personified.

The religious said furtive prayers and crossed themselves and told their beads. The superstitious fondled luck charms and avoided black cats and ladders.

In an overcrowded field of two-year-olds at Jamaica race track a filly with "13" on her saddlecloth broke her leg and was destroyed. The gamblers shuddered and nodded wisely. The filly's name was "Showgirl."

Simpering chorus boys with marcelled hair swished and made jokes about the horror. At stage doors, they shrilled to each other, "Watch out for Waldo, dearie! Lock your door tonight!"

Broadway had known the threat of Death before. During Prohibition guns had blazed in night clubs and on the side streets and the blood of those who defied the mob had soaked the carpets and the gutters. But gangsters could be bought and dealt with. You bought protection from them. You cut them in. You played ball. If you were kidnapped you were ransomed before they packed you in cement and sank you down with the garbage and rusted junk beneath the river.

Waldo was no mobster. Waldo was crazy as a bedbug. And bedbugs are not amenable to bribes and deals.

Waldo was there, only he could not be seen. He was that man who sat beside you in Child's pouring syrup on his pancakes. He was the old bum whose quivering, sore-crusted hand begged a nickel of you. He was the enormous young man in the braided uniform who stood outside the movie and cried "See the all-talking, all-color, all-horror Drama with Dracula and Frankenstein on the Giant Screen in Three Dimensions." He was the prissy little man who mumbled "Standing room only tonight" from behind his box-office wicket. He was the bulge-bellied man with warts who hissed, "Hey, Sister! Hey, Sister!" at a stenographer from the Bronx. He was the trembling, red-eyed drunk in the Astor Bar.

"Find Waldo!" the papers roared at the police commissioner.

"Find Waldo!" the police commissioner roared at old Inspector Sansone.

"Find Waldo!" old Sansone roared at Lieutenant Romano.

"Waldo," Romano whispered to himself. "God damn his stinking soul to hell."

12 Early Thursday morning the skies over Broadway wept silver tears for Waldo's dead.

Bart Hardin stirred in the big chair by the window where he had fallen into a half-drunken sleep. The hell-glow of the neon sign no longer shone upon his face. The misty world of rain outside the windows cast dun-gray light into the room and in the heavy gloom the twin marble figures that supported the mantelpiece loomed as startlingly white as naked ghosts. Even the Crossroads of the World was almost deserted now. Wet newspapers flapped crazily in the drenching wind. The few passers-by scurried on with heads bent low as if they were pursued by some fearful presence. The dim light was kind to Hardin. There was a spiky beard now on his jowls and his pale eyes were blood-flecked and watery. The dove-gray vest with the yellow flowers was rumpled and stained with whisky. The black tie had been pulled askew beneath the wilted collar of his shirt. Beside Hardin's chair the Irish bottle had been overturned and its contents splotched a smelly pool upon the rug. The first things of which Hardin was conscious were the foul taste in his mouth and the throbbing splinters of pain in his temples. Then his swimming eyes focused on an object in the gloom—the girdle that a murdered girl had worn. Finally he realized that it was a sound which had split the murky veil of alcoholic sleep. Beside his chair, Old Bones was growling. The dog was directing low rumbles of sound at the door of the apartment. The bell of the apartment buzzed and Bart realized that he had heard the buzzing before and that this was what had awakened him. He slapped Old Bones lightly on the ear, said, "Quiet, boy." He shook his head and rose from the chair, knuckling the corners of his inflamed eyes. He made a light, called out, "Yes? Who is it?"

He heard a muffled voice through the thick panel of the door. "Romano. I want to talk to you."

Bart crossed the big and dimly lighted room and unbolted the door. Romano was alone. He was unshaven and very sleepy-looking. The blue-black beard on his swarthy face made Bart think of movie mobsters.

Bart said, "Come in and sit down. I'll be right with you. I got stinking and passed out in a chair."

Romano said, "That ain't like you, honey boy."

Bart went to the bathroom. He stripped himself naked to the waist, filled a bowl with cold water, stuck his head deep into it. He splashed water over his shoulders, chest and arms. He rubbed himself briskly with a thick crash towel. He washed his teeth and gargled with an amber fluid. He ran a comb through his pale gold hair. He found a small bottle and took three Empirin compound tablets. He donned a seersucker robe and returned to the living room. Romano was sitting in an overstuffed chair, staring at the girdle on the mantelpiece. He said, "The joint smells like a distillery and looks like a cat house."

Bart picked the girdle up from the mantelpiece, tossed it into Romano's lap, said, "Maybe that's evidence I killed her. Psycho killers sometimes take souvenirs, I hear. The girdle belonged to Waldo's latest victim."

Romano inspected the girdle briefly, abstractedly, tossed it aside, said, "We got lots of evidence, only it don't mean much. Take you, now. You got her girdle for a souvenir, but you were with me when the squeal came in and you'd been sitting in that trap a long time before I came and before that, even, you were eating in full view of a lot of witnesses at the Saddle and Whip. What we got from the p.m. so far is she probably wasn't chilled before nine at the very earliest and likely much later, maybe just a little while before that janitor's wife stumbled in on the corpse."

"Apparently I'm a suspect," Bart said. "You seem to have checked my movements."

"Uh-huh," said Romano, yawning. "We checked. You're one of the ones she mentions in her little book. Her diary."

"She kept a diary?"

"Quite a diary. Lots of names in it, including yours. She called you the Blond Beast. Kind of cute. Last name she mentions is Waldo. Last thing she wrote was 'Ten P.M. Help! Waldo is coming!' If she wrote the time right, then she was killed a full hour later than the earliest time the medical examiner sets. She was killed about the time you were on your way to that Salome trap."

Bart said, "That's in her own handwriting? How on earth could she have known Waldo was coming and why didn't she holler copper if she did?"

Romano shrugged. "I'm just a dumb cop, honey boy. I never could get it straight even what the difference between 'induction' and 'deduction' is. But it's her handwriting, that's for sure."

Bart said, "If Waldo got there about ten he must have

killed her pretty quick, or kept her from answering the phone, anyway. It's funny the things that stick in your head. I called her from a drug store last night. I remember looking at my watch just before I called and I remember it was seventeen minutes after ten."

Romano said, "Now ain't it funny you should remember the exact time like that? But maybe it helps. Taking together the time in the diary and the time you say you called her apartment, it figures she was chilled some time between ten and ten-seventeen. That checks with what we've got so far from the p.m. boys okay. Of course, Waldo could have been keeping her still at the point of his knife when you called. Only he didn't use a knife this time. He used a hammer."

Hardin pressed the palms of his hands against the side of his aching head, said, "Isn't that out of line? Waldo using a hammer?"

"Uh-huh," answered Romano. "Kinda. Psychos usually follow a pattern. But sometimes they change it a little in an emergency. Jack the Ripper did. He killed most of 'em in an alleyway but he killed one poor woman inside her room." He glanced at Bart, said, "Haven't you got some hair of the dog? You look God-awful."

"I'll live," said Bart. "I've lived through worse than this. I never drink till four and it's barely eight. I haven't been up this early since I was a marine. Old Bones kicked one bottle over but there's another crock if you want a shot."

"Uh-uh," said Romano. "I'm not hung. I'm just pooped. Sorry to disturb your slumbers in the chair, but there's more names in the book than yours. Some of 'em from the *Broadway Times* office. I want to find out what time I can catch 'em."

"Who?" asked Bart. The name of Pops Taylor had occurred to him immediately. He had no reason to believe Pops knew Angelle. He might have seen her at the office, that was all. Then he knew the reason. Gert had mentioned yesterday that Pops was growing goatish at an advanced age. Bart said, "Who? Our distinguished drama critic, Cole Denham?"

Romano regarded Hardin with narrowed eyes, said, "That name popped right out, didn't it, honey boy? Why?"

"You'll find out anyway soon enough," Bart answered. "Denham met Angelle in Baltimore a year or so ago. The producers of some musical flew all the New York critics down for an out-of-town tryout as a publicity stunt. Gave 'em a party with all the fixings, including girls from night spots. Dear old Cole got a little stewed and told Angelle she ought to come to New York so he could get her a job in the bigtime. She took him up and he had to make good. Talked Hymie Keppel into giving her a place in his line."

"You think there was anything intimate between 'em?" Romano asked.

Bart said, "It would be kind of hard for any man who doesn't use rouge and lipstick to know Angelle without there being something between 'em, I guess."

"Denham's name is in the book, all right," said Romano, "and I want to talk to him. But there's somebody else up at your office I want to talk to even worse."

"Who?"

"That oversized young character with the stop-light hair you sent down to Manhattan West with Waldo's letter. The one you call Li'l Abner."

"Orville Cartwright?" asked Bart. "You've flipped, copper. He's just a kid. He wasn't in Angelle's league. He might have seen her in the office but he couldn't have known her."

Romano had the little black book out. He flipped the pages, said, "Lemme read you something Miss Brann wrote. It's dated a Sunday, just about a month ago. 'Whew, whatta night! I guess I'm to blame, though, for luring that young punk they call Li'l Abner up here and pretending I wanted him to move some furniture for me. He's so big and young and innocent I thought I might get a few laughs teasing him when I ran into him on the street tonight. I'd seen him at the *Broadway Times* and kidded him a little. Well, he came up, and maybe I teased him some, but never again! He went berserk. I mean NUTS! Jeez, you'd think it was the first time he ever found out girls and boys are different. I had a hard time getting him out and Hymie Keppel's costumes aren't going to cover the bruises those big hams of his made when he grabbed at me. Never again! But never!!!' "

Bart said, "I wouldn't have thought Orville was the type to play rough."

"This is a funny squeal," said Romano, "only I'm not laughing. We got all kinds of suspects with motives, maybe, handed to us on a silver platter, or anyway inside a little black book. We got you. You don't impress me as the jealous-lover type, but you're in the book and you've got her girdle. You left the Saddle and Whip around ten and you didn't get to the Salome Club till about ten-thirty. You could have ducked down the street a block or two, done a fast chill and walked into Hymie's place and ordered an Irish, only I doubt it. We got Denham. He's got a rich wife and if he was playing around, this girl could have made him right uncomfortable. We got Orville, and Miss Brann wrote it down in black and white that he's the psycho type who blows his stack when he sees a little bit of stocking above the knee and that he'd been up to her place before. Also we got Latti, the super of the apartment. Several times she wrote down she was afraid of him. She called him 'creepy.' She says in the diary he'd propositioned her about taking her picture in the altogether. He looked so hot we checked him already. Long time ago when he was a kid, he was a photographer for the old *Graphic*, back in the days of the composograph. After the *Graphic* folded, he got a suspended sentence for trying to peddle obscene photographs. Then, during the late part of the Depression, he pops up as janitor in a high school. He did a rap on the island that time for propositioning the female students about posing for him without their clothes or doing worse things than that even."

Romano brought a mashed-up pack of cigarettes out of his pocket, lit one, said, "Christ, a cigarette tastes bad when all you've had for breakfast is a hamburger with onion." He spit out tobacco shreds, said, "Latti got married a few years ago and had one of those late-life kids. The kid is six or seven. They were having a birthday party for the kid last night. Otherwise, Latti'd be pulled in as a special-consideration suspect. After all, it was his hammer. Trouble is, there were eight guests at the party and every damn one of 'em will swear Latti was passed out cold from eight o'clock on, right in front of 'em on the living-room couch."

"You mean everybody got drunk at the birthday party of a six- or seven-year-old kid?" Bart asked.

Romano grinned. "You're not a *paesano* like I am, honey boy," he said, "or you'd know that's an old Italian custom. The poor kid cuts a cake and gets his presents and is hustled off to bed, then all the old folks get roaring drunk on dago red to celebrate his birthday."

The lieutenant inhaled smoke, expelled it, made a wry face and snuffed out his cigarette. He said, "We got suspects with motives, but that's what we don't want. Psychos like Waldo don't kill for motive. Usually, they don't even know the ones they kill, except kind of casually, maybe. This Latti might fit, but his alibi's as iron-clad as a battleship. Now we got something else to consider. It happens more often than you might think that some guy takes advantage of a series of psycho kills to chill his wife or girl friend and get it blamed on the guy the newspapers call a 'fiend.' Trouble is, whoever wrote that letter to the *Broadway Times* knew that Waldo killed Geraldine McLennan. Only Waldo himself knew that."

"You knew it," said Bart. "Other cops knew it. Mark Clements knew it."

"I didn't kill Angelle, honey boy," said Romano gravely. "Honest I didn't. We'll question Clements but I doubt we get much. All we got against Clements is he's a sick alcoholic. He was a good cop once. I listened to a bug doctor lecture one time, maybe it was at the police academy. He said an alcoholic was a neurotic but almost never a psycho. We're looking for a psycho. The worst kind of psycho. And the toughest kind of criminal there is to find."

Romano sighed. "It's not a nice job I got myself," he said. "Old Inspector Sansone, the toughest cop in town, left word for me. I called him and he gave me one of those 'or-else' pep-talks. He'd got one himself from the commissioner and I guess the commissioner had got it from somebody even higher up. I'm not quite fifty, but I feel like I been around forever. I can remember this street way back when Helen Morgan used to sit up on top of a piano. I been on the captain's list a long time and I'm getting closer to the top of it every year, but maybe I'll be back in uniform before my number comes up now. I guess my kid could always clerk at Macy's instead of going to Marymount. I feel like a guy named Sir Charles Warren."

"Who?"

"Sir Charles Warren. He was commissioner of Metropolitan Police in London back in 1888 and he was forced to resign because he couldn't catch Jack the Ripper. I read quite a lot about the Ripper in the library last year when these Waldo kills first started coming up, because I kind of thought Waldo was imitating Jack, only he was working in bright light instead of dark alleys. But all the reading I did didn't help me much. I questioned maybe three hundred psychos and maybe fifty of 'em confessed he was Waldo, but none of 'em really was."

Romano rose and began to pace around the big, gloomy room. Javelin thrusts of rain speared against the window panes. The bulldog smelled Romano's ankles, wagged his stubby tail.

The lieutenant said, "Old Bones knows me. He's an old dog and I'm an old cop. I been here before, drinking Kentucky whisky with your old man when you were in the big war and the little one. We used to sit here looking at those crazy statues beneath the mantelpiece, and we'd talk about the old days and what we'd do when we retired. If I don't get Waldo this time maybe I could raise minks. They breed fast and I hear there's money in 'em. I was a tough cop once. I wasn't any hero, but I was never scared of hoods. Hoods are yellow. All of 'em. I ain't smart, but I always knew that. I got a medal for bringing in the Harlem baby-killer singlehanded when I was off duty and wasn't packing any metal but the buckle on my belt. I roughed up Lenny Fassio, the town's boss mobster, in a night club once. He had six torpedoes with him, all heeled. You weren't supposed to live if you did that. I'm living. Hoods don't scare me. But Waldo scares me. Psychos like Waldo scare the holy hell out of me because they don't play according to the rules."

Romano fumbled for another cigarette. "I got a daughter who was eighteen just last month," he added.

Bart said, "I can't figure the hammer and the lye. Waldo uses a knife. He doesn't dissect his victims expertly, like a surgeon, as Jack the Ripper did, but most of them were horribly mutilated just the same."

Romano nodded. "I ought to know. I saw his victims when they were fresh killed, remember? A psycho like that has to have death and horror just like an ordinary man has to have sex. I can't understand it, but that's the way it is. Well, a hammer can kill as sure as a knife. And the things lye does to a human face aren't pleasant. Waldo had his death and horror, all right, last night."

Bart winced. He said, "You got anything else? Anything besides the little book?"

Romano said, "Not much. The body didn't tell us much. She must have bleached her hair just before she died. It was still wet underneath her shower cap. She wasn't any natural blonde."

He looked at Hardin. Hardin made no comment.

"She was a healthy kid," Romano continued. "No operation scars, just the mark of her girdle. No false teeth. Not even any fillings. She wore falsies. Not the kind you think. False fingernails, the kind you buy in dime stores. She bit her own down to the quick. She was quite a housekeeper for a chorus girl. She'd had a busy night. She bleached her hair. She took a bath—the shower curtain was still wet. And she really scrubbed and polished that flat of hers. Not a smudge of dirt anywhere. The identification boys couldn't even find a recognizable fingerprint in the place, except Mrs. Latti's on the phone. Of course, Waldo came after everything was scrubbed. No prints on the hammer or the doorknob, though. They were wiped clean. Probably he wore gloves, anyway. She'd been using lye to flush her sink. Maybe that's what gave him a new idea, kept him from using the knife." He shook his head. "It all adds up to nothing much."

"It's funny about the falsies," Bart interposed. "The false fingernails. They fooled me all right. She wore her nails long and red and she had a nervous habit. She was always taking an emery board out of her bag and shaping them with it."

"That's not unusual," Romano told him. "You're a cop, you learn that people who've got something they want to hide are always calling attention to it one way or another, like they're daring you to notice. I knew a guy wore a toupee on his head. He was always smoothing it with his hand."

Bart said, "Quit stall-walking. I'm hung and you make me nervous. Sit down. Maybe I can tell you something that will help."

Romano dropped heavily into a chair, sighed, said, "You want to help? I thought you were mad. I thought you said you were going to nail me to the cross."

Hardin pressed fingers against his aching temples. He said, "I spoke out of turn. I saw too many corpses, maybe, in what you call the big war and the little one. When I saw her there on the floor with her face all burned, I flipped, I guess. She was up here just the night before. That's when she left the girdle. You'll be crucified, all right. Not by me, maybe, but by everybody. The press. The commissioner and Inspector Sansone. And the public. The public's scared to death and when it's scared it's got to have a victim. I know you're a good cop and a decent man. My dad was fond of you and he was a good judge of men. I know you do your best."

"Yeah," said Romano. "Yeah, thanks. Only this time my best ain't good enough, it seems. Why does it have to be Waldo they hand me? Why can't it be some nice, simple hood who blasts his victim's guts out with a Tommy gun and wraps him up all neat in cement and drops him in the river? With that I can deal."

Bart thought a minute. At last he said, "I can tell you a little bit about her. Not too much. Her name wasn't Angelle Brann. It was Annie Branowski. She came from Sparrows Point, a steel town outside Baltimore. Her father was a drunken bum who worked in the mills when he was sober enough. Her father and mother are both dead. She had a sister who must have been a bitch, and I think she said the sister died, too. She did time in a Maryland reform school. I don't know what one, but it should be easy to check. She was there about ten years ago. She worked in clubs in Baltimore. She was mixed up with a hood when she was a kid, but I don't know his name. He got a stretch for a holdup. She came to town just about a year ago and she's worked at Keppel's trap ever since."

Romano made notes in a little book. "Thanks," he said. "It might help a little. You couldn't tell me something about Waldo, could you?"

Bart thought of Mark Clements, drugged by whisky and knockout drops in a Turkish bath, and of the knife wrapped in paper that lay there in the shadows on the mantelpiece.

"Maybe," he said. "But not just now. There's something I've got to check first."

Romano opened his mouth to answer, but no words came out. The bell of the apartment was buzzing urgently. Romano rose alertly, seated himself in a chair placed in the darker gloom by the fireplace, out of the line of vision from the door.

"You expecting visitors at eight-thirty in the morning, baby doll?" the detective asked softly.

Bart crossed to the door, opened it.

Cole Denham, the drama critic, stood at the door.

The usually neat and well-pressed little man was haggard and disheveled.

Denham said, "I'm sorry to disturb you, Hardin. But I'm afraid that I'm in trouble, bad trouble, and I need advice." He paused, bit his lip. He said, "I'm afraid they're going to arrest me for murder, Hardin."

Romano's voice came out of the shadows.

"Why, honey boy? Why are they going to arrest you for murder? Did you kill somebody, maybe?"

13 Denham lurched like a skittish yearling colt. He ducked back into the hallway. Hardin grabbed his arm, said, "There's nothing to be afraid of, Denham. Come on in."

He drew the resisting little man into the apartment with gentle force. He closed the door, switched on more light, said, "Lieutenant, this is Cole Denham, drama critic of the *Broadway Times*. Cole, meet Lieutenant Romano of Homicide, Manhattan West."

Denham stood speechless for a moment, blinking his heavy-lidded eyes. At last he said, "What is this, Hardin? A joke or a frame-up?"

Hardin said, "Why would I try to frame you, Denham? I didn't ask you here. You must have seen Romano before. He's been around Broadway for years."

Romano still sat placidly in the chair, rubbing his fingers over his black-spiked jowls. He said, "I know Denham. At least I've seen him around. Nobody framed you, honey boy. Bart didn't ask me here, either. The both of us are interrupting his beauty sleep, in fact. What's this about you getting arrested for murder? It sounds interesting."

Denham said, "I came here to ask your advice, Hardin. If I have to make a statement to the police, I want a lawyer present."

Romano was scratching his hand over the brier patch that grew beneath his chin. He said, "Well, now, honey boy, the thing is you already have made a statement in front of the police, only you didn't realize it at the time. You got a right to your legal eagle just like every other citizen, of course. If you stand up on your hind legs and holler for your rights, though, I'll have to take you down to the station and charge you with something or hold you for questioning and let you call your lawyer from there. And I'm awful tired and sleepy. If you'd sit down and be comfortable right here and tell me what you meant when you said you were afraid of getting arrested for murder, it might save me a trip." He turned to Bart. "Why don't you give your friend a shot of Irish?" he asked. "He looks like he could use it. He's all wet, too."

Bart poured the whisky, handed it to Denham, said, "It's not my fault, Denham. You blundered in like the bull in the china shop. Romano's a reasonable man, but he's a cop and if you've got something to hide you'd better clam up until your mouthpiece gets to you. I'll level with you right off. Romano's investigating Angelle's murder. He was going to talk to you, anyway, later on because your name's in her diary. He knows you met her in Baltimore and that you got her her job with Hymie. If you're guilty the best thing to do is keep your mouth shut tight."

Denham lifted the whisky to his mouth with a trembling hand, drank it neat, collapsed into a chair. For long moments the room was silent except for the insistent sound of rain against the windows. Denham was making futile gestures at smoothing the wrinkles in his soaked clothes. At last he spoke.

"I don't deny knowing Angelle Brann or getting her a job in New York," he said. "I don't deny my connection with her. I have a perfect alibi for at least part of last evening, too. If she was killed after nine o'clock, I have an alibi that's unbreakable."

Romano yawned. "So you think you need an alibi?" he said. "Just what alibi you got?"

"From nine o'clock until nearly midnight I was at the home of Martin Land on East Sixtieth Street. He is attorney for the *Broadway Times,* but I was there to consult him on private business."

"You chose yourself a good mouthpiece," Romano said. "Marty Land's the smartest cookie's been on Broadway since Bill Fallon played the hot spots. Will Marty testify you were there all that time?"

"I see no reason that he shouldn't," Denham answered testily. "He didn't arrive himself until after ten-thirty. But his servant let me in at about nine and knows I waited in the living room until Land got home."

"This servant stay in the same room with you?" Romano asked.

"No, of course not. He was in and out several times, serving me drinks, emptying ash trays."

"I know Marty's place," Romano said. "It's a little private house near Madison. I been there myself. Marty's got a habit. Every time he beats a murder rap for a hood he gives a little party at his house for the homicide cops on the case, just so there'll be no hard feelings, maybe. The living room's got French windows just a few feet above the street, with a little iron balcony in front of them. It wouldn't be too tough to un-latch one of the windows, walk out on the little balcony and drop to the street. It wouldn't be too tough to get back in through the unlatched window, either."

Denham snorted contemptuously. "Are you really serious, Lieutenant? Any man seen climbing in and out of windows of a private house in that neighborhood at that time of night would be arrested."

"Not unless somebody hollered copper," Romano said. "You'd be surprised how few New Yorkers holler copper. They get used to seeing goofy things."

"Nonsense," said Denham. "Besides, the servant was in and out all evening."

"How many times?"

"At least three times. I had three drinks. Probably oftener."

Romano stifled another yawn, said, "Just for the sake of argument, though, he could have missed a guy going out and coming in and he might not have wandered in while the guy was gone. Why'd you go to see a legal eagle at that time of night, anyway?"

Denham hesitated. Finally he said, "I guess I'll make a kind of statement to you, Lieutenant, since there is an unprejudiced witness present. Land was leaving for the Adirondacks for a few days anyway on the one o'clock train this morning, so I couldn't call him if I wanted to. I went to see Marty Land last night because I was being blackmailed and I wanted legal advice. I was being blackmailed by Angelle Brann."

"Oh?" said Romano without apparent interest. He took a small notebook and a pencil stub from his pocket, said, "You don't mind if I scribble a note or two. Just to refresh my mem-ory, like they say."

Denham said, "Don't write this part down, if you want the truth. It's compromising to me personally but it is not evidence that I'm implicated in a murder. I'm willing to talk frankly, but I don't want what I say printed in newspapers that my sick wife might see."

"I ain't a reporter, honey boy," Romano said. "I'm too dumb for that. I'm just a cop. What you say to me won't get in a newspaper unless it's a legitimate part of the record of a murder squeal."

Denham looked uncertain. He pushed the moist, soiled-snow locks back from his forehead. He looked at Hardin.

Bart said, "Don't look at me, Denham. All I can tell you is that I won't print it unless it's news that's relevant to the brutal murder of a kid I liked. I've warned you that Romano's a cop. He may have a sleepy look, but he's a damned shrewd operator. Don't talk if what you say can hurt you."

Denham said, "My only guilt was that I had intimate relations with Angelle Brann and I'm a married man. My wife has been an invalid almost since the day that we were married. Angelle was one of the party girls they engaged in Baltimore to entertain the New York critics they flew down for the tryout of a musical show. I got paired off with her and I liked her. She was gay and warm and human. And she was young and pretty. I was drinking, like all the others. Angelle spent the night in my hotel room and I guess I got a little maudlin and promised I would get her a job if she came to New York. It was just one of those vague promises men make when they've drunk too much, but a few weeks later she appeared. That was about a year or so ago. I'd never been involved in anything like that before. I'd met Hymie Keppel of the Salome Club—he's had an interest in several Broadway musicals—and I half-promised him I'd try to get his publicity in the *Broadway Times* if he'd hire her. It was unethical and I hated doing it, but I did.

"Hymie gave her a trial. She could dance well enough and she had a good body and she's been in the Salome line ever since. I'm fifty-two, but I don't feel I'm quite an old man yet. Angelle seemed willing enough to continue our relationship in New York. I visited her on numerous occasions, but I was very discreet. At first she asked for nothing. Then she started borrowing small sums, twenty-five or fifty dollars. Then she said she was losing money to Moe Selig, the bookie, and she had to have a hundred or so to pay him off. I could handle that out of my salary if the calls weren't too frequent, and associating with Angelle was worth the price. My wife inherited money, but she owns all our really valuable assets in her own name and I can't touch any of them except with her permission. Last Monday Angelle came to me at the office. She said she had to have two thousand dollars by early Wednesday evening—last night, that was. I told her I couldn't possibly raise such a sum on such short notice. I earn enough to keep me going, but any large sums would have to come out of my wife's accounts. Angelle seemed desperate. For the first time since I'd known her she became abusive and angry and she threatened that if I didn't have the money by eight o'clock last night she'd write my wife or call on her in person. She said she kept a diary and that there was plenty about me in it and she would show that to my wife.

"There were other people in the office, and I was afraid they might overhear. I agreed to meet her at eight o'clock last night at a little Basque restaurant I'd read about in *Gourmet* magazine. It's on Fifty-first between Ninth and Tenth and has mostly a foreign clientele, so I thought it unlikely we'd see anyone we knew. Tuesday I managed to get the money. The bank wouldn't be fast enough in negotiating a loan. Moe Selig is not only a bookmaker, he's a loan shark on the side. I got it from him at the loan shark's usual rates of six for five. I've still got the money."

The little man handed a brown envelope to Romano. Inside were twenty hundred-dollar bills.

"Angelle didn't show up," he said. "I waited there outside the restaurant for her. At eight-thirty I called her apartment and she didn't answer. I called the club and she hadn't gone to work. I called her apartment again a little before nine. I was frightened what she might do. My wife is an invalid. The shock of learning about this might kill her. I decided I needed help, a lawyer. I thought at once of Marty Land because they call him the Main Stem Mouthpiece and he's the paper's lawyer. I took a cab to his house, but he'd gone to a dinner party. When his servant learned I was from the *Broadway Times*, he said I could wait.

"I waited. Land finally arrived. He said there was nothing I could do but wait for her to make another move, but that when he came back from the Adirondacks he'd see her himself and try to put the fear of God into her. Or at least the fear of the law.

"I left Land around eleven-thirty and walked toward Broadway. I hadn't eaten and I was going to some place for scrambled eggs or Welsh rarebit. I was very disturbed. I called my home and told the servant to tell my wife not to worry, that I was spending the night in town. I often do. The servant said there'd been no visitors and no calls, so I thought I had another day of grace at least. I bought a copy of the *Mirror* —they were shouting an extra—and there was Angelle's picture, the one they have in the lobby of the club, right on page one, with the story of her murder. I tried to call Land back, but he'd left for his train. I drank a lot and just wandered. I didn't know what she might have written in that diary, of course.

"Finally I checked into the Tremont on West Fifty-third. I tried to sleep and couldn't and when I couldn't stand it any longer I came down here to ask Hardin what he thought I should do."

"That's all?" asked Romano. He handed back the envelope with the hundred-dollar bills.

"That's all," said Denham, "except this. I admit I might have had a motive for killing her, justification, even. But Waldo killed Angelle Brann. You might believe I killed Angelle but I don't think anyone could believe that I'm a madman who killed those other four women, too."

"It's like I was just saying to Bart here," said Romano sleepily. "We got plenty of people with motives. And what we want is somebody who don't have any motive except he's nutty as a Hershey bar."

Denham rose. He seemed dazed, unsure. He glanced from Hardin to Romano, said, "What do you plan to do?"

"About you?" asked Romano. "Routine stuff. Check with Moe Selig about lending that money. He'll tell me even if lending it wasn't legal. I'll check with the servant about the time you were at Marty's house. I'll check with Marty, too, if I can reach him."

"I can help you there," said Denham. "He's staying at the Old Stone Inn at a place called Fork Ridge."

"Thanks for being helpful," Romano said. "Thanks for being frank. Just stick around in case I want to ask any questions."

Denham hesitated, started for the door, turned back. He said, "Lieutenant, am I a suspect in this murder?"

Romano sprawled in the chair, stretched out his legs, yawned. He said, "Honey boy, I don't go around suspecting people. I've just got to ask 'em questions and maybe sometimes send 'em to the electric chair."

"Go back to your hotel and try to sleep, Denham. You can come in as late as you want today," Bart said.

"I will," the little man replied, his small hand fluttering toward the soiled-snow locks of hair. "I'll get in some time this afternoon and do my daily stint and finish up the Sunday feature."

He left, closing the door carefully behind him. Old Bones growled. Romano yawned.

Bart said, "He said something significant."

"He didn't know?" asked Romano.

"He couldn't have known," Bart replied. "It's not possible."

"Then he said something significant," agreed Romano. "So maybe my kid won't have to clerk at Macy's after all. Maybe she can get herself some culture up at Marymount. Only trouble is, if he's it, he's Waldo and not some guy who just pinned on the card for a red herring. And Waldo shouldn't have a motive good as his."

Bart said, "Psychopaths who kill and maim are guys like Denham or me or you most of the time, until the craziness comes on them. They lead normal lives when they're not possessed by whatever it is that hits them. Anybody who leads a normal life can run into a situation where murder seems the only way out. A psycho could do that in his role as a normal man. If no one suspected him of being psycho he might kill for motive and leave clues leading to the other part of his personality, the crazy part, and think that in itself would be an alibi. The cops might suspect him of the kind of murder for motive a normal man would commit under pressure, but they'd never tag him for the psycho kills."

Romano nodded, "One murder for business instead of pleasure," he said. "I was thinking about that. But it's not too easy to believe. That significant crack he made could have been just a slip of the tongue or poor memory. And he's got an alibi. If the story of the servant and Marty Land check with Denham's, that theory of mine about him slipping out the window will be as silly as it sounds. No D.A. would take it in front of a jury. Besides one of his main reasons for killing her would have been to keep their relationship quiet. He knew she mentioned him in the diary. But the diary was left there on the desk, within arm's reach of where Angelle was murdered. Why wouldn't he have taken it?" Romano rose, picked up his battered hat, said, "I got to talk to other people. Where can I find this young character Cartwright?"

"He lives with his mother in the Village, in a flat on Cornelia Street," Bart answered. "They came here from some little town in Jersey a year or so ago. The old lady is the doting sort and gets hysterical about her boy. She calls the office if he's a few minutes late getting home. Why see him there and bring his mother into it? He'll be at the office by noon."

Romano thought about it. He put the battered hat on his head. He leaned down, patted the dog, said, "You're a game mutt, Bones, living up here above a flea circus." He turned to Bart, said, "You did me a favor not running that letter in the paper. I guess one good turn deserves another. You sure he'll show up?"

Bart nodded. "He'll show up. He'll show up even if he's Waldo. And he's not."

Romano crossed to the door, opened it. "Okay," he said. "I'll drop around your office noontime." He yawned. "I hope I stay awake till noon. You know what disease a homicide cop should catch?"

"What?" asked Bart.

"Insomnia," the lieutenant answered.

14 Bart Hardin hadn't felt worse since the time they'd piled him on a litter and jolted him over the pitted trail that led south from the Yalu. It wasn't just the liquor that he'd poured into himself or the fact that he had slept for only a few hours bent double in a chair. Hardin had the horrors, not the vaguely jittery horrors of the common hangover, but the peculiar horrors that senseless acts of violence and sadism inspire in normal men. The urge to kill, to inflict pain on another human being, was a thing that he could understand. It was a sudden engulfing emotion he had known himself more than once. He had known it when he was in the boxing ring and an opponent's jab had crushed and bloodied his nose and caused hot, pointed wires of pain to thrust into his temples. His one thought then had been to hurt back as hard as he could. He had known the urge to kill when *sake*-sodden, screaming Japs had sought honorable suicide in the banzai charges on a dozen isles and atolls and when the Chinese moved out at last from behind the little hills of North Korea in terrifying force, their ridiculous brass bugles cackling like a madman's laughter in the night.

But the wanton enormities, the calculated cruelty of the criminally insane, cannot be answered with fist or gun or bayonet. Such evil is beyond all comprehension and it repels belief.

The horror of Waldo was that Waldo might be anybody. Deep down, as faint as some dim racial memory, there was a little bit of Waldo in every human being. Sometimes, once in every hundred thousand lives, perhaps, the evil that repels belief comes floating slowly to the surface and briefly it is there, visible and naked, like some Mesozoic monster spawned suddenly from the uncharted caverns of an ancient sea.

It's no mere accidental mingling of chromosomes and genes that produces a Waldo, Hardin thought. It's people who produce him. The people who swarm on Broadway and millions of other streets in a million other cities, heedless, contemptuous, callous, preoccupied with their own small aims and appetites in their own small lives. It's the unforgiving mother and the self-righteous father and the belittling teacher and the silly girl who laughs derisively at her sweating, awkward swain. These are the real forces that produce a Waldo. They beat down his pitifully small ego until he can no longer stand the world of the present in which he lives and he retreats into the dark past he finds buried in himself and there, in the forbidden depths, he discovers man's forgotten lusts and the evil that repels belief.

When the evil comes clamoring from the depths like some flailing, half-drowned swimmer fighting to the surface of dark water, the press trumpets that another "fiend" is loose.

And almost always, Hardin thought, the "fiend" is some meek human being. Like Denham. Or Clements. Or Taylor. Or Li'l Abner Cartwright.

They've come in every age, the fiends, Bart reflected. They were the witches and the demons of the old times. In the

Middle Ages they had legal status as Grand Inquisitors and headsmen on the chopping blocks in the city squares and torturers in the dungeons of old castles. Jack the Ripper was not the first. He had illustrious predecessors in the noblemen de Sade and Gilles de Rais, who was called the first Bluebeard. But they're coming oftener now, the fiends, Bart thought. They're coming oftener in an age that saw the atom dust of Hiroshima.

Despite the chill dampness of the morning Bart stripped off the robe and climbed into the miniature swimming pool of black onyx that had been Flo Matthews' bathtub. He turned on the needle shower his father had installed when he moved into the apartment years before. He stood shivering as the ice-cold rapiers of water slashed his bare flesh. He dried himself with a rough towel, shaved. He took a benzedrine tablet and wondered how it might react with the Empirin compound he had already swallowed. At least, he thought, I'm not showing any tendencies of acute alcoholism. Not yet. I don't want a drink and there's a gnawing in my guts that means I'm hungry. It was bad enough to have to live and work on Broadway, the quivering core of a neurotic world. When you sought the escape of booze or dope you were finished. Maybe Waldo's way was the ultimate in escapism.

He dressed carefully. In deference to the damp and gloomy morning, he selected the most somber of his eleven floral waistcoats, It was a charcoal silk with dark red rosebuds. He found an English raincoat and put on a shapeless felt that he reserved for rainy days.

He strapped the harness on Old Bones and walked him. Old Bones disliked rain. And he was not used to the indignity of being awakened so early. He balked at the leash and took malicious delight in delaying the natural processes he was supposed to perform as Bart stood in the soaking rain.

Hardin had seldom seen Forty-second Street at this hour of the morning. Most of the shops that displayed tawdry wares were still closed, for they remained open until after midnight. In a dismal bar across the street a lone sailor lifted beer to his mouth with a shaky hand. There weren't a dozen people walking on the Crossroads of the World, although the hour was almost nine. Near him a girl still wearing a low-cut evening dress sought a taxi vainly. She had no protection from the rain which smeared her make-up and plastered the satin to her full young body. She looked as if she'd had a hard night. Bromberg's Flea Circus and Fun Arcade was closed. Bart wondered what time Bromberg woke up his fleas for their first matinée. Where did fleas sleep, anyway? Did Bromberg have a pack of long-haired collie dogs to serve as bedrooms?

Old Bones grudgingly finished his appointed tasks and Bart returned him to the apartment where the dog immediately curled up at the marble feet of Klaw. Bart left the apartment again and made for the Copper Skillet on Broadway near Forty-fourth. A tall waitress with dark hair and pointed breasts curved the oily rosebud of her mouth into a smile for him.

"Still going to dancing school, Felice?" Bart asked the girl.

"Yeah, Mr. Hardin," Felice replied. "But maybe I better quit now that Waldo character is loose again. That Waldo goes for dancers."

Bart hoped Felice would qualify as a showgirl on some-body's casting couch before too long. At twenty-five or twen-ty-six, hoofers were old on Broadway. Even the waitresses hired to lend sex appeal to the Copper Skillet didn't last much longer. Bart ordered ham and eggs and Felice served them in the small copper skillet in which they had fried, detaching the handle. After he had finished his third cup of coffee, Bart felt better. He overtipped Felice, as usual. Felice said, "Thanks, Mr. Hardin. I wish all the characters who come in here was generous like you. You know, Mr. Hardin, it would help a lot if I could get a mention in the *Broadway Times*. Those characters that hire showgirls pay a lot of attention to the *Broadway Times*. I could be awful nice to you if you run a piece about me in the paper, Mr. Hardin."

"I'll just bet you could, sugar," Bart answered, grinning. He left the restaurant and walked up the main stem to the Karnak Baths. A very old man built like a mastodon was making his painful way toward the desk of the little lobby, his bent hogshead of a body supported by two sturdy canes. His name was Banko and he had been a top-class wrestler in Greco-Roman days.

"Howzit, Banko?" Bart said.

The old man raised his thick neck with obvious effort, said, "Things ain't good, Bart. I sit up all night playing gin with the boss, Soljer, and I lose a week's pay. I been saving up to buy a new kind of brace I see advertised in a physical-culture magazine, but I can't afford it now, and the pain's been bad. Me, who took the best as was at catch-as-catch-can, handing out towels to fags and puking drunks in a Turkish bath and not enough dough to buy a brace to ease my hurting back."

"You on duty here last night?" Bart asked the old man.

Banko said, "Soljer was supposed to be, but he wanted to play cards and my back hurt me so I couldn't sleep, so I come down and played with him in the little office. Not much else to do. Sports and spenders used to come to Turkish baths to sweat out the grape they'd drunk from ladies' slippers and fighters and jockeys used to come to take off weight. But not now. Low-down drunks and queers, that's all we ever get."

"I've got a couple of drunks upstairs now in charge of the Old Top Sarge," Bart told him.

"You in on that? One of 'em got loose last night," said Banko. "Soljer and I didn't see him go out. The Old Sarge come down looking for him. But we saw him come in all right. He's that skinny guy looks like a lunger that used to be a cop. I was at the desk when he come in and he was sobbing like a baby. The rams, that's what he had. He had a tabloid in his fist with the picture of that babe that Waldo bumped and he says to me, 'I know her! I love her!' he says. 'I saw her just before she died!' He's real squirrel meat, you ask me."

"That all he said?" asked Bart. "What else happened?"

"That's all," the old man answered, "except that crippled up like I am, I had to take him up on the elevator and try to get him in his room."

Bart took bills from the right-hand pocket, said, "You just earned a little toward that brace. What's the room?"

"Three-twelve," said Banko. "I'll take you up."

"Never mind. I'll walk."

Banko thanked Bart for the money, but there was a hurt and disappointed look upon his face. Suddenly Bart knew why. He had forgotten to ask the usual question.

"Who was the best, Banko?" Bart asked, grinning.

Banko's old eyes shone with the look of remembered things.

"The Zybysko boys were good," he said, "and so was Strangler Lewis. But Joe Stecher was the best. Joe Stecher was a man. He wasn't a fat-bellied bum with dyed hair and perfumed armpits like the clowns which call themselves wrestlers today. Joe Stecher was the champ. He was the best."

The old man raised his thick neck as high as possible and jutted out his chin. "Joe Stecher broke my back," he added proudly.

Bart went up two flights of steps, paused at one of the numbered doors of the cubicles that served as rooms in the Karnak Baths. He was surprised to hear a typewriter clacking busily from behind the door. He knocked. The Old Sarge opened the door. He was fully dressed and the Medal of Honor adorned his neck. Bart noted that the pale blue ribbon of the medal was growing grimy. The Old Sarge's mastiff face looked haggard, but it beamed with pride. Eddie O'Grady tugged at his Napoleonic forelock, said, "The Old Sarge accomplished his mission, Captain. Graham's already writing up the story for you."

The tiny room was close and stank of stale, alcoholic sweat. The Old Sarge had pulled his cot away from the door. The cot and the two beds took up almost all the floor space. Fritz Graham, clad only in his underwear, had wedged his bulging belly into a corner. He was pounding a typewriter that perched on a table with peeling paint. On one of the beds Clements was lying, staring at the ceiling, gasping for breath. He looked as if he might have died a long time before without benefit of an embalmer.

Sweat was pouring from Graham's pink face, his fat, flabby body. He did not even bother to wipe it off. He glanced over his shoulder at Bart, said, "Last night, when we were sweating it out down in the baths, Clements told me the story. It was connected and coherent and convincing. I couldn't write it then, but I remembered every detail when I woke up and early this morning the Sarge gave me a drink or two and I sat down to write it. It's almost finished, Hardin. It's a good yarn, too."

Three or four typed sheets lay beside the typewriter. Bart picked them up. There were many typos. Words and sentences had been X-ed out. But the whowhenwherewhathow was there in the lead. It was concise and vivid and the facts were clear. The facts about a dissolute woman named Geraldine McLennan who took a madman to her room. The facts about a drunken cop who arrived too late. The story flowed as a good newsman's copy should flow. Graham had been a fine reporter once. Bart supposed that once you had the gift, the knack, it never left you completely no matter how much booze and bitterness ate into you.

"How much more?" Bart asked Graham.

"One more paragraph," the perspiring man replied. "Then I write 30 at the end. Then you pay me for it and I go out and get a drink. A big drink. The biggest drink in town."

He pounded the typewriter again. A couple of minutes later he sighed deeply, tore the sheet from the roller, handed it to Hardin. He rose, rapidly donned his rumpled clothes. He held out his hand, said, "Money, Hardin. It got written. Pay me off."

Bart pocketed the copy. He handed bills to Graham. He said, "There's part of it. I'll give the rest to the Sligo Slasher this afternoon. He can dole it out so you won't blow it all in one place."

Graham looked at the money, shrugged, said, "It's enough for a drink, anyway. The biggest drink in town." He nodded toward Clements. "What about him? He's sick. The green giraffes are looking through the window at him."

Graham mopped sweat from his face with a dirty handkerchief, hurried from the room, the money still clutched in his hand. The Old Sarge stood near the door, respectful, anxious.

"Did the Old Sarge do all right?" he asked eagerly. "Did he, Captain?"

Bart said, "You did fine, but I may have one more job for you before you report for work at Moe Selig's. The book doesn't open until noon, anyway. You go downstairs and talk to Banko in the lobby. I'll call you."

Eddie O'Grady left the room, his chest expanded as proudly as that of a recruit who has been commended by the company commander for good work on K.P. Bart turned to the man on the bed, said, "You conscious enough to know who I am, Clements?"

Clements nodded miserably, coughed, said in a cracked voice, "Hardin. For Christ's sake give me a drink, Hardin."

Hardin opened drawers in the small chest, found the bottle O'Grady had bought to taper off his patients. There was about half a pint left in the fifth, he judged. He rinsed out a dusty tumbler, filled it half-full of whisky, splashed in water. He handed it to the gasping man on the bed. "Sip," he said. "There's not much more."

Clements grabbed the tumbler in two hands that trembled as violently as dry leaves in the wind, gulped half the whisky, coughed, gagged and immediately gulped the other half. His head dropped back on the sweat-soaked pillow and he exhaled in a drawn-out sigh as his quivering body relaxed. The thin man said, "I've been in hell before when I was like this. But I never felt quite so bad. I'm muddled. I think I did things, then I'm not quite sure."

Bart didn't tell him about the knockout drops. He said, "What do you think you did, Clements?"

Clements said, "Some of it's pretty clear, at least I think it is. After we got broiled down in the steam room we came up here and O'Grady gave me a drink or two and I passed out cold, early in the evening. Then I woke up, I don't know what time, and Graham and the Sarge were sound asleep. I was crazy for a drink. I couldn't wake up Graham or O'Grady and I couldn't find the bottle. Then I found the Sarge had the bottle in bed with him. He was sprawled over it and clutching it and I was pretty weak and sick and couldn't get it loose from him. His bed was across the door, but I leaned over him and undid the latch and the door opened outward. I got into some clothes. Maybe they were mine, I don't know. Anyway I found some money, bills and change, in another pair of pants, and I took it. I pushed the door open and crawled under the Sarge's cot and got out of the room. After that I was in a lot of ginmills, drinking. I don't know which ones. I don't think I went to the Slasher's, though, because I was afraid of meeting you there, and I didn't want to lose the stake you'd promised Graham and me. Some time or other I found my money was giving out and I got frantic. I found a liquor store that was still open and bought the cheapest alcohol I could.

A bottle of Sneaky Pete, domestic sherry. I gulped from it right on Broadway, in doorways, with crowds of people all around me."

Clements' breathing became labored again and sweat poured from him. He said, "Please, Hardin, I've got to have another shot."

Bart shook his head. "No. Not now. Finish the story and I'll give it to you."

Clements struggled to an upright position, sat on the edge of the bed, his head pressed between his hands. "The rest is all confused," he said. "Like a crazy dream. I'm not sure it even happened."

"Tell me about it, anyway," Bart urged.

"After I'd drunk about half the wine, I got one. of those screwy ideas a drunk thinks up. I'd met a girl a few days before, or maybe it was a week or two before—I can't keep track of time any more. She was one of your girls, Hardin. I'd seen you with her at the Slasher's place. Her name was Angelle. I didn't know her last name until I saw her picture in the tabloid and read that Waldo had murdered her. I know that part's right. The paper with her picture in it was still on the floor beside my bed when I woke up this morning."

"You saw Angelle last night?" Bart prompted.

Clements shook the aching head that was pressed between his hands. "I'd been up to her place the other night, whenever it was I met her. She'd come into the Slasher's a little tight, kind of blue, and we got to talking. She felt sorry for me, I guess. She found out I'd had no solid nourishment in days and she insisted I come up to her place for scrambled eggs. She and Graham and the Sligo Slasher are the only people who've treated me like a human being for months. To all the others I'm just something that ought to crawl back into the woodwork."

"What happened at her place?"

"Nothing happened except she fed me and we talked and we drank a little gin she had. She gave me a couple of bucks for a flop, too. She was jittery. She told me she was afraid of Waldo. She even hinted she knew who Waldo was."

"Who'd she say he was?" Bart asked eagerly.

"She wouldn't say. Just said she was scared of him, that he might try to kill her. I thought she was just tight. Now I know better. That's twice I've just missed catching Waldo."

Bart said, "What about last night? Think hard, Clements. Did you see Angelle last night?"

Clements said, "I can't think hard. I can't think at all. I need a drink. All I know is I got this crazy idea I should go up to her place and share the rest of my bottle with her because she'd been kind to me. My mind was all fogged, but I could remember the house she lived in clear as anything. It was on Forty-ninth. So I started over there."

"And you saw her, Clements?"

Clements shook his head decidedly. "I didn't see her. But I think I saw the man who killed her, maybe. I think I saw Waldo."

Bart held his breath, afraid to ask the obvious question of the tortured man.

Clements said, "I'm finished, Hardin. Done for. My mind's gone. I remember vaguely going to her house and as I just about reached it, there was a shrill sound, like police sirens. I saw a man coming out of the doorway—fast. He seemed to be trying to get away before the prowl car came. I thought I recognized him."

Clements paused, moved his head from side to side between his hands. The silence in the room was heavy. Rain washed against the streaked window pane. From outside the mounting noise of Broadway rose.

"All I can remember about the man is this, Hardin," Clements said at last. "I had the impression at the instant I saw him that he had some connection with you and with the *Broadway Times* and with the Sligo Slasher's. With my head in this state, I can't remember who he was, but I think I knew him. I think he must work for the *Broadway Times* and must drink in the Slasher's and that I've seen him there and know his name."

"What does he look like, man? Think!" said Hardin.

"I can't tell you what he looked like. That's all I remember. Just the impression. I don't know if he was old or young or short or tall or fat or thin. I can't recapture it. I was very drunk. But I remember the impression. He had some connection with you and with the *Broadway Times* and with the Sligo Slasher's place. If I could only get some liquor and drink myself sober, I might remember who it was. The name might come back to me."

Bart smiled wryly. There wasn't a drunk, he reflected, who didn't think he could drink himself sober. And sometimes, oddly enough, it even worked. Sometimes, at a certain stage of intoxication, an alcoholic had a sudden flash that amounted almost to total recall. Clements must have experienced that yesterday, when he'd related the entirely coherent story that Graham had just written.

Clements was saying, "A prowl car pulled up, and I faded. After what happened to me, I don't like seeing cops. Too many of them know me. I found I still had a little change, so I guess I drank in bars again after I finished the wine. Then I read about the murder in the paper and saw her picture and I think I started sobbing like a baby. She'd been kind to me.

Not many people have been kind to me recently. I wish I was a cop again. I wish I had another chance at Waldo. For God's sake, Hardin, let me have a drink."

Bart said, "In a minute, Clements. There's something else." He took an elongated, paper-wrapped parcel from the patch pocket of the English raincoat. He tore off the paper. He tossed the thin carving knife, with "Salome Club" stamped on the handle, onto the bed beside Clements.

"Where'd you get it, Clements? You had it on you when the Old Top Sarge undressed you this morning."

Clements stared at the knife. There was the fascination of sheer horror in his sunken eyes. He did not touch the knife. He said, "My God, was there blood on it? My God, I didn't kill her, did I?"

The bronze flecks swam in Hardin's eyes like tiny fish in milky water. "Did you, Clements? Did you kill her? Where'd you get the knife?"

Clements said, "I didn't kill her. I couldn't have. No matter how drunk I was. I loved her. Not the way you think. Not as a woman. As a human being who was kind to me."

"The knife, Clements. You had the knife," Bart said relentlessly.

Clements' head dropped between his shoulders. His voice was barely audible. "I got it from her. From Angelle. Not last night. The other night, or other week, whenever it was I was there. She was morbid. Talking crazy. She said something about the dead coming back to haunt her. She said she knew who Waldo was. She said Waldo was going to kill her. Then she took the knife out of that big pocketbook she carries. She said she'd stolen it so she could protect herself from Waldo. I was afraid of what she might do to herself with the knife. So I took it from her."

Clements raised his head, looked into Hardin's grim face, said, "That wasn't the only reason I took it. I'm at the end of my rope. I've tried suicide before, but I bungled that like I bungled everything else. I carried the knife around, wrapped in paper. I thought I might get drunk enough sometime to get the courage to cut my throat. Don't stall me any longer, Hardin. That's all I know. I've got to have a drink."

Bart poured whisky into the glass. "It won't help, Clements," he said. "You're beyond the help of whisky. You need a hospital."

Clements drank, sputtered. He said, "I've got no money. Bellevue won't take just plain drunks any more. They stopped that while I was still a cop. You have to be committed to the bug ward as a mental case and even the bug ward's hard to get into now. If a cop finds a drunk lying in the gutter nowadays about all he can do to get him in a hospital is kick him in the head so he'll have blood on him."

Bart said, "There's a souse trap up on Central Park West. Dr. Ridley's place. Half of show business goes there to sober up. They lock your clothes up and give you sedatives and spoon-feed you with paraldehyde and shoot you full of vitamins. It costs a hundred and a half for a week. I can't afford it, but I'll stake you to a week there, Clements. I'll call and make arrangements. Then I'll have the Old Sarge take you up."

Clements' lifeless eyes searched Bart's hard face. He said, "You'd do that? You'd do that for me?"

Bart said, "Not for you. Not because I'm a do-gooder who wants to help his fellow-man. Most of the fellow-men I know are lousy, chiseling bastards. But I want the information locked in your rumdumb brain, and I'll pay for it. I want to know who Waldo is."

15 It was ten-thirty by the time Bart reached the old firehouse that was the office of the *Broadway Times*. Even so, Bertha, the phone girl, batted her mascaraed eyes in surprise at his early arrival. All the editorial employees except Pops Taylor came to work around noon. Pops lived in a beat-up hotel that was two clean sheets and a towel or so above a flophouse on West Forty-ninth, next door to the Church of the Theater. He could have afforded far better accommodations, but he preferred to blow his weekly salary on cards, dice, horses, aspirin tablets and the drink that made the aspirin tablets a necessary item of his diet. Pops came in early because he suffered from headaches and insomnia and had nothing whatever to do with his mornings since his wife had died. Bertha was on duty because the business office kept the civilized hours of nine-thirty to five-thirty.

Bertha said, "My goodness gracious, Mr. Hardin, what happened to you, getting here so early? The flea circus burn down? Anyway I got a couple of messages for you already. Mr. Taylor called and says he's got some dreadful disease I never heard of and he won't be in till late if he gets in at all, so please see his desk is covered. Wait a minute, I wrote it down what he's got, poor man." She consulted a note pad, said, "Migraine. Is that catching, Mr. Hardin?"

"Pretty infectious, sugar. Everybody's got it nowadays. It means a headache."

"Well, my goodness gracious, why couldn't he say so?" asked Bertha. "Mr. Hardin, there's also a *lady* waiting for you. I told her you didn't come to work till noon, but she said she'd wait and she barged right into the editorial, I couldn't stop her." Bertha's nose tilted as high as her fashionably uplifted bosom as she accented the word *lady*.

"Who is it?" Bart asked.

Bertha said, "All she'd tell me was that her name was Gert, and if you'll pardon the personality, Mr. Hardin, I think she's a little bit drunk or screwy or something. She says she wants to tell you who Waldo is!"

"Well," said Bart, "that would be a right interesting thing to know."

He entered the barnlike city room which was deserted except for a tall girl in a red print dress and a floppy hat who sat on the edge of a straight chair near Cole Denham's desk. Bart nodded, opened the door to his cubbyhole office, said, "Come on in and park it, sugar."

Judging from the pinpointed pupils of Gert's eyes and her air of repressed excitement, the pusher the Broadway hustler had met in front of Mickey Walker's the day before had sold her a bindle big enough to last awhile. Gert sat down, looked at the photographs of thoroughbreds and showgirls on the walls, said, "Jesus, how'd those horses get in this cat house?"

Bart said, "I hear you're seeing Waldo when you mainline the H these days, sugar. Maybe you should cut down the dose."

"I think I saw Waldo last night all right. I know a girl just across the street from where I was saw Waldo. Waldo killed her."

"Where were you?"

"I had a halfway date with a punk who thinks he's a heavyweight contender. In Greeley's ginmill on Forty-ninth just across the street from the house the doll got chilled in. The muscle punk didn't show. I guess his manager decided naughty girls like me are bad for athletes. So I stayed around drinking Alexanders. When I can't eat, I drink Alexanders. They've got cream in 'em. They're very nourishing."

"Between the H and the Alexanders it's no wonder you saw Waldo," Bart commented.

"I told you yesterday that old pappy guy who works for you was a wrongo," Gert declared. "Pops—whatshisname?— Taylor? Well, he come into Greeley's. He was plastered like a Hollywood bungalow. He's a bug, Bart. A real, life-size bug. He started mumbling about how he'd won a lot at stud and I could have it all if I'd only be a daughter to him. A Daddy Browning type, no less. Imagine me, a daughter, with corkscrew curls and a set of rompers, maybe! Anyway, when I wouldn't let the jerk adopt me, he started playing with matches. He kept setting little pieces of paper on fire in ash trays and mumbling to himself about how all life came out of fire. When the paper burned up, he'd say that what he called 'gray, cold ashes' were like old age. Then he'd strike another match and touch the burned paper and make it glow a little and he'd say it took the fire of youth to bring the spark of life back to the ashes. It don't sound like much, but honest to God, it was scary, Bart! To get rid of him I patronized the ladies' powder room and when I come back, he'd taken it on the MacArthur, like the soldiers say. I went up and stood by the window so I wouldn't miss any customers in case they come strolling by, and I saw the old goat going into the house across the street, the house where that doll got herself chilled. Right after that a guy who looks like he can pay for company asks me if I want to take a walk and I say I do, and we leave. But I can tell you this. That Pops Taylor was acting bugs last night and he went into that house just about the time that poor kid was murdered. He was looking to adopt a daughter and, you ask me, he 'adopted' her the hard way."

Bart grinned, said, "You're a good kid, Gert, and an honest hustler. You might even make a fine daughter for dear old Pops. But your mind works like a junky's. You think a nice old man like Pops is a psycho killer because he gets drunk and plays with matches and maybe wants to pat a young girl's behind and wish it well. So he went into the house where a kid was killed. There are a dozen other apartments in that house, most of 'em occupied by show business people and Broadway grifters. Pops likes to gamble. Maybe there was a game going."

"The mood that old goat was in he wasn't looking for a game they play with dice or cards," Gert asserted. "He was looking for the kind of kid they found beat to death with her face burned off by lye."

"What time did you see Pops go into the house?"

Gert shrugged. "I wasn't punching a clock on him. Between ten and eleven, give a little, take a little."

"Well, thanks for coming in," said Bart. "Old Pops is sick today but I'll ask some leading questions when I see him."

Gert scratched at her bare arm with blood-red nails as long and sharp as the talons of a Manchu. "He should be sick," she said. "After what happened it makes me sick just to think about him. Okay, buster. You don't believe a word I say. So maybe I'm a hustler and maybe I'm a junky, but I know what I see. Do me just one favor. Tell that old man to stay away from me. I know a lot of men. Some of 'em do nasty things when the door is closed, and I can take 'em in my stride. But I want no part of Mr. Waldo Taylor, thank you."

73

Gert rose and left the office in a huff. She strode across the big city room, her buttocks undulating with the semi-circular motion peculiar to street-walkers and sailors.

Bart looked after Gert and shook his head. He wondered where she'd come from and what had made her what she was. Broadway crawled with women like Gert, only most of them weren't quite as honest. The others didn't stand on street corners and peddle their favors as a huckster peddles cabbages from his cart. Gert at least was forthright. The others got themselves kept by rich and ageing men with neurotic wives or they were "on call" for visiting buyers at a hundred bucks a night, with dinner and the theater a prelude to the same thing Gert sold for the price of a dingy room in a beat-up brownstone. Probably Gert had come from a broken home, like Angelle Brann, and had wanted to be a showgirl, too. But Gert wasn't made of the same tough fiber as Angelle. She'd taken to the streets and the junk. She was almost thirty and soon the streets would not be Broadway and its environs but the dark and brawling slums on the fringes of the Bowery and the garish, twisting lanes of Chinatown and the uptown streets where little men with dark faces and gold teeth would appraise her as she passed and finger the two dollars in their zoot-suit trousers and wonder if Gert was worth all that. Maybe it would be better after all if Gert met Waldo.

Bart spun the swivel chair toward his desk and his brow wrinkled. Something was missing. His typewriter wasn't there. Sometimes Orville Cartwright took spells of being officiously efficient. Maybe he had found the typewriter jumped three spaces after you hit an N and had taken it back to wait the service man.

Bart walked through the city room and turned up the corridor to the morgue. He paused as he heard a typewriter clattering. The door to the morgue was closed. Bart pushed it open silently. Red-haired Orville was hunched over a typewriter, laboriously pecking at its keys with two big fingers. Bart said, "You're down kind of early, aren't you, kid? Is that my mill?"

Orville jumped guiltily. Crimson seemed to drain downward from the follicles of his flaming hair into his chubby cheeks. "Mr. Hardin!" he exclaimed. "I didn't expect you in till noon. I had an important letter to write so I came a little early and borrowed your machine. The one I had in here for the repairman is over at the Karnak Baths. I'll take this typewriter right into your office, Mr. Hardin."

"Never mind," said Bart. "Finish up your letter. I don't need the mill right now. And you can pick up the one at the Karnak when you get time. Old Banko has it at the desk."

Bart made his voice as casual as possible. "Orville, you knew Miss Brann who was murdered last night, didn't you?"

Orville's wide and effeminately pretty face was an interesting chromoscope. Crimson flowed from it and for an instant the boy was ghastly white. Then the blood returned in mottled purple patches.

"It was a terrible thing, Mr. Hardin," said Orville, shaking his red mop. He stood up with an elaborate and elephantine pretense of unconcern and sat on the edge of the desk so that his big body shielded the paper in the typewriter. "I chatted with Miss Brann a time or two when she was here to see you or Mr. Denham," he said. "Of course I didn't really know her, though."

"Ever go up to her apartment?" Bart asked.

"Why, yes, now you mention it, sir, I did. I guess she must have told you. I met her on the street one Sunday night and she spoke to me and then she asked me if I would move some furniture for her."

"What happened?"

The chromoscope had turned from purple to bright red again. "Why, nothing, Mr. Hardin. Except I moved some furniture and she gave me some kind of gin drink and thanked me and I left." Bart thought he had never seen such naked guilt on a human face, but Orville's guilt seemed ludicrous, like that of a small boy caught elbow-deep in the plum preserves. "Did—did I do anything wrong, Mr. Hardin, sir?"

"That's what I'd like to know," said Bart. He left it at that. Orville didn't want to talk, so he'd leave him to Romano. It was 'throwing raw meat to lions, leaving poor Orville to the cops. Orville's weak and absurdly pretty face was a vivid chart of his emotions and confusions.

Bart returned to his office. Lank Pete Cruise, the photographer, was waiting, chewing on a cold cigar with yellow teeth. Pete said, "Bertha told me you got up early today. I come in to develop some prints I had left over from last night. I got something to tell you. You know this Latti that was janitor at the girl's house?"

Bart said, "Heard of him, that's all."

Cruise said, "If it's the Joe Latti I think, he's a creep. Papers said he used to be a photographer. I worked with him years ago. He liked dirty pictures. Every cameraman's got his own collection. I got one myself locked up somewhere. But Joe Latti was different. He didn't just want pictures of broads who were willing to pose with their clothes off. He wanted candid shots of nice young girls and he took a lot of 'em and even tried to sell 'em. He was always hanging around corners on windy days with a Leica in his mitt. He got fired off the paper because they caught him hiding in the ladies' room with a candid camera. A mind like that could make a Waldo."

"Nice character," said Bart.

"Yeah. Sweet and lovable. Just thought you ought to know." Pete undraped himself from the chair on which he'd been sitting cross-legged, ambled off. Two large men were walking through the city room toward Bart's office. Romano's battered felt was on the back of his head. Grierson was as stolid-faced as usual. Romano sighed, dropped into a chair, said, "Hello, honey boy. I thought you might be here account of I got you up so early. You haven't got a cup of black coffee in your hip pocket, have you? I can't stay awake much longer." The lieutenant untied his shoes and loosened the laces. "A cop's feet are like a fighter's legs," he said. "They go first."

Bart told Romano what Pete had said about Joe Latti. Romano nodded heavily. "Yeah," he said. "We had that one pegged as a dirty name right off the record. Also it was his hammer the dame was hit with. But we can't even have some fun and rough him up. He had eight guests last night. Solid, middle-class Italian *paesanos,* mostly his wife's friends and relatives, from East Side, West Side, the Village and the Bronx. And every one of 'em will swear on a stack of *lassagna* recipes that Latti was passed out on that couch from eight o'clock till after his wife found the body and put in the squeal."

Romano added, "That's the trouble. We got a lot of people but we got nobody we can take in front of twelve solid citizens because the D.A. is particular about having what he calls a case. I been right busy since I left you, even with my hurting feet. I talked to that man of Marty Land's. He says that Cole Denham got there just about the time he said he did and didn't leave until nearly midnight. He says he was in and out half a dozen times or more and Denham was always sitting in the same place, didn't even get up to go to the can. He remembers particularly that Denham was there at ten exactly, because he was serving him a drink and the clock was striking. Seems this man of Land's listens to a babe called 'Everybody's Sweetheart' who makes love to men listeners over the radio, and he wanted to hurry back to the kitchen to tune her in on his portable at ten. You ever hear that dame? She calls you 'Sweetie' and she's got more sex appeal in her voice than these babes on the wall got when they shake their this-and-that. Anyway, if Denham was there at ten, he was up in the Sixties while Waldo was climbing the stairs on Forty-ninth, according to that last entry in Angelle's diary."

Romano yawned. He said, "I hope you don't feel hurt, honey boy, but I had you tailed. You're a right sweet guy sending Clements up to that pink-elephant zoo on the park.

He was a good cop before he started taking little nips for snake bite. You get anything out of Clements in the Turkish bath before the Old Sarge took him over to the jitters doctor?"

"I found out about the Geraldine McLennan kill. I know it was Waldo and not the boy friend that cut her throat."

"Yeah," said Romano wearily. "I couldn't keep you from putting it in the paper now, I guess. It can't hurt much, anyway. We got about all the break we could expect already from that angle, and it doesn't do us any good, not enough to go before twelve good men and true. There's something I forgot to ask you at the flea circus this morning. You ever hear of a dame named Prudence Dean?"

Bart shook his head. "Sounds like the by-line on a cooking column," he replied.

"Yeah. Angelle mentions Prudence Dean in the diary several times. She seemed to admire this Prudence Dean a lot. Every time Angelle thinks she's done something naughty, like taking Orville up to her apartment and teasing him, she writes, 'Oh, why can't I be good and sweet and nice and moral like Prudence Dean' to kind of scold herself, I guess. I thought she might have mentioned this Prudence Dean to you."

Bart said, "No."

"I wish I could find this Prudence Dean," the lieutenant continued. "She's not in the city directory and she doesn't have a driver's license. Maybe she's a friend Angelle knew down in Maryland."

Bart said, "Why don't you advertise for her? They say it pays to advertise."

"What, honey boy?"

"Let the papers know you want to question her about Angelle. They'll run it in connection with the Waldo story. If Prudence is as good and sweet and moral as Angelle says she is, she shouldn't object to coming forward voluntarily. I'll run a bold-face page-one box myself, but be sure to give it to the others. Prudence Dean doesn't sound like a gal who would be in show business or a chick who plays the horses." Bart made a note about the box.

Romano said, "You know, honey boy, sometimes you're right smart. I can't think of anything else to do right now. You don't mind if I sit here, do you, and just rest my feet and wait till twelve o'clock when Li'l Abner Cartwright comes to work?"

Bart said, "I don't mind you giving your dogs a rest, but Orville's here already. He came in early to write a letter."

"It wouldn't be another Waldo letter, would it?" Grierson asked.

"I hope not," Bart replied. "He's writing it on my typewriter."

The tramp of heavy feet echoed in the deserted city room. Bart leaned over the roll-top desk, peered out the door. He said, "Here comes Orville now. Don't get too rough with him. He's kind of delicate."

Orville lumbered into the little office, clutching Bart's standard-sized typewriter in one big paw, said, "Excuse me, gentlemen," placed the machine on a stand beside the roll-top desk.

Romano looked the youth over sleepily. He said, "Hello, honey boy. There's sure as hell an awful lot of you."

"It's pituitary," Orville explained seriously. "The glands are very funny things, sir."

A stamped and addressed envelope protruded from Orville's pocket. On it the word "PERSONAL" was capitalized and heavily underlined.

As Orville started for the door and Romano made no move to stop him, Grierson spoke. "Your name Orville Cartwright?"

Orville nodded. "Yes, sir," he replied politely.

"We're policemen," Grierson said. "We'd like a few words with you."

Orville said, "Oh, I remember you, sir. I gave you the letter I took to Lieutenant Romano at Manhattan West. I'll be glad to talk to you in just a minute, but I've got to do something first." He walked through the door. Grierson yelled, "Hey, you, Junior! Wait a minute!"

Orville kept on walking and increased his speed as he headed across the big city room. He did not even look back. Grierson lunged through the door, sprinting after Orville, yelling "Hey! Hey, you!" Orville was running now, head down, like a fullback bucking the center of the line. Bart darted into the city room. Romano followed him, stumbling over his loosened shoelaces. Bart took a diagonal course across the city room, on an angle from that which Orville and Grierson were pursuing. Romano followed, still tripping on his laces, breathing hard and muttering curses. Bart cut through a door to head Orville off at the gate beside the phone desk. As Bart suddenly appeared and Orville and Grierson came thundering out of the city room, Bertha's black-fringed eyelids fluttered and her uplifted bosom heaved tumultuously beneath her sweater. A bewildered little man wearing rimless glasses came out of the business office and stood staring with his mouth wide open. When Orville saw the exit was cut off by Bart, he veered course suddenly and charged up the stairs to the composing room. Grierson, who had won the 220 once at a K. of C. track meet, was right after him. As Romano stumbled up, gasping profanities, Bart jerked his head, said, "This way," and returned to the city room.

They had hardly entered the barnlike editorial department

before Orville came shinnying down the fireman's brass pole as gracefully as a sack of flour plummeting from a second-story window. Grierson was still right after him. Orville landed on Pops Taylor's swivel chair in the slot of the horseshoe copy desk and Grierson landed on Orville's shoulders.

There was a resounding crash. The swivel chair shot forward on its rollers. The enormous horseshoe table overturned, spewing stacks of paper, copy spikes, wire baskets and telephones to the floor. The chair whirled from under the grunting contestants and they fell to the floor, wrestling.

Romano shook his head, said, "Ain't it great to be young and frisky?"

Grierson jerked Orville to his feet, hit him a meat-ax blow across the mouth with the edge of his right hand, said, "So you wanna play tag, Junior? Okay, you're it."

Orville staggered back. There was a look of astonishment on his girlishly pretty face. Blood showed on his mouth. He dabbed at his mouth with a clean handkerchief. He said, "I think you loosened my bridgework, sir. You've got no right to hit me."

"Oh, no?" said Grierson.

Orville said, "I was only going to mail a letter. A *personal* letter, sir."

Orville's voice rose to an hysterical falsetto when he emphasized the word "personal."

Grierson shoved Orville roughly, jerked the letter from his pocket, ripped the letter open. The detective said, "I'm a queer. I get my kicks reading other people's mail. Especially personal letters."

Grierson began to read the letter. His face was still blank, but somehow there was a look of gloating to it. The eyebrow shot up to the point where his hat had been before it dropped off during the chase.

Orville dabbed at his split mouth, said, "You can't do that, sir. It's unethical."

Grierson's eyes darted over the typed page. His eyes began to shine. It took him awhile to read it all. He handed the letter to the lieutenant, said, "Read that. Well, well, who ever thought that Waldo would be so young!" He turned to Orville, said, "So you got a little nance in you? So you and this boy friend over in New Jersey used to play house, did you? You and this chum of yours used to plan a perfect murder, did you?"

Romano began to read the letter. Faces of employees of the business office were appearing at the doors to the city room. Romano nodded toward them, said to Bart, "Get 'em out."

Bart shouted at the faces, "Get out of here! Get back to your goddam chisel sheets and adding machines. This is the city room and I'm the guy that runs it!" The faces disappeared. Bart walked across the room, closed both the doors. Romano finished reading the letter, handed it to Bart. He said, "Let's go in your office and sit down. My feet hurt something awful."

Grierson shoved Orville toward the office. Bart and Romano seated themselves. Orville remained standing, dabbing at his mouth. Grierson stood close beside him. Bart read the letter Orville had typed on his machine. It was addressed to a Paul Sturgis in Hohokus, New Jersey, Orville's home town.

Dear Paulie

I guess you'll be surprised hearing from me after all this time but Im implicated in this murder of a Broadway glamor girl & maybe the police will find out youre a friend of mine & I want you to use discreton if youre interviewed. I mean the ANGELLE BRANN case. This Waldo character killed her last night you know. Well I have a very important newspaper positon now & I get to know all these Broadway glamor girls including her & she asked me up to her place one night & I think she wanted to have intmate relatons the way she acted, feeling my muscles & putting on a neglegee & all that. Well I would not be a gentleman if I said what happened so I will just leave it to your imaginaton knowing me of old, ha ha.

I know she kept a diray because I found one on her desk & she grabbed it when I picked it up & said maybe she would put my name in it. I mean the police may have this diray & they go a lot by psychology nowdays, I mean what you did when you were young & all that & so maybe theyll poke around the high school & find out you & I were buddies 3 years ago when we were kids about 14.

Well I mean, dont tell them all the crazy things we did & talked about. Whats the use. I mean, like when we used to go to the old shack & talk about the girls in school & get steamed up imagining how it would be to have them there in the shack in their bathing suits or underware. I mean, whats the use, we were only kids & it didnt mean a thing. And dont tell them how we got that book about the Loeb & Leopold case & planned a perfect crime killing that little snotnose kid Joey with the freckles, the one who put the stink bomb in our shack & filled our swim trunks with itchy powder. If the police knew how we stole a butcher knife & threatened Joey they might think Im the pyscho type like Waldo & killed this babe. We werent serious, it was just a gag, so whats the use I say.

80

I know youre inteligent & will catch on. Maybe they wont even interview you but if they do just remember the old saying, Discreton Is Better Than Vallor.

Your pal,
Orville Cartwright

Bart handed the letter back to Romano. He said, "A newspaper copyreader's job is getting tougher every year. It's this progressive education. They don't teach kids to spell any more. If Orville here wrote the Waldo letter, he's gone back a hell of a lot in spelling and punctuation during the last twenty-four hours."

Romano said, "Yeah. That's one reason I like the parochial schools. They stick to reading and writing and 'rithmetic." Romano sighed and began to tie his shoestrings. "Broke one, damn it, gallivanting around," he said. He turned to Orville, said, "Maybe you'd like to tell us where you were last night, kid. Between the hours of nine and eleven, say."

Orville dabbed at his bloody mouth. "I paid thirty-seven dollars for this bridgework just about a year ago," he complained. He looked searchingly at Romano and his face flooded crimson as the blood on his mouth. "If I tell you, will my girl find out?" he asked.

"I don't know your girl," Romano answered.

"Her name's Miss Helen Larsen. I was at a picture show, but I don't want her to find out I was."

"Why, honey boy? You do something naughty in the picture show?"

Orville shook his head. "No, sir. But she broke a date with me. She said she had to rehearse for a play she's in and I guess she did but I was mad, so I told her if she broke the date I was going out with a Broadway showgirl and I don't want her finding out I just went to a picture show by myself."

"What show you go to?" Romano asked.

"The Art Theater on Eighth Street, not far from where I live. They had a J. Arthur Rank film. It was a kind of melodrama about a murderer. I admire English pictures. They're intellectual, different from this corny Hollywood junk."

"You're a hell of a speller for an intellectual," said Romano. "You know about what time you got to the show?"

"I know exactly. I don't like getting in the middle of a picture. There's a paper called *The Villager* that runs a weekly timetable of all the neighborhood shows. The last show began at 9:14. I ate dinner with Mama, then I walked over there and I had time to drink a cup of black coffee they serve free in the lobby before the last show began. I got there just a little after nine and I wasn't out until eleven-twenty."

81

Romano sighed. He said, "I hate to have to move around on my poor sore feet but we'll have to take you down to Manhattan West and have you dictate a statement. At least, it's quit raining."

Orville said, "Can I go out and straighten up the mess we made first, sir? Mr. Taylor will be mighty mad if he finds his copy desk turned over like that."

Romano said, "Sure, honey boy. Grierson, you helped to make the mess. Help to clean it up."

Grierson glared at Romano. Then he said, "I've got to find my hat, anyway." He followed Orville into the city room.

Bart said to Romano, "It's about eleven-thirty. At four o'clock I'm going over to the Slasher's for a drink. If Orville's not back by then to walk my dog, I'll want to know why. It won't take a third degree to make that chump talk in four hours and a half."

Romano said, "I'll be in touch, baby doll."

He walked into the city room. Orville and Grierson had made some semblance of order out of the shambles. Grierson had found his hat and was wearing it. He accompanied Orville to the morgue for his coat. Orville left the deserted city room in custody of the two detectives. Romano was walking with a tired limp.

Bart returned to his desk and spread Fritz Graham's copy out in front of him. He did not begin to read it at once, however. He sat thinking about Orville and Waldo. He couldn't believe the big, awkward oaf was really Waldo. Orville was an overgrown kid with ridiculous pretensions to intellectual interests who couldn't spell "cat" or put a subject before a predicate, a typical product of the modern educational system that puts all the emphasis on the end and none on the means. Socially conscious do-gooders would describe him as a big, mixed-up boy. That was fine, except it was the big, mixed-up boys who gang-raped girls in city parks and forced their escorts to look on with switchknives at their throats. It was the mixed-up kids who smoked reefers and mainlined H and ran down old ladies with their hot rods just for kicks. Maybe it was the fault of the child psychologists who warned parents against thwarting Junior even if he wanted to set fire to Grandma. Maybe the wars were coming too close together lately. Or maybe it was the looming shadow of the big, fat bomb that was going to drop some day and blow the whole damned world to hell and gone.

Bart shook his head. He picked up a copy pencil and tried to concentrate on Graham's story of the strumpet who took a madman to her room. Suddenly his eyes narrowed. He opened the bottom drawer of his desk. He fumbled beneath the shirts and bottle and cards and dice and brought out the photostat of Waldo's letter. He laid the photostat beside the copy paper on which Graham's story was typed. He switched on the glaring bulb of a gooseneck lamp. He picked up a magnifying glass he used sometimes to check the agate type in the past-performance proofs.

Bart was no identification expert, but there couldn't be any doubt about it. It wasn't only the high A. The two samples had too many other points of similarity to admit coincidence.

Waldo's letter and Fritz Graham's copy had been typed on the same machine.

Orville Cartwright had had that machine back in his morgue for a week or more.

16 By midafternoon the city room of the *Broadway Times* hummed and crackled with the disciplined confusion of putting out a daily paper. Desk men barked "Copy! Copy boy!" then remembered that there wasn't any copy boy today and carried their stories and heads to the chute that ran on ropes to the copy-cutter's desk in the composing room. Pops Taylor hadn't put in an appearance. A rim man who wore thick-lensed glasses sat in his slot at the horseshoe desk. The winner of the sixth at Jamaica was of little moment today, anyway, Bart thought. This was an all-Waldo edition of the paper, with two juicy exclusives smack on page one. One was the photostat of the letter Bart had suppressed the night before. The other was the story Clements had told to Fritz Graham in the Turkish bath.

The banner line in 72-point had already been set and the proof of the shrieking streamer was curled on the roll-top desk. "TERROR HITS BIG STREET AGAIN!" Also on the desk was a proof of the bold-face box requesting Miss Prudence Dean to get in touch with the police. There was a bare space on the wall where Angelle Brann's photograph had hung. The photograph was at the engravers' now, being made into a halftone for page one. There was little room tonight for race horses and their doings in the *Broadway Times,* although the gamblers would be waiting at the newsstands for their past performances in spite of famine, war or Waldo.

Bart walked into the city room. Cole Denham hadn't taken the day off after all. He was sitting at his typewriter, still pale and rumpled, laboriously typing out his copy about Libby Holman and Clifton Webb and the *Little Shows* that had bedazzled Broadway nearly a quarter-century before.

Bart said, "Couldn't sleep?"

Denham had a paper cup of water on the desk beside him. He took a small bottle from his pocket, shook a white pill from it. He swallowed the pill, poured water after it. He said, "I don't think I'll ever sleep again. I've been taking sedatives all day, but my nerves are like hot wire."

"They checked your story," Bart told him. "It seems kosher. You can relax."

Denham said, "It's not the murder. I know now they couldn't charge me with that, no matter how hard up they are for a suspect. I got hysterical, I guess. But they can take me down and question me and let the newspapers know about it just to prove they're efficient and aren't neglecting any possible angles. My wife is a very sick woman. I was foolish, very foolish taking up with that poor girl at my age. It would be awful if my wife found out."

My wife is very sick, thought Bart. She's very rich, too. And Denham has tastes he can't afford on a drama critic's salary.

Denham said, "I understand the police are questioning Orville. I hope they aren't too rough on him. He's rather a sensitive boy, you know."

"I didn't know that you and Orville were chummy," Bart replied.

"I rather like him," Denham answered. "He's interested in the arts. So few young people are nowadays. I've taken him to an opening or two when the extra ticket wasn't being used and I've got passes for him and his girl friend to other shows from time to time. Once or twice I've taken him to Sardi's for coffee after a show, and we've talked a bit."

And I bet you sat at the table right beneath that caricature that Zito drew of you, preening yourself for Orville's benefit, Bart thought. Suddenly he remembered Grierson's crack about Orville "playing house" with his boy friend in New Jersey and he wondered just how close a relationship there might be between the boy and the middle-aged drama critic whose wife had been sick since their wedding night.

Denham was saying, "Of course, Orville *did* know Angelle. In fact, he made a rather unpleasant scene in her apartment one night. She told me about it."

"What kind of scene?" asked Bart.

"I expect it was Angelle's fault, really," Denham answered. "She was rather charmingly amoral, you know. I've no doubt she provoked the boy, after she'd got him up there on one pretext or another. Anyway, Orville rather lost his head, I'm afraid. He made advances that were—er—somewhat physical. Angelle suffered some minor bruises, she said."

You think Orville's a nice, intelligent, sensitive boy, but you just couldn't wait to tell me all about him attacking Angelle, could you? Bart thought. He said, "Angelle didn't bruise too easy," and walked off toward the turf desk.

He nodded to the man who sat in the slot. The man's eyes were monstrously magnified by the thick lenses of his glasses. He made marks on flimsies from the leased wire, looked up at Bart. Bart said, "Howzit, Tilden?"

Tilden said, "Same as usual. Horses running all over the place. Some are winning. Most are losing. You hear how old Pops is feeling?"

Bart shook his head. "Uh-uh. I think I'll call him. It's not like Pops to let a headache get him down."

Bart returned to his office and called Pops' hotel, a cave of sad-faced mien that glorified in the name of the Buckingham Chambers. When Pops came on the wire, it was immediately obvious he had taken a few to ease the misery of his migraine.

"How're you feeling?" Bart asked.

"Man," said Pops, "you should dig me. I look like Frankenstein's great-uncle."

"You get drunk last night, Pops?"

"Man, I had myself a do, I did. I was ambling and gambling. I had my pot-gut full of rotgut. I was shuffling off to Buffalo like old Bill Robinson, only I wasn't skipping the gutter any. I was Nero burning Rome down to the ground."

"What happened, Pops?"

"Most of it's not too clear. I was skunk-drunk. After we put the paper to bed there was a stud game going with the printers in the composing room. I sat in and inside an hour I had all the money in the game. I couldn't get anything in the hole but aces. So I started drinking and I met a girl and I asked her to be a daughter to me, I think, but she wouldn't, so I went out looking for another game. I know a race-horse tout calls himself Colonel Shelby. He lives on Forty-ninth and usually there's action of some kind in his flat. I went there, but when I was about to ring the bell, police cars came up, so I figured they were raiding the joint and I scrammed. I don't know what time I wound up in my pad."

Very neat, thought Bart. It explains everything quite nicely just in case somebody saw Pops coming out of the house on Forty-ninth or going in there. Nobody could dispute his story, either. Nobody but a girl named Angelle Brann, maybe, and Angelle Brann was lying in a refrigerated place on Twenty-ninth Street where the customers don't talk or even move.

"Maybe I'll drop by tonight and hold your head," said Bart.

"Maybe you'll find me," Pops answered, "unless I find a game first. Or maybe they'll have me stuffed by then and on exhibit in Macomber's Funeral Parlor in Columbus Circle."

Bart hung up. He made desultory marks on proof sheets that were stacked on his desk. He noted absently that somebody had again inserted the bum joke about Miss Jane Russell and Three-D into the "Big Street" column. Suddenly he realized that now all the copy about Waldo and his murders was written and headlined and edited he had no further interest in the night's edition. He sat staring at the vacant space on the wall where Angelle's almost-nude photograph had hung. Angelle's body was swathed in a city-laundered sheet now. Mercifully, the sheet was pulled up over her lye-scorched face. But Bart could see the scarred face in the blank space on the wall. The eyes were accusing and they asked a question. The eyes asked "Why?"

And there wasn't any answer.

Why were so many Waldos loose in the land? Why should sweet and soft and healthy young animals like Angelle have their flesh ripped with knives and bludgeoned with hammers? Why did women fear to walk the lighted streets at night? Why had all the city's parks, built for children's play and old folks' relaxation, become dark, fearsome, Gothic stretches inhabited by muggers and murderers and perverts who waited silently?

When had it happened? When had the world gone suddenly sour? When had the human mind ceased to function as a thinking instrument and become a repository of insanely violent lusts or of trembling, abject fear? What hour of what day had the universal brotherhood of Suspicion been activated? How was it possible for a man like Bart Hardin to sit there and wonder if a bumbling, seriocomic adolescent lout like Orville or a precise and pedagogic little man like Denham or a sick and wasted human being like Clements or a cheerful, pot-bellied foxy grandpa like Pops could be a psychopathic murderer?

The eyes in the blank space on the grimy wall asked many questions, and Hardin had no answers.

He thought of Broadway, the world he knew best. When had it changed? Was it during the Great Depression of the Thirties when the apple-sellers came? No, thought Bart, it wasn't then. There was a peculiar dignity to the apple-sellers. It took courage for strong men to stand on corners, wearing the last vestiges of their pride in the form of overseas caps and little campaign ribbons, offering beggars' wares to earn money for their children's milk. There was even a peculiar sort of courage implicit in the bankrupt rich man who drank the last of his bonded booze and stuck a flower in his buttonhole before he stepped into space from a twentieth-storey window.

Broadway had been brash and loud and slightly vulgar

even in his father's day, but its exhibitionism was gay and pleasant then, like the colorful stridency of a circus. Its flashing lights were as naively self-assertive as the studs and stickpins of Diamond Jim Brady. Now, thought Bart, Broadway was a sinister place, full of craven people who walked in fear. Fear was a new and terrible force that grew like a cancer at the core of the world. People could not put a name to their fear any more than the cops could put a name to Waldo.

The eyes stared from the blank space on the wall. You're a man, they said, a man with mind and muscle. Why do you sit there impotent? Bart's clenched fist hit the desk a resounding blow and on the other side of the partition, Cole Denham jumped nervously.

"You wanna smash," Maclaren had said. But smashing did no good. Smashing only bruised your knuckles.

Heeltaps sounded outside the office, slowed down, paused uncertainly. "Oh, how do you do, Mr. Denham," said a girlish voice. "I wondered if I could possibly see Mr. Hardin for just a minute?"

"Good afternoon, Miss Larsen. I'm sure any man would welcome such charming company," Denham answered gallantly.

"Oh, thank you, Mr. Denham. I—I suppose it's really too much to hope, but Orville thought you might drop around to the Church of the Theater to see me in the Drama Club show tomorrow night."

"He asked me, Miss Larsen, and I'm terribly sorry I can't. There's a Broadway opening. A very special opening. A friend of the paper's owner is the star. However, I promised Orville to attend your dress rehearsal this evening."

"Well, I told Orville you were much too important for such an amateur thing, anyway." The girl's voice was disappointed.

"I'm not important, Miss Larsen," Denham said. "I'm just a little man who writes little pieces for the paper." He raised his voice, called through the partition, "Hardin! There's someone here to see you."

Bart rose, called, "Come in."

Bart greeted the lovely youngster with a smile. "Hello, honey," he said. "You look upset, but it's becoming to you. Take a chair."

Helen Larsen sat down, smoothing her skirt over her knees. She said, "I went back to the morgue looking for Orville. He isn't there and I'm worried."

"Orville's all right," Bart assured her. "He had to go out for awhile."

"The police have him, don't they, Mr. Hardin? I know they do."

"Why on earth should you think that?"

Helen said, "It's all my fault." She dabbed at her blue eyes with a bit of wispy lace. "Poor Orville's so jealous. He thinks I've got a crush on Mr. Arnold, the director of this show I'm in. It's so silly. Why, Mr. Arnold's nearly thirty."

Bart winced. Helen added hastily, "I don't mean thirty's *old*, of course, it's just mature. I mean, a woman sees a man like you, Mr. Hardin, she doesn't think of him as old or young, she just thinks of him as kind of ageless. I mean she doesn't expect him to be a raving beauty like a matinée idol or something, she just thinks of him as kind of *male*. I mean, no matter what his age is, he just seems kind of, well, strong and dependable and all. . . ."

Bart grinned. "Maybe I'm not pretty, honey," he said, "but I wear pretty vests. And I'm over thirty, too."

"Well, anyway, Orville wanted to pick me up at the rehearsal for this show we're giving tomorrow night in the Church of the Theater on Forty-ninth Street. But Mr. Arnold said we'd be very late because we had to get the rough edges off and all, so I told Orville not to try to wait for me. His mother goes simply crazy if he gets home late. Well, he thought I had a date with Mr. Arnold or something and he said he was going out with some chorus girl. Some *floozie*, he said. I didn't pay any attention because he's always trying to impress me how attractive he is to sophisticated showgirls and actresses and all and you'd think, honestly, they were just fighting to *seduce* him, really now, I mean. We had a fight down here at the office and he called me again when he was through work and said he had this date with some older woman who had been making passes at him. He said she did the dance of seven veils or something at a place called the Salome Club. Well, we rehearsed so late I didn't get up till nearly noon and that's the first I knew about this murder. Orville told me the woman he had a date with was named Angelle Brann! I tried like mad to get him on the phone and when I couldn't I came down here."

"You tell this to anybody?" Bart asked.

"No, Mr. Hardin. No one but you. The police couldn't drag it out of me with wild horses. I expect Orville told them another story."

"I bet he did, too, sweetheart," said a voice.

Romano was standing in the doorway, his hat on the back of his head, sweat running down his swarthy face. He nodded affably to the girl, said, "You're mighty pretty, sweetheart. I got a daughter looks something like you, only she's brunette. She's going to Marymount this fall if I only keep my job. You go to school?"

Helen said, "I attend the Academy of Dramatic Arts."

"That's nice," said Romano. "You act real good and Mr. Hardin will put your picture in the paper." He turned to Bart, said, "You need a dog-walker? I got one just outside for you."

"What's the pitch?" Bart asked.

"This Orville character should play the horses," Romano answered. "It starts raining atom bombs, he'll get caught in Mammoth Cave. He's got an alibi every other suspect offers and not one in ten thousand can ever prove. The one about going to a picture show alone. Orville proved it. They got girl ushers at this Art Theater. There was one on duty Orville had met in some Village coffee shop. After she seated the customers for the last show she sat right alongside him in the last row till the show was over. He waited for her and after that they went to the Rienzi Coffee Shop on MacDougal Street and talked about something called Existentialism, which I will bet Orville cannot spell. Anyway, we checked the girl and we checked the coffee shop and I got another suspect the D.A. will never take before twelve good men and true."

"You mean he didn't have a date with Angelle Brann at all?" asked Helen, her face flushing prettily.

"Not unless he took her to the picture show," Romano answered.

Orville's flaming hair loomed above Romano in the doorway. "Helen!" he exclaimed, looking vastly pleased. "The police have been grilling me all day."

"You!" flared Miss Larsen. "Why, you nasty, dirty liar, you! Don't ever speak to me again!"

She pushed her trim young body past Orville's bulk and flounced out of the office. Orville gazed after her, his mouth hanging open.

"I just don't understand women," Orville said. "I don't understand them at all."

"Honey boy," said Romano, "that remark is not original."

Bart tossed a key to Orville, said, "Go down to my flat and walk Old Bones. It will take your mind off things."

Orville said, "Yes, sir, Mr. Hardin, but first I'd like to ask a question of the lieutenant here." He rubbed his bruised mouth. "Don't you think the city should pay for my new bridgework?" he inquired. "Thirty-seven-fifty is a lot of money."

"Don't push your luck too far," Romano advised him. "You resisted an officer in the performance of his duty and you beat a rap all in one day. Don't sue City Hall."

Orville shook his head. "It wasn't ethical for that detective to hit me," he declared. "It wasn't ethical at all."

Orville left the office. Romano sighed, sank into a chair and untied his shoelaces. He said, "It didn't take much pressure to make our boy come through with a straight story, except he kept interrupting himself to claim he ought to have a lawyer present. Seems he's interested in ethics. He drove Grierson nuts. I had a hard time keeping Grierson from slapping him around a little. These young cops are so damn energetic. They got no patience, that's what it is. You been around as long as I have you get patient. Anyway we called the Eighth Precinct in the Village and they contacted this usherette and she bore out his story, time and all. They even checked that Rienzi Coffee Shop on MacDougal. It's an Existentialist joint where the boys wear beards and berets and the girls wear pants and everybody talks about some character called Jean-Paul Sartre, whoever the hell he is. Orville talked a lot about him. Seems he's kind of a hero to the younger set, like Jesse James and Buffalo Bill used to be to me when I was a kid. Anyway, they knew this girl well at the Rienzi and they remembered Orville-boy because he's so big and his hair's so red. You wouldn't have a can of foot powder around, would you? Once I get this Waldo out of my hair I got to take time off to see a chiropodist."

"No foot powder," Bart said, "but there's a crock of Irish in the bottom drawer."

"No good for aching feet," said Romano, plucking at the laces of his shoes and sliding them off at the heels. "This Orville admitted he went up to Brann's apartment. She 'lured' him up, the way he put it. Made me think of one of those old Theda Bara silents about the vampire and the fool there was. She went into the bathroom and put on something sexy-looking and Orville-boy thought that was a signal for him to make a grab. So he grabbed and she bopped him in the kisser. Also she scratched his face, he says. Says he had scratches for a week. You remember seeing 'em?"

Bart nodded. "I remember. He came in with his face scratched up about a month or so ago. Only he told me he tangled with an unfriendly alley cat in the Village."

The phone rang. Bart answered it.

A strange voice said, "Mr. Bart Hardin? This is Dr. Ridley's Sanitarium. I understand you're interested in a patient here. A Mr. Mark Clements."

"Interested enough to guarantee his board and lodging, if that's what you mean," Hardin answered.

"Mr. Clements has, ah—disappeared, Mr. Hardin. We missed him about half an hour ago. Of course, we use no forcible restraint on patients, but we do lock up their clothes. Mr. Clements was under sedatives and appeared entirely calm. He seems to have left his room, however, and to have gone into an orderly's quarters. The orderly was taking a bath. Mr. Clements appears to have donned the orderly's white uniform and to have taken his wallet and left the sanitarium."

"That's all he took?" asked Bart.

"No. He took something else, apparently. An odd thing for him to take. A lumbar needle."

"What's a lumbar needle?"

"It's a needle used for spinal taps, to draw off the spinal fluid and relieve pressure on the brain. We sometimes use it on patients who are disturbed, especially those who have fallen down and suffered head injuries that might result in concussion. It's a very large type of needle, about five inches long, I'd say."

"You mean it could be used as a lethal weapon?"

"A lethal weapon, Mr. Hardin? We hardly think of it as that. You don't believe that Mr. Clements is violent or dangerous, do you? If he is, you should not have sent him here. We don't take violent patients."

Bart said, "With a five-inch needle in his fist, Mark Clements may be the most dangerous man in New York City.

"Mark Clements may be better known as Waldo."

17 The clock on the Sligo Slasher's wall showed seven minutes to four when Bart Hardin hurried through the door. Tony Maclaren said, "Hello, ya Protestant bum. Ye're seven minutes early and ye're all outta breath. Have an Irish to relax ya, then wash yer feet and take a nap."

Bart said to Maclaren, "You seen Mark Clements today?"

The little man shook his head. "Not since the Old Top Sarge dragged him outta here yesterday afternoon to give him a bath."

Fritz Graham was at the far end of the bar, his belly resting comfortably against the mahogany, his pink face beaming alcoholically. Graham said, "If it's not my benefactor, the boy editor of Broadway. What gives, Editor? You looking for another beat?"

"You seen your collaborator this afternoon?" Bart asked him.

"Clements? The last time I saw Clements he was playing ring-around-a-rosy with a purple hippopotamus in a Turkish bath. I saw the Top Sarge a minute, though. He told me you'd sent Mark up to Old Doc Ridley's plush-lined Chamber of Horrors on the park."

"He got out. He stole a white uniform and a wallet and a five-inch lumbar needle and he took off like the bird with the big behind."

"A lumbar needle? What the hell would he want with that? I had one stuck up my spine once back in the days before Bellevue got exclusive and still took common drunks as patients. A lumbar needle is not a pleasant thing."

"Maybe he wants to kill somebody with it," Bart answered. "Maybe he wants to kill some young girl like Angelle Brann."

Graham looked blank. He said, "You've flipped, Editor. Mark's a low-down drunk like I am. But the only person he'll ever kill is himself. I always thought his trouble was that he's too gentle a soul to be a cop."

"He just missed Waldo twice," said Bart. "It's too much of a coincidence. Nobody else even got that close to Waldo once except the women that he killed."

Graham thrust his tongue between his lips and blew his breath out in a loud Bronx cheer. "Not Mark," he said. "Mark Clements isn't Waldo. I might be Waldo. I'm stewed and flabby and fat, but I'm tough. I could be Waldo. You could be Waldo, Editor. You wear funny-looking vests and you don't throw your weight around too much, but you're tough, too. You could be Waldo. But not Mark. Mark's soft. Whoever Waldo is, there's one thing certain. He's tough. Right down to the core."

Bart said, "There's nothing certain about a psycho. They come in all patterns."

Maclaren said, "Ye're all tight inside, ya Protestant bum. There's a drink there on the bar for ya. Toss it down and unwind yerself."

Bart glanced at the clock, said, "I've got three minutes to go."

Graham gave a short laugh. "The stickler for discipline," he said. "Never take a drink till four and you never become a bum like fat Fritz Graham. Iron will power you've got, and you prove it to yourself every day, don't you, Editor? Some day something's going to happen. It'll happen at ten o'clock in the morning or two o'clock in the afternoon. Something's going to happen that'll tear the guts out of you, and when it does you'll reach for the bottle and pull out the cork and pour it down without bothering with a shot glass, whatever time it is. I controlled my drinking once. I did my work and then I did my drinking. But something happened and now I do my drinking and to hell with work. Hardin's still got money to deposit for me, Maclaren. Fill it up."

Bart said, "I'll wait till four o'clock. It's a kind of habit." He gave Maclaren the rest of the money he owed Graham.

At four exactly he took the first one. He was in no hurry to leave. As far as he was concerned, the paper had already gone to bed, except for the race results which Tilden, sitting in for Pops, would handle adequately enough. The paper's columns were filled with Waldo just as the minds of Broadway's people were filled with Waldo. Waldo was more than a shadowy menace bent on murder. Waldo was a symbol of the vague fears and uncertainties that motivated the jumpy citizens of a jittery street. There was nothing more he could do about Waldo. If Waldo was a wild-eyed drunk in a white hospital uniform who brandished a long, sharp needle, he should be easy to find. The police knew Clements and they knew that he was on the loose. He had been one of them just a few months ago. Romano had set the bloodhounds after Clements already. All over the Times Square district men in plain clothes were wandering in and out of bars and cheap hotels and other haunts that Clements might frequent seeking a crazy lush in a white duck suit. Hardin thought of Romano's silently accusing eyes when he had told him of Clements' relations with Angelle and of the knife that had been stolen from the kitchen of the Salome Club. Probably he should have turned Clements over to the cops instead of sending him to Dr. Ridley's souse trap on the park. But Bart had thought that Clements had a vital piece of information locked in his addled brain and he doubted that the blows and blustering of police interrogation would force the lock. All men guessed wrong at times, he thought. If they didn't, there'd be no horseracing.

After an hour had passed, Bart pushed back his empty glass and refused another on the house. He said to Tony Maclaren, "If Clements should come in, don't let him out that door, Maclaren. Call me or call the cops, but keep him here."

Maclaren's right slashed through the air viciously and he grunted. "The bum won't go through the door," he said. "I'll hit him with the right cross that broke the jaw of Froggy Fanton, the lightweight champion of France. On St. Patrick's Day of 1920, it was, in the second minute of the eleventh round."

Bart left, walked up Eighth Avenue. James Lennox, the old actor who had been a friend of Bart's father, was waiting outside the *Broadway Times* office. His shiny and mended blue serge was creased to razor sharpness and his ancient pearl-gray felt was set at a jaunty angle. In his buttonhole was a flower from old Bessie's basket and it was only slightly wilted. He seemed as proud and excited as an ingenue reading her first notices. He held a manila folder under his arm.

"Bart, my boy!" Lennox exclaimed happily. "I inquired for you inside and the young lady at the desk informed me you had gone out for a spot of tea. Afternoon tea is a gracious, old-fashioned custom we see too little of nowadays. I found it most refreshing during my days in the theater. Always had a kettle on the gas ring in my dressing room."

Bart grinned, said, "I hate to disillusion you, but the kind of tea I take gives you alcoholic halitosis."

Lennox presented the manila folder to Bart with the flourish of a college regent conferring an honorary degree upon a celebrity. "It's finished, Bart!" he declared. "My little jottings about the great Richard Mansfield and the Broadway of another time. I hope your paper may find them of some historical value."

Bart took the folder, said, "Let's go inside and I'll look your copy over."

As they passed Cole Denham's desk, the drama critic called to Bart and proffered him a small envelope. "The theater sent your tickets over with mine for the Arlene Lash opening tomorrow night," he said. Bart nodded, pocketed the envelope, waved Lennox into his cubbyhole office. He sat at the roll-top desk and opened the folder. There were many sheets of paper inside covered with writing so precise it appeared to be copperplate. Bart glanced through the pages. The old man's phrases were florid and stilted enough to be worthy of the purple ink in which they were written. If he used the copy, much of it would have to be killed and all of it would have to be rewritten. But it could be used, he decided, as a Sunday feature on some rainy day when the paper was wide-open. The rounded sentences and lush adjectives re-created a forgotten street on which tall, proud men walked with lovely women on their arms.

Bart said, "It's fine, sir, fine. I'll use it some day very soon. I'll give you a by-line, too, and run a little biographical introduction about your achievements on the stage. Also, and more important, maybe, I'll make you a space-rate voucher for the cashier and you can cash it right away."

He found a voucher pad and filled it out for a generous sum. The old man's eyes were shining. Bart knew that poor as he was, the money would mean less to Lennox than seeing his name printed again in a Broadway paper. Lennox looked at the slip unbelievingly and said, "Are you quite sure it's worth all this? It seems such a large sum, Bart."

Bart said, "The *Broadway Times* has never overpaid a contributor yet."

He took the theater tickets from his pocket, checked the location of the seats. "How long has it been since you attended a Broadway opening?" he asked the old man.

Lennox said, "Why, Bart, I *played* in a Broadway opening

not so long ago. It was in one of those Federal-project plays during the Depression. I didn't have many sides, of course. I played a butler."

Bart handed Lennox one of the tickets. He said, "Maybe you'd like to catch Miss Arlene Lash in *A Borrowed House* tomorrow night. She's a *protégée* of Maddox Slade who owns this rag. Maybe she can't act, but she's got one hell of a chest expansion. Sorry I can't give you a ticket for a friend, but I'll have to put in an appearance myself for a little while at least."

Lennox said, "You're very good, Bart. I really don't have friends any more, except you and a few people in old actors' homes that I visit occasionally. It would be very wonderful to go to the theater again. I seldom do, because these modern house managers don't extend professional courtesies as they used to. But I'm really afraid my evening clothes are a bit out of fashion."

"Don't let that worry you," said Bart. "The only tails and top hats on Broadway nowadays are worn by the sandwich men who carry signboards. Young guys are likely to wear sports shirts to openings and dolls appear in blue jeans."

The old man left, muttering effusive gratitude, clutching the ticket and the voucher as if they were winning numbers in the Irish Sweepstakes.

Bart began to dummy in the slug lines of stories, mostly about Waldo, on layout sheets ruled into eight columns. "WALDO," "MURDER," "LETTER," "EX-COP," the slug lines read. He examined the engravers' proofs of the cuts of Waldo's letter and of Angelle Brann's cheesecake photograph. He was looking at Angelle's picture and thinking of the black satin girdle on his mantelpiece and of the girl's funny, high-pitched voice and of the silly pet name "Blond Beast" she'd given him when Orville came trundling into the office. Orville laid a key on Bart's desk, said, "I took Old Bones out for his walk, sir, but he was kind of mean and peevish. He was sleepy. You must have got him up too early."

"Old Bones and you have something in common," Bart replied. "The cops bothered you both today."

Orville handed Bart a letter, said, "Miss Bertha sent this in, sir. It just came special-delivery mail."

The envelope was addressed by typewriter to "Editor, The Broadway Times." It had been posted in Times Square at nine-thirty that morning.

Bart ripped the envelope open, glanced briefly at the letter. His hard face froze. Orville said, "What's the matter, Mr. Hardin, sir? Is something wrong?"

"Speaking as a newspaperman," Bart answered, "everything is fine. I've got myself another beat on the hottest story since

95

Harry Thaw shot Stanford White. This letter is from Waldo."
The letter read:

Editor,
The Broadway Times
Sir:
    You did not take my previous communication
seriously enough to publish it. I trust the events of
last evening have proved I am no idle boaster.
    I strike again on Friday night. Another young girl
will die between the acts of a theatrical production.
    This is fair warning.

                              Respectfully,
                                  "Waldo"

Bart reached for the phone, touched it, paused. There was
something familiar about the typing of the letter. It had not
been typed on the same machine as the first one. This was pica
type. The other had been élite. There were no high A's. But
the typing had certain peculiarities. The machine skipped and
spaced after the letter N. Bart turned to his own machine, inserted paper in the roller, typed "Now is the time for all
good men to come to the aid of the party." He tore the sheet
out, laid it alongside Waldo's letter. He again switched on
the gooseneck lamp, picked up the magnifying glass. The letter
had been typed on his own machine. That typewriter had been
in Orville Cartwright's morgue early in the morning, just as
the machine had been in the morgue at the time Waldo's first
letter was written. Bart glanced up at Orville Cartwright who
still stood beside the desk, his face as blank as usual. Bart
said, "Stand by a minute." Then he picked up the phone, said
to Bertha, "Get me Pete Cruise fast. Then get me the skipper
in the composing room. Then get me Lieutenant Romano at
Manhattan West."
    To Pete Cruise he said, "I'm sending up another Waldo
letter. I want a fast print made and I want the print sent
through to engraving marked 'Extra Rush.' I want the cut in
an hour and a half. I'm getting on the street early, even if I
have to fudge-box the late race results or leave 'em out. Give
the letter back to Orville to take to the police."
    To the skipper in the composing room he said, "There's
a makeover on page one. New banner line and new story.
Cut of that Waldo letter goes to page three in place of that
shot of Al Vanderbilt's horse. New cut coming for page one.
We lock the forms at seven and to hell with the horse players."
    To Romano he said, "A new love letter from Waldo just
arrived. You'll have it in half an hour. It was unquestionably
written on my own typewriter, but that doesn't mean much.

The office is never locked. Broadway reporters wander around all night and they drop in here at any hour they please to write up the gossip they've collected. Also Maddox Slade is the clubby sort. He likes theatrical people to feel this office is a second home for them, that they can come around any time to chew the rag and relax. Figures we get news tips about the Street that way. Only thing worth stealing is in the business office. That's locked up after hours. There's a watchman, but he spends most of his time taking naps. I'll read you the letter."

Bart read the letter to Romano. Romano said, "Why couldn't he have waited a little while longer? I was just going home to soak my feet."

Bart folded a piece of copy paper. He shoved the letter and envelope inside the paper with a pencil, said to Orville, "Take this up to Pete Cruise and tell him to use rubber gloves when he handles it. Be careful yourself. You get your fingerprints on it, Romano will send you to the electric chair."

"They're already on the envelope, I guess, sir," said Orville.

"I'll alibi you for that," Bart promised. "Wait around until Pete is through shooting the letter. Then take it down to Lieutenant Romano at Manhattan West. And don't let Grierson knock any more of your teeth out. Tell him you'll sue if he does."

Orville left, holding the letter gingerly in the folded paper. Bart swiveled his chair to the typewriter that skipped three spaces every time you hit the letter N and banged at it with two busy fingers, writing the story of Waldo's latest threat. He picked up a fat pencil and copy-read the story. Then he wrote a new banner line, double-decking it:

WALDO WILL KILL BETWEEN
THE ACTS TOMORROW NIGHT

At the top of the story he wrote "! ! ! EXCLUSIVE ! ! !" and marked the word for 24-point bold-face caps. He wrote drop-heads and jump-heads. Then he climbed the steps to the composing room with the copy and the heads in his hand. He supervised the make-up of the paper.

A little before seven the cut of Waldo's letter arrived from the engraver and was dropped into the already leaded form. The make-up man turned a crank and locked page one and the wheeled type table was pushed off to the stereotyper by a begrimed galley boy. Bart returned to his office, called the pressroom and ordered an extra-heavy run. The *Broadway Times*, he suspected, was going to be a sellout tonight. The floor trembled as the old press started up in the basement. Minutes later an ink-stained youth slapped a bundle of papers stamped "SAMPLE COPY" on Bart's desk. Bart scanned the paper, marking minor typographical errors for correction in the replate.

It was the livest edition of the *Broadway Times* since Arnold Rothstein had been shot down in the Park Central Hotel, back in his father's day, Bart reflected.

He didn't realize that the most important item in the paper was a small, bold-face box requesting one Prudence Dean to get in touch with the police.

18 The elevator boy tapped lightly on the door of Mrs. Belknap's terrace apartment. Prudence Dean opened the door immediately. The elevator boy said, "The old lady asleep? Here's the paper you wanted, Miss Dean. Had to go all the way to Lexington Avenue to get it."

Miss Dean said, "She's asleep, but she sleeps very lightly. I don't want to waken her." Miss Dean spoke in a husky whisper.

The elevator boy said, "Can't figure you reading a paper like the *Broadway Times*. Wouldn't ever dig you for a horse player, Miss Dean."

"I'm interested in the theater," Miss Dean replied. "Being companion to an elderly lady is a twenty-four-hour job and I never even get to go to a picture show any more except on my day off. So I read about the theater."

The elevator boy proffered change from the dollar bill Miss Dean had given him to buy the paper. Miss Dean said, "That's all right, Henry. Keep the change."

The boy said, "Aw, that's too much tip, Miss Dean. The rich people here don't tip like that. No reason you should. You work for a living same as I do. Glad to do you a favor any time." He forced her to take the change.

Miss Dean said, "Well, thanks, Henry. Thanks and good night."

The elevator boy thought that Miss Dean might look like a square from Delaware but that her heart was in the right place and she was regular. Only poor folks, he mused, ever tipped enough. This big apartment house on Fifth Avenue, right across from the Metropolitan Museum of Art, was full of millionaires who spent their time worrying about the income tax and Henry was lucky to get an occasional quarter from any of them, no matter how polite and obliging he might be. This Miss Dean wasn't anybody's dreamboat, but she

was all right just the same. She wouldn't look so square and
dumpy if she didn't wear those aunty's-panties clothes that
reminded him of the uniform they forced his kid sister to wear
at the convent school. He couldn't see any reason for those
big, round, black-rimmed glasses, either. They made Miss
Dean look like a frightened barn owl. If she'd only get herself
a flashy set of threads and frizz her straight dark hair a little
and put on some war paint instead of chalk-white talcum
powder and buy a set of those slant-eyed glasses with rhine-
stones in the rims Miss Dean might get by in a crowd even
though she wouldn't be a slick chick exactly.

Miss Dean returned to the dimly lighted and enormous living room of Mrs. Belknap's tower apartment. The rather
dowdy young woman in the shapeless clothes and goggle-like
glasses seemed ludicrously incongruous in this rich setting of
crystal and needlepoint and satin and gold-leaf and velvety
Persian rugs. She sat down on a fragile little love seat upholstered in pastel pink satin and appeared about as out of place
as a mouse that has settled itself upon an old-fashioned, lacy
Valentine. The love seat was her favorite piece of furniture,
however. When she sat there she felt as if she were perched on
a little pink cloud, way up in the sky, an illusion that was
heightened by the fact that she could look out the huge picture
window. Far below was spread the black-green reaches of
Central Park and the twinkling never-never land of nighttime
New York. Miss Dean liked nothing better than to sit on
her fluffy pink cloud and gaze down on the fairy scene beneath her and play the Swiss music box that Mrs. Belknap
had brought back from one of the European holidays she had
enjoyed with Mr. Belknap when he was alive. The music box
played a tinkly tune called "Angels' Choir" and when the
machinery was set in motion two exquisitely carved little
angels on top of the box began to swirl about in waltz time.
Miss Dean took a childish delight in the music box and the
waltzing angels, but she could not wind it up now. It was not
quite nine o'clock but the elderly lady she served as companion had already retired for the night. Mrs. Belknap had
had a bad day with her heart condition and they'd had to call
in the doctor and she had missed her usual afternoon nap.

Miss Dean switched on a silk-shaded lamp beside the love
seat and started to open the paper that the elevator boy had
bought for her. Then she suddenly folded the paper again
and hid it beneath a cushion of the love seat. She walked
down a hallway and peered through a half-opened door into
a bedroom in which a tiny night light was burning just brightly enough to cast a soft and hazy radiance over the old woman
on the canopied bed. Mrs. Belknap's wrinkled, patrician face
was relaxed and her eyes were closed in sleep. Her breath

99

made tiny, peanut-whistle sounds as it issued through her parted lips.

Prudence Dean stood at the door and watched the old lady's fluttery breathing. She made no sound, but she was praying inside herself. "Please, God," she was saying, "make her feel all right when she wakes up in the morning. Please, God, don't let her die or get sent to a hospital. Let her stay here so I can take care of her. Please don't let her die, even if she's awfully old. She's sweet and kind and good and I love her, God. I love her like she was my mother."

Miss Dean tiptoed down the hallway to the living room. She took her paper from beneath the love seat, sat down, unfolded the *Broadway Times*. She shivered as the big, black, frightening words of the headlines leaped out at her: "WALDO," "KILL," "TERROR," "MURDER."

Such words did not belong in this quiet and softly lighted room with its precious mementoes of a gentle lady's tranquil life.

Miss Dean did not turn immediately to Cole Denham's drama column as her expressed interest in the theater might indicate she would. Instead she read avidly every word of every story about Waldo and his murders and the murder of tomorrow that he threatened.

Miss Dean was deadly afraid of Waldo. She tried to tell herself that here in this abode of the rich and the protected her fears were nothing more than hysteria and she was a practical young person who did not sympathize with hysterical females. This building was guarded by stout doors and locks and bolts and doormen and elevator men and a superintendent and a manager and the Holmes Protective Agency. But just the same, Miss Prudence Dean was afraid of Waldo.

Miss Dean had read all the stories about Waldo with the rapt and shocked and guilty attention of a holy nun perusing the ritual of a Black Mass when she suddenly caught her breath and held it for a long moment before exhaling with a hissing sound. Miss Dean's own name was printed there right on page one. "ATENTION PRUDENCE DEAN," the headline said. It was a very small headline indeed in relation to the ones about Waldo. Beneath her name appeared a brief notice to the effect that the police would like her to come forward, as she had been mentioned in the diary of the late Angelle Brann. Miss Dean was terribly upset. Angelle Brann had not been the type of young woman with whom a gentle lady's companion should have any connection whatsoever.

Miss Dean crossed to a library table and picked up a copy of the *World-Telegram and Sun* which Mrs. Belknap had delivered to the apartment each evening. She had already read the stories about Waldo in the paper, but now she scanned every page, clear back to the comics and classified ads, with engrossed attention. She heaved a sigh of relief when she discovered that there was no mention of Prudence Dean in the paper. She must remember first thing in the morning to pick up the *Herald Tribune*, which was also delivered to the apartment, before the maid took it in with Mrs. Belknap's breakfast tray. Miss Dean thanked her stars that this was Thursday, the standard maid's day off in New York City. She had important business to transact immediately and the presence of a maid would complicate things greatly.

Now that she knew the police were seeking her, Miss Dean was even more afraid of Waldo. She was afraid that the police might inadvertently lead Waldo right to her. Her fear of Waldo had a very sound basis, indeed, Miss Dean reflected. Besides the psychopathic murderer himself, Miss Dean was the only living person who knew Waldo's real identity.

Miss Dean crossed the room again and picked up the telephone. She extended a stubby forefinger on which the unpainted nail was cut short and square and hooked it into the slot marked "Operator."

When the operator's metallic voice sounded in her ear, Prudence Dean said very softly: "Give me the police."

19 Bart Hardin had finished his dinner earlier than usual because the urgency of the Waldo story had caused him to put the *Broadway Times* on the street almost an hour before its regular time. It was barely nine o'clock. He stood now outside the Saddle and Whip watching the crowds do a St. Vitus dance to the unmelodic symphony of the traffic. Several denizens of Broadway with padded shoulders and hats a size too large for them were standing there beside him. None of them ever went inside the restaurant but they stood outside every night. They reminded Bart of his father's description of a Broadway phony: "He eats at the Automat and picks his teeth outside the Saddle and Whip."

Hardin had dined on excellent English mutton chops washed down by still ale drawn from a cask, which was a specialty of the house, but he felt none of the pleasant lassitude that should result from a good and hearty meal. The raw ends of his nerves tingled as they had when he was on a night patrol in Korea and he could feel that the enemy was all around him even though he could not see him. He was haunted by the specter of Waldo. His pale, restless eyes searched the crowds for the flicker of a white hospital orderly's uniform and he snorted with laughter, thinking of himself as a small boy in a haunted house whose bugging eyes peer through the gloom seeking the flash of ghostly vestments. He thought also of Pops Taylor's crinkled old face fringed by its monkish tonsure and he wondered if Pops were still lying on his bed of pain and eating aspirin for his sins.

Hardin had a strange feeling that Waldo—whoever he was —was within yards or even feet of him there in the ceaselessly shifting, gawping crowds. He was wrong.

Waldo was some five blocks east of the spot where Hardin stood at the moment, eating his dinner in a small café and reading the Broadway Times. *Waldo was staring at the name of Prudence Dean on the first page of the paper and his eyes were speculative.*

Bart decided to visit Pops at his pad on Jacobs Beach. He walked to Forty-ninth and turned west. Just past the Church of the Theater was the Buckingham Chambers, an old building whose crumbling brick was crusted by generations of city muck. Bart entered the lobby and wondered why a man who made a fair salary should choose to live in such a squalid dump. The lobby was tiled and it reminded Bart unpleasantly of an uncleaned public toilet. It even smelled like one. Behind the scarred desk sat a man with liverish spots on his face who wore a sickeningly chartreuse sports shirt. The man was studying the past-performance pages of the *Broadway Times*.

Hardin said, "Howzit, Grulik?"

Grulik looked up, scowled, said, "What gives you got this Waldo all over the paper? Who wants Waldo? Where's the horse news, Editor? This Waldo don't help a man to win himself a bet. So who's Waldo, anyway? He's a guy who chills himself a few Broadway chippies. Too damn many chippies cluttering up the streets, who cares? Is Waldo running in the daily double at Jamaica, maybe?"

Bart said, "Is Pops Taylor still upstairs counting the lavender crocodiles on his ceiling?"

Grulik shook his oily head. "Uh-uh. Some character called up and told Pops the juice is on for the floating crap game again. He took off like a madam with a vice cop on her tail."

"The hell you say! I thought Moe Selig was going to mix the floater so long as the D.A. let his books alone."

"First I've heard of any floater action in the past three months," said Grulik. "But this steerer called up about a hour ago and said that Moe was calling all shooters again."

"Who was the steerer that called?" Bart asked.

"You mean steerers got names now?" said Grulik. "How

the hell should I know? Just a character who called up on the phone. Pops is down on the sucker list of every smart in town."

"He tell you where the game was?"

"Sure. In case I wanted to pass the word along to other shooters. Maybe you."

"Not me," said Bart. "With the bankroll I've got in my jeans tonight I couldn't sit in a fast parchesi game. But I might kibitz. Where is it?"

"In a room at the Karnak Baths, according to the character. Room 312."

"That's not possible!" Bart exclaimed. "I was in that room just this morning. It's so small you couldn't get more than three shooters in if you moved out the furniture."

Grulik shrugged. "Three's a crowd, if they're packing cabbage," he declared. "Pops is packing. He did a Canfield at stud last night, I hear."

Bart said, "Well, a Turkish bath's a good place for shooters to get cleaned." He left the Buckingham, walked to Eighth Avenue, crossed the street and headed north. Old Tom Trigg, the Negro who had been a promising heavyweight in an other era, was standing outside Madison Square Garden, all ginned up and looking for a handout.

Bart thrust change into the big, brown paw, said, "Tom, you look like you're hurting for a gin."

"*Always* hurting for a gin, Mist' Bart," the old man said. "I slug myself with gin I feel as good as ole Jack Johnson used to feel when he landed that snaky left of his."

"Tom," said Bart, "if the word was out about the floating crap game, you'd get it, wouldn't you?"

"If the rumble is out, I get it sure," said Trigg. "Mist' Moe know old Tom can make hisself a buck steering shooters to the floater."

"The rumble out tonight?"

"Ain't no rumble 'cause they ain't no floater," said Tom. "Ain't been no rumble now three-foah months anyway. Minute there's a rumble, ole Tom hears it. You craving action, I could send you to a certain back room where a wheel is spinning and they ain't no Double O for the house, Mist' Bart."

Bart said, "I heard the shooters are over at the Karnak Baths tonight."

"Mist' Bart," said the old Negro, "you been listening to a man that's talking through the hole in his haid. You mean they running a crap game in a steam room now? I see Mist' Moe jes this afternoon, and he's in company with Mist' Lenny Fassio, the big boss hisself. They both speak to me right friendly and stake me to a little flop and eating money and don't neither one give me a rumble about the floating game. They start up that floating game again, the D.A. man close down all the books and numbers business in town."

"A man hears lots of stories on this street and most of 'em are lies," said Bart. "Thanks, Tom."

"When the rumble's out for the floating game you'll be the first ole Tom tells," said Trigg. "You one sport knows a ole man got to have his gin."

Bart walked back toward Jacobs Beach. He stopped at a red-fronted tobacco store and purchased a cigar. In deference to his financial condition, which was always acute on Thursday, the eve of payday, he bought a fifty-cent cigar instead of a dollar perfecto. It was his idea of economy. Outside the store he encountered old Bessie, the flower seller, hurrying along with her freight of wilted merchandise to catch the theater crowds during the first curtain break.

"Hello, handsome!" Bessie screeched. "I missed you this afternoon, but I saved your bachelor button." She thrust a purple cornflower through his lapel. Bart dropped change into her cup and reflected that his involved economy was upset again. "I'm happy as hell, tonight," old Bessie cackled. "I'm the happiest broad on Broadway. You know why? Because I'm old as Mrs. God and I got a mole on my chin and only four teeth in my head. There's many a young doll on Broadway that envies old Bessie tonight. Waldo's got the young dolls scared right out of their pretty panties. But he don't scare old Bessie. Not even Waldo wants old Bessie any more."

Bart walked up Jacobs Beach, turned into the blinding blaze of Broadway. Shipping clerks in pearl-gray sharpy suits ogled plump stenographers and commented audibly upon their more interesting anatomical points. An elderly couple from Keokuk gazed wide-eyed at an enormous animated electric sign that depicted a dancing cat. A sightseeing barker with two bored shills in his bus chanted, "Leaving right away, folks. Chinatown, the Bowery GREEN-itch Village." A filth-caked panhandler spat at the heels of a passing policeman. A sailor said to his buddy, "Not in there. They got fifteen-cent beer just around the corner." An old man wearing a sandwich board that advertised a pawnshop gazed entranced into a haberdasher's crystal-bright window where twenty-dollar sports shirts were displayed.

From the newsstands the *Broadway Times* and other papers shrieked "Waldo!" In a soda fountain dancers with ochre-stained faces drank Cokes between the stage shows of a picture house and chattered about Waldo. "I think I'll stay home with a case of cramps tomorrow night. He could climb right in through our dressing-room window. The catch is broke." "He's an agent, that's who he is. He's some damn ten-percenter with a casting couch."

Bart Hardin hardly noticed the people who pressed around him on all sides. He searched the street for a faceless man. He felt that Waldo was almost close enough to touch. He was not far wrong.

Waldo was a block or two away now. Waldo was talking to himself. His lips moved soundlessly as he repeated the name, "Prudence Dean, Prudence Dean." His sleepy eyes appraised the young girls who passed by. "I must meet this Prudence Dean," Waldo told himself.

Bart Hardin turned into the Karnak Baths. Soljer, the beefy man with the lamb's-wool eyebrows, was at the desk, engrossed in a comic book that concerned the adventures of a fanged fiend with hairy ears and bright green eyes.

Bart said, "Howzit, Soljer? You been on duty long?"

Soljer said, "A little while. It's Banko's night, but his back is aching and he went up to his pad to try to sleep."

"There's a rumble out," said Hardin. "I hear you're playing host to the floating game tonight."

Soljer's mouth gaped open, displaying nuggets of purest gold. "Those cops!" he exclaimed. "Those lousy, stinking cops! First they say I got hoods, then they say I got fags, now they say I got shooters. What they think? They think maybe I drained the pool downstairs so the characters could bounce the dice?"

"They didn't say that," Bart told him. "They said the game was in Room 312, where I had those two lushes cooling out."

Soljer laughed until tears streamed from the little eyes beneath the heavy foliage. "Those cops!" he said. "Those stinking cops! If there's a game in 312, poor old Banko won't get much sleep. His pad is right next door in 314. You wanna know who's in 312, just for laughs? One of the rumdumbs you sent around, that's who. He came here this afternoon looking for a pad and he had money so I give him the one he just moved out of. He's a real gone hipster, that one is. Thinks he's young Doc Kildare now. He's flying around in a ice-cream suit and he had something looked like a hypodermic needle sticking out of one pocket and a fifth of rye sticking out of the other. Some characters you send me, Editor."

Bart stared hard at Soljer. "You mean Mark Clements is in Room 312?" he asked.

"I guess that's the name. The cop that looks like a lunger. The one got bounced on his fanny off the force last year."

Bart said, "Give me a passkey, Soljer. Give it to me quick. Then holler copper. Holler loud."

Soljer said, "Why should I holler? I don't want a copper. I don't even want the ex-cop that I got."

"Give me that key!" Bart demanded. "Is Pops Taylor up there with Clements, Soljer?"

Soljer's lamb's-wool eyebrows knit together. "Pops? He come in a while ago. Said he was going to see a friend. He took the stairs. I don't know where he went."

"The key!" barked Hardin. "Quick, Soljer. Give me the key and call the cops."

Soljer handed Bart a key on a large ring, said, "What the hell! What's up there, you're so lathered up?"

"Waldo, maybe," Bart said, starting for the stairs.

Soljer's fingers touched the phone. He said aloud, "Hoods, fags, shooters, the cops say I got. Now the man says I got Waldo."

Bart Hardin took the stairs two at a time. On the third floor he raced down a dimly lighted corridor. He listened at the door of 312 for a second. He could hear no sound. He turned the passkey in the lock, pushed the door open.

Pops Taylor lay on the threadbare carpet of the room, his rabbity old face aghast with naked terror. A weird figure in white clothing was bending over him, thrusting Pops' head back, holding a long, thin needle at his throat. Mark Clements' ashen face turned slowly as the door opened. The needle's point pricked the skin of Pops' throat as his assailant moved. A small crimson bubble began to well around the needle's point. Pops made a gurgling sound as he stifled the scream.

Clements' deep-sunk eyes were bright and mad. Clements said quite casually, "Don't come closer, Hardin. If you do I'll stick the needle through his throat. I'll pin him to the floor with it."

Hardin tried hard to keep his voice even. He said, "Why should you, Clements? Pops is an old man and he's harmless."

Pops gasped, "Please . . . please . . ." His beseeching eyes that seemed to look on death rolled in their sockets, pleaded with Bart.

Clements said, "He's not harmless. They gave me a little glass of stuff at the sanitarium. At first it made bells ring inside my head. But it cleared the fog. I remembered everything. I remembered who it was I saw running away from Angelle's house last night. It was this bastard. He killed the girl who was kind to me. This son of a bitch is Waldo!"

"No, please!" Pops' voice was hardly audible. There was a pink streak on his throat from the tiny prick of the needle's point.

"You don't have to kill him, Clements," Bart said. "Just hold him for the cops. If you catch Waldo you'll be reinstated on the force. You can start all over again. Not many men get a second chance."

"I'm done," said Clements. "I'll never make a cop again.

They fired me because I missed Waldo once. I've got him now. I'm going to kill him. Angelle was kind to me and he killed her and burned her pretty face and now he's going to die. But he's going to suffer first. The needle's going in slow. Slow, so he'll feel every inch of it."

The connecting door to the next room was a yard behind Clements. It was opening slowly. Bart tried hard not to look at it. He hardly dared to breathe. The door was fully opened now. The doorway was filled with the huge, bent form of broken-backed old Banko, teetering on his two stout canes. Banko's great-barreled body lunged farther and farther forward, balanced on the canes. Suddenly the two canes clattered to the floor. Banko's broken body smashed down on the floor beside Clements. At the same instant, one great, loglike arm swung through the air, encircled Clements' scrawny neck, closed like a vise. Clements was hurtled through the air, fell over Banko. Banko's left hand closed over the right wrist and the pressure was increased. Clements' tongue protruded from his mouth. His eyeballs bulged like those of a praying mantis. Clements slashed the long, thin needle wildly through the air, seeking Banko. Bart's size-ten blucher smashed down hard on Clements' thin wrist. The wrist cracked and the needle rolled away.

Bart said, "Okay, Banko. Don't squeeze any harder. He's almost dead."

Pops Taylor still lay on the floor, gasping, his horror-stricken eyes regarding the tableau. The eyes moved upward in their sockets. Old Pops had fainted dead away.

Heavy footsteps sounded in the corridor. Two uniformed policemen crashed into the little room. One said, "What the hell? What goes on here?"

Bart pointed to the recumbent figures of Pops Taylor and Mark Clements, said, "Hold these men for Lieutenant Romano of Homicide. Then help me up with this old man. He's crippled. Get his canes there."

They righted old Banko, sat him in a chair. He was breathing heavily. Pops Taylor made no sound. Clements whined like a wounded kitten.

Bart poured a stiff drink from a bottle on the dresser, handed it to Banko. He grinned. "Who was the best?" he asked the old wrestler.

Banko drank, said, "Joe Stecher. Joe Stecher was the best. But, by God, he never win a fall with a broken back."

20 At the first knock, Prudence Dean opened the door an inch or two, peered out to make sure it was a policeman and not Waldo. The policeman was not in uniform. He was a middle-aged man and swarthy, with rather classic features. He wore a battered felt on the back of his head. There was a tiny necklace of sweat beads at his hairline. Miss Dean thought he was rather handsome in a rugged sort of way, but he seemed dead on his feet now. She said, "Lieutenant Romano?"

When the swarthy man nodded and answered "Yes, ma'am," politely, she took the door off the safety chain, opened it, motioned him inside. She put a finger to her lips, said, "Mrs. Belknap is sleeping. Please don't make any noise." She did not lead Romano into the softly lighted living room. She took him down a short hall, pushed open a door covered by richly tooled leather that led into a small room. The room was paneled and shelved and lined with books in rich morocco bindings. The sofa and chairs were upholstered in dark red leather. The desk and tables were scrubbed oak. The andirons in the fireplace were fashioned in the shape of Napoleonic grenadiers and the single painting in the room was a Meissonier battle scene.

Romano sank into one of the cushioned chairs with a deep sigh. He said, "This is nice. This I like. It would be great just to sit here the rest of my life and read all these books and get real smart. Comfortable, too."

Miss Dean had closed the tooled-leather door. She opened it an inch, said, "I'll leave it open in case she calls. We can keep our voices down. This was Mr. Belknap's study when he was alive. He was a very educated man. Education is wonderful, don't you think? I'm a college graduate myself."

The lieutenant said, "That's nice. I got a daughter a little younger than you, I guess. She's going to college in the fall. To Marymount. At least I hope she is. College costs a lot nowadays. Where'd you go to school?"

"The University of Maryland," Miss Dean replied. "I took up social sciences. That was the field I worked in before I became a lady's companion. Social sciences. It's very interesting."

"You look pretty young to have had so much experience," said Romano.

Miss Dean said, "It's my round face. People with round

108

faces always look younger than they really are. I'm almost thirty."

"No!" exclaimed Romano. "I'd never have believed it. Let's see now, this friend of yours, Angelle Brann, the one that Waldo killed, was about twenty-five when she died, according to our best information. That about right, far as you know?"

Miss Dean pursed her small mouth that was innocent of lipstick and thought a moment. "About," she said. "I was twenty, just out of college, when I first knew her. She was one of my first cases. I was working for a social-service agency in Baltimore and she had just been paroled from Hickory Knoll. That's a reform school for girls in Baltimore County. She was about sixteen then, as I remember. Lieutenant, you told me over the phone that you found my name in her diary. Tell me, what did she say about me?"

"Nice things," Romano answered. "She mentioned your name just a couple or three times. Said she wished she was a good, sweet, moral girl like you. Things like that."

Miss Dean shook her head and lowered the eyes behind the big, round spectacles. "Poor child," she said. "Such an awful end for her. She had a most unfortunate life, Lieutenant, but she wasn't really bad. She was sweet, really. Kind and generous."

"We hoped you might be able to give us some information about her," Romano said. "We don't know much."

Miss Dean said, "I'm afraid I won't be too helpful. Her real name was Annie Branowski. She grew up in the steel town called Sparrows Point, a part of Greater Baltimore. Her father was a worthless drunkard. Her mother was an invalid. Both had died by the time that I knew Annie. She'd had a sister, but the sister died, too. The sister was a bad sort, apparently. A religious fanatic. She got herself involved with some crooked preacher, one of those fakes who take advantage of ignorant, superstitious people. I don't remember his name, but he was always in trouble. He made his followers handle live rattlesnakes, and one of them was bitten and died. And he was arrested for soliciting money under false pretenses. Annie said her sister gave this man all the money she could get together. She said her sister even gave him money that might have saved her mother's life if she'd bought medicine with it."

"What was the sister's name?" Romano asked.

Miss Dean bit her lip, rolled her eyes up under the black-rimmed goggles. "Let's see," she said. "Molly, that was it, I think. No, it wasn't, either. Something like Molly, though. Polly! Polly Branowski."

"I'd like to hear more about Angelle herself. Annie, I mean."

Miss Dean said, "She was about fifteen, I think, when she ran away from home. You couldn't blame her too much for that. It couldn't have been a pleasant atmosphere for a young girl, though she should have stayed, of course, and taken care of her poor mother. She took up with some nasty little man. A kind of gangster, I guess he was. I can't recall his name. One day she was riding in a stolen car with him. She didn't know the car was stolen. They stopped at a gas station. She thought he only wanted gas, but he pulled out a gun and held up the attendant. A State Police car came by. They must have recognized the stolen car because they stopped, and they caught this gangster right in the act. He went to prison and Annie was sent to Hickory Knoll as a juvenile delinquent."

"You met her when she came out?" Romano prompted.

Prudence Dean nodded. "She was one of the cases they assigned me. I tried to persuade her to use the vocational training she'd had in the school. They'd taught her typing. But she wanted to be a dancer. She fell in love a little later on. A fine, educated young man. A real gentleman. He was a college student. But this horrid sister, Molly—Polly, I mean —showed up and told the young man all about poor Annie's unfortunate affair and the time she'd served. He joined the Army and was killed. I saw Annie from time to time in Baltimore, and she was pretty bitter. She danced in cheap night clubs. Then she came to New York. She wrote to me a time or two, and I answered her, of course, and I should have looked her up when I came here myself. But I only took this job recently, and it's quite confining. Mrs. Belknap is sweet and lovely and very understanding. But she's nearly eighty and she's led a sheltered life and it might shock her to learn that her confidential companion had a friend who danced in a night club like the Salome. When I read the police wanted to talk to me tonight I almost fainted."

"It's funny you even saw the item," Romano answered. "I meant to give it to all the papers, but so much has been happening I forgot. The *Broadway Times* is the only sheet that ran it. I can't imagine a young lady like you reading the *Broadway Times*. It's all right, of course, but like they say on the Street, it's all about horses and hoofers."

Miss Dean dropped her eyes. "I have a confession to make," she said. "One of the reasons I came to New York was to be near the theater and the museums. The museums are educational, don't you think? But my real secret passion is the theater. I was in a play in college and I never got over it, I guess. I suppose my real ambition is to play the

116

balcony scene from *Romeo and Juliet*. I'm just a frustrated actress."

"You'd make a fine actress, I'm sure," said Romano gallantly.

Miss Dean shook her head. "Oh, no," she said. "Actresses should be beautiful. I'm just an ugly duckling."

Romano entered a conventional demurrer, but privately he thought Miss Dean didn't do much about preening the ugly duckling's feathers. Those wide black rims on her glasses couldn't help to improve her eyesight any. They only made her round face look grotesque. And his own kid wouldn't wear the kind of clothes Miss Dean had on to a Hard Times party.

Miss Dean said, "So I read all the reviews in the daily papers, and I read show-business papers, too, like *Variety* and the *Broadway Times*. That's how I happened to see my name. I'm awfully glad you didn't run my name in the regular newspapers. Mrs. Belknap might have seen it, and it would upset her terribly to know I was connected with the victim of a murder."

Romano rose wearily from the chair, picking his hat up from the floor beside him. He said, "Well, you've been a good citizen coming forward voluntarily like this when you found out we wanted to talk to you. I can't think of much else to ask you. Is there anything else you can tell me?"

Prudence Dean said, "No, I'm afraid there isn't. I'm afraid I've told you all I know, Lieutenant."

She said that with a certain mental reservation, with her stubby, short-nailed fingers crossed.

She hadn't told him the name of Waldo.

21 By Friday night the Big Street ran a fever. The neon tubes were huge thermometers, crimson ribbons recording Broadway's soaring temperature. The glaring signs were lighted charts that traced the pounding pulse and measured the giddy blood pressure of Times Square as the time drew near for Waldo's kill.

Grim-faced cops galloped by like Cossacks on great-rumped chestnut horses. Green and white prowl cars scraped the fenders of bright yellow cabs. Harness bulls planted their big feet solidly on cement as they walked their beats in pairs, their cold eyes searching and appraising, their hands inches from their gun butts. Detectives in blue serge and gray tweed and charcoal flannel stood in theater lobbies and in stage-door alleys, watching, waiting. Plainclothes men wearing corduroys and sweaters and overalls mingled with stagehands and electricians in the wings. Other policemen in ill-fitting dinner jackets sat in orchestra pits, although they could not read a note of music.

Including the Bellefonte, on Forty-sixth, where *A Borrowed House* was opening, there were fifteen plays and musicals in Broadway houses that Friday night. There were cops inside and outside the theaters where each was playing. That was not all. The commissioner, Inspector Sansone and Lieutenant Romano had mustered the full strength of New York's Finest to meet Waldo's public challenge. The picture houses that featured stage shows were covered, too.

Waldo had always killed on Broadway. But his latest letter had merely said he would murder between the acts of a theatrical performance. There were cops at the Provincetown and Cherry Lane and Circle in the Square and other arty little theaters in Greenwich Village. There were cops at the Italian Amato Opera House on Bleecker Street. There were cops at the Yiddish Theater on the Lower East Side. There were cops at the Chinese Theater on Doyers Street.

The cops were everywhere.

Everywhere except the place that Waldo had chosen for another murder.

Half an hour before curtain time Bart Hardin and Pops Taylor and Lieutenant Romano stood outside the Saddle and Whip, watching the fevered milling of the crowds. The scene was a surrealistic nightmare, Bart thought. He saw the shifting crowds as thousands of disembodied eyes floating in the white-hot blaze of Broadway's lights and the eyes danced and sparkled with the insane excitement of the diseased. The unblinking eyes were bright with the lecherous anticipation of forbidden experience.

Bart cursed under his breath and spat contemptuously at the sidewalk.

This was no ordinary theater crowd. It was no mere crowd of people come to amuse themselves with the tarnished pleasures of a tawdry street because tomorrow was a Saturday and they could lie late abed.

This was a throng of sadistic sightseers lured by the fascinating prospect of a madman mutilating a young girl before their eyes. Bart felt slightly sick. It had been predicted that fear of Waldo would keep the timid customers home and that the theaters would be deserted. The theaters were about to have their greatest night in recent history. Ever since the evening before when the *Broadway Times* had hit the street with Waldo's letter crowds had besieged the box offices of every house in town and had stormed the ticket brokers seeking choice seats for a Roman Circus. Even the worst flops on the Street had their SRO signs out. The possibility of brutal murder between the acts as an extra added attraction was too much for perverted human nature to resist.

"It looks like New Year's Eve," Romano said.

"Or Election Day," said Pops.

"Or Walpurgis Night," said Bart.

"Thanks for the dinner," Romano said to Bart. "I ate too much, though. I didn't stick to any salt-free diet. They say if a man don't sleep he's got to eat to keep his strength up. I've slept about five hours in the last forty-eight, mostly in a chair, so I guess I needed a heavy feed for what's in store tonight. I hope it wasn't like the condemned man's last meal. They tell me most of the boys at Sing Sing order steak, but one smart guy I sent there for Murder One wanted pheasant under glass. Me, I had steak."

"You think it was a condemned man's meal?" asked Bart.

Romano said, "This is it. This one is the pay-off. If Waldo hits tonight and I don't nail him this time, I know a warehouse in the Bronx that's advertising for a watchman. The hours are pretty long and you couldn't send a kid to college on the pay, but it's got social-security benefits. Oh, well. This job was a good one while it lasted, but it was hell on fallen arches."

Pops Taylor said, "I enjoyed the meal, too, Bart, and I guess I needed it." He fingered a patch of adhesive at his throat. "I didn't get much sleep myself, between a gone character sticking a needle in my throat and Romano's boys firing questions at me in a back room all night. Seriously, Lieutenant, you didn't dig me for a crazy bopster like Waldo, did you? A nice old man like me?"

Romano said, "I don't know yet if you are Waldo. I think I know who Waldo is, but I can't be sure. Hardin thinks that he knows, too. Waldo made one little mistake. But it's not enough to send him to the hot squat or the booby hatch."

"If it's Clements, there won't be another kill," said Pops. "They've got Clements in a strait jacket in a locked ward down at Bellevue."

"Yeah," said Romano. "Poor Mark. He tried so hard to get in Bellevue for the cure. He finally made it the hard way, fighting snakes. I hear the D.T.'s he's come down with are something special."

Hardin said, "Like Romano says, Waldo may have made just one mistake. That's the only hope. It may pay off tonight. If Waldo's who we think he is, we know where to find him tonight. I've arranged for that. Also, we can even guess what girl he plans to kill."

113

"Listen, Lieutenant," put in Pops Taylor. "I want to ask a favor. Just in case this Waldo's not the character you think he is, will you put one of those cops of yours right on my tail? Will you have him stick close to me and make a note of everything I do? If there's a kill, I don't want your crazy hipsters giving me another third degree. I want an alibi."

Romano shook his head. "Can't spare a cop for it, honey boy," he said. "You'll have to hire your own witness tonight. If there's a riot up in the Bronx or a gang war on Staten Island, I don't know what we'll do. The able-bodied cops are all right here on Broadway."

Bart said, "It's a quarter after eight. I'm going to stroll down to the Bellefonte on Forty-sixth. I probably won't stay long, but I've got to put in an appearance. My boss, Maddox Slade, is angel of the show. His protégée, Miss Arlene Lash, is the star, of course."

"Yeah," replied Romano. "I'll come along. Might as well start there. I got stake-outs at fifteen theaters to check before the first-act curtain. And that don't even count the picture houses."

Pops said desperately, "Can I come along with you, Bart? I want somebody with me."

Hardin shook his head. "You haven't got a ticket. And the opening's a sellout, along with every other show on the Street tonight."

They left old Pops scanning the faces of the passers-by desperately for an acquaintance who might provide him with an alibi for the evening.

Hardin and Romano melted into the glaze-eyed crowds and drifted toward Forty-sixth. Many times they heard the name of "Waldo" mumbled. The electric belt of letters that circled the triangular midriff of the New York *Times* Building to flash the latest news had Waldo's name in lights every sixty seconds. "WALDO DUE TO STRIKE AGAIN TONIGHT," the electric letters warned.

At the Bellefonte Theater an inconspicuous man wearing a pepper-and-salt suit and a hat with a turned-down brim stood in front of an enormously enlarged, chesty photograph of Miss Arlene Lash. Romano said to the man, "All set?" The man said, "Yeah, Lieutenant. There's a guard outside Lash's door and a policewoman inside her dressing room. She put up a squawk, but I think she kinda likes all the attention."

Romano nodded, said to Bart, "I'll see you later, honey boy. I got to do some checking." He walked up the narrow alley that ran beside the theater. The lobby and the sidewalk in front of the Bellefonte were already crowded with chattering groups of people. A surprisingly large number of them were in evening dress. Bart imagined that many of them were society friends of Maddox Slade and had come with passes supplied them by the angel of the show. All dressed up for their ringside seats at the bloodletting, Bart thought. He saw Maddox Slade talking to Cole Denham. Slade's hair was white, his eyebrows so black you suspected he must dye them. His smugly handsome face was smooth and pink and when he smiled his expensive dentures were as snow-bright as his hair. His dinner jacket was faultless. He sported a dark red cummerbund over a paunch that was barely noticeable. Denham wore the usual well-draped serge and the white shirt with the flaring collar. His face was gray and haggard and his eyes were bloodshot. Gray locks hung over his high forehead. His eyes were so heavy-lidded that he seemed half-asleep as he conversed with the owner of the *Broadway Times.*

Slade greeted Bart with a show of warm friendliness that was so habitual with him Hardin considered it affected. He extended a well cared for hand, said, "I'm so glad you could find time to come tonight, Hardin. I think you'll see a fine performance on the part of our little friend."

Little where? Bart wondered. Miss Arlene Lash was a tall young woman and she protruded.

Bart disregarded the pleasantries. He said, "I think you made a big mistake tonight, sir, not allowing me to hold a staff to put out an extra when I called you on the phone. Waldo means business. If he kills again, it's big news for a Broadway paper and we should have it. The Waldo stories in last night's edition gave us our biggest circulation in the history of the *Broadway Times.*"

"Now, now, Hardin," Slade said placatingly, smiling to show his gleaming dentures. "You did a fine job last night and you're to be congratulated. But we mustn't carry this Waldo thing too far. Hysteria, you know."

Bart said, "The trouble is that Waldo's carrying it too far."

"I know, I know," Slade replied. "But look at it this way. The *Broadway Times* is a paper that deals with sports and entertainment. Personally, I would rather see a story about that fine horse of Jock Whitney's on page one, or a tribute to a talented actress like Miss Lash, than to read the unpleasant news about a lunatic. After all, it's not our job to frighten people away from Broadway, you know."

Hardin snorted. "You think Waldo's frightening 'em away?" he asked. "Take a look at those ghouls on Broadway. They're thick as blowflies on a dead horse. Waldo, not Miss Lash, is the star tonight."

Slade placed a fatherly hand on Bart's shoulder. "You're a fine editor, Hardin," he said. "I'm very proud to have you on the staff. But you're young and a little rash. There's a lot of bitterness, a little violence, even, in you. I don't want it coming out in the pages of the paper." He chuckled genially. "You'll grow more mellow as you grow older, just as Denham here and I have done. Isn't that right, Cole?"

Denham's tired, lizard-lidded eyes scanned the pinkly pleasant face of his employer. "At least you learn to compromise," he said.

An elegantly gowned dowager tittered politely. "My goodness, who *can* that person be?" she inquired of her companion. "He looks like something out of Dickens."

Bart followed the direction of her condescending gaze, saw old James Lennox timidly entering the lobby. Bart said, "Excuse me, I see a friend," crossed to Lennox, greeted the old man. Lennox was dressed in a dinner jacket cut in the style of twenty years before. It was scrupulously cleaned and pressed but it was growing greenish at the seams. The stiff shirt bosom was slightly yellow with age. Smoked pearl studs showed bravely in the shirt front and the old actor carried a gold-headed stick. "This is quite a night for me," Lennox confided. "I used part of the money you paid me to get my studs and stick out of the pawnshop. The studs were given me by Walter Hampden when I appeared with him in *Cyrano* and the stick was presented to me by the management of the old Empire when I played my twenty-fifth production at that hallowed house."

People were jostling each other now, forming a wavy line in front of the doorman. Bart and Lennox queued up, presented their tickets. As they stood waiting for an usher, Cole Denham came by alone. Denham said, "You're left center, are you? I'm fifth row right as usual." He looked at the standees who had already lined up behind the railing, said, "If I were a kind man, I'd give this extra ticket to one of them. But I'm not quite as mellow as our dear employer thinks. Alex Woollcott used to say that the only advantage of being a drama critic was having an extra seat for your coat and hat." He moved off to find his seats.

In the immemorial custom of Broadway, the curtain was fifteen minutes late in rising. Even so, latecomers thronged the aisles and piled over those who had been seated after the house lights went down. *A Borrowed House* was supposed to be a mannered and sophisticated comedy in the tradition of Noel Coward, but it missed fire on almost every score. Bart supposed the new-school playwright had sought effect through understatement but the dialogue lacked both subtlety and sparkle and the lines fell entirely flat. Miss Lash was as abundantly bosomy as a Hollywood heroine, and as completely wooden. The audience laughed politely when the actors paused expectantly. Bart squirmed uncomfortably in his seat. Old Lennox, however, seemed entirely enthralled, content to sit and bask in the reflection of the footlights. He smiled happily. Only once did he lean toward Bart to whisper, "These modern actors don't know how to project their voices. They throw away their lines."

The curtain on the act fell at last to the claque's clapping of a first-night audience. Lennox said he had given up smoking years before and would not accompany Bart to the lobby for the intermission. Bart wondered if the curious stares of the dowager and others had made the old man sensitive about his appearance. He shouldn't be, Bart thought. He may appear old-fashioned, but he looks like the last surviving gentleman.

Bart encountered Romano in the lobby. Romano said, "He's here. Do you think he'll make his move this intermission?"

Bart said, "Yes, he's here. But I don't know if he'll make a move at all. We can't be sure he's Waldo."

"It's better if I keep out of sight," said Romano. "I'm going backstage again." He moved off up the alley. Sleek men and expensively gowned women surrounded the beaming Maddox Slade. They oh-ed and ah-ed and praised Miss Lash in tones as phony as a seven-dollar bill and Slade showed his glistening dentures and seemed to love it. Denham slipped out of the theater, carefully skirting the group around Slade. He said to Bart, "My God, I've got to praise this thing! I've got to think up adjectives about that woman. I can think up a lot, but our boss wouldn't like any of them." He shivered with disgust, lit a cigarette, said, "I've got to have a drink before I can stand another act of this. Thank God there's a bar just up the street." He pushed through the crowded lobby, disappeared among the throngs on the sidewalk.

Bart looked around him. Romano was not in sight. He saw the detective in the pepper-and-salt suit mingling with the crowd, but the man did not know him. Bart started for the street. He was blocked by a restraining hand. Maddox Slade said, "Well, what do you think, Hardin? Doesn't our Miss Lash have talent? I think we have a real discovery."

"I'm sure she must be very talented," Bart replied. "She's pretty, too."

He sought to push by Slade. Slade said, "What's the matter, boy? You're all tense. You should learn to relax."

Get out of my way, you grinning idiot, Bart thought.

He said, "I want to get a drink before the curtain's up again. Excuse me, sir."

"You have to drink between the acts?" asked Slade. "That kind of drinking is compulsive, dangerous, Hardin. You should watch it."

Bart said, "Sure, I'll watch it," and pushed on past. The nearest bar was half a block up the street, almost to Broadway. Hardin threaded his way through the crowded street, entered the bar. His eyes searched the length of the bar. Cole Denham was not having his drink here. Bart left. There was another bar across the street, on the corner of Broadway. Bart crossed against the light, dodged traffic. He went into the second bar. This was a larger place, full of people. It took Bart some time to determine that Denham was not here, either. But he might have been. He might have come here, had a quick drink and walked back to the theater while Bart was searching for him. Bart started out of the place. Someone bumped into him, said, "Hey, watch it, buddy." Bart looked up. He had bumped into a very tall, slightly drunken young soldier. The soldier had flaming red hair. He was almost as big as Orville Cartwright. With the red hair he looked something like Orville.

Suddenly Bart's body became rigid. Orville Cartwright! Helen Larsen! He pushed the protesting young giant aside and slammed through the door. He started to turn up Broadway, then realized he would never make it in time through this crowd. He turned back west on Forty-sixth, walking very fast, almost running, bumping into people without apologizing. As he passed the Bellefonte Theater he noted that the audience was streaming back inside for the second act.

When he gained Eighth Avenue and headed uptown he began to run on the comparatively deserted thoroughfare. People turned to look at the running man with the pale gold hair and the gaudily flowered vest.

"Too late!" Bart Hardin told himself. "Too late, like the troops that might have saved the marines trapped at the Chosin Reservoir."

22 Waldo glanced at his watch. According to his calculations, he had arrived in time. It had all been planned carefully. There were always irksome delays in such matters. But the schedule was not too far off, he assured himself. He could still do the thing as he had planned. He must keep to the shadows now. He had plotted the way. He moved as silently as possible. There was no real darkness in the area of Broadway but here the afterglow of the lights was crepuscular. At last he reached the little plot of ground with marble statuary that was his destination. He looked about him. It was rather like a small graveyard, Waldo thought. Appropriate enough for what must be done.

Waldo stood still, breathing hard, for a minute. He took gloves from a pocket and pulled them on his hands. He took

a small bag from another pocket and drew a folded plastic
raincoat from the bag. He shook out the thin stuff of the coat
and donned it. Sometimes there was so much blood. Waldo
fumbled with a little envelope with his gloved hands. He took
a small card from the envelope. There was a pin attached to
the card. The card read "Compliments of Waldo."

Waldo moved up close to the building now, flattened himself against the wall. He inched toward a lighted window. He
could see several figures moving about inside the building.
One of them was the girl. The thing to do now was wait until
the last possible second, when the girl would be slightly re-
moved from the others.

The girl moved toward the door. Waldo moved sidewise
down the wall toward the door. When he had almost reached
the door, he took the knife from his pocket and unclasped it.
The door was open a crack. Waldo opened it wider, put his
face against the crack. The girl was about five feet from the
door.

Waldo called through the door in a husky whisper.

"Helen! Helen Larsen! Come here a minute, Helen!"

23 Hardin almost collided with a filthy crone in wid-
ow's weeds who bore a shopping bag filled with
treasures from a garbage can. She shrieked after him, "Everybody's crazy! People ain't got manners any more!" Hardin
raced on. His dark jacket flew back to reveal the embroidered
flora of his vest. A hanger-on in front of a cigar store shouted,
"Hey, guys! Get a load of the galloping flower garden!" Just
before he reached Forty-eighth he came close to plunging
on his face. He drew up short, cursing. A group of Hell's
Kitchen urchins had stretched a rope knee-high across the
sidewalk. "Toll gate, mister! Toll gate!" they shouted. "Nickel
to go by!" Hardin jumped over the rope, ran on. Oaths known
only to moppets of the West Side slums pursued him. Just past
Forty-eighth Bart was halted again, more effectively this time.
A blue-coated bulk was planted solidly in front of him. It was
an old cop, with a tough, beery face. Grizzled strands of gray
hair hung beneath the visored cap. Hardin knew most of the
cops on this beat. He did not know this one. He must be one
of the many policemen sent to augment the Broadway patrol
because of Waldo.

"Ahright, ahright," the old cop growled. "Slow down, fancy
boy, and tell me where the fire's at."

The old cop's malty breath blew in Hardin's face. Bart panted curses at him. The old cop took a handful of Hardin's jacket in a paw as big and red as a pound of sirloin. He shoved Hardin. Hot rage burned Hardin. He wrenched free. His left shoulder lurched back. His right arm crooked, dropped a clenching fist to his hip. The old cop's raw-steak paw was clutching a nightstick now. He raised the nightstick, said, "So you're tough, you fancy bastard. Back up against the wall. Back up, or swallow teeth."

Hardin regained control of himself, gasped, "I'm a news-paperman. The *Broadway Times*. Let me reach and I'll show a card."

The nightstick was shoulder-high. The old cop said, "Up against the wall." The left hand thrust suddenly, hard against Hardin's chest. "Quick, or swallow teeth, smart boy."

Hardin backed against the wall. A small knot of people had formed around the cop and the man in the flowered vest. The group of urchins who had been operating the toll gate came shrieking up.

"He's a cheap bum! Slug him, copper!"

"Hit him! He pushed a old lady off the sidewalk!"

"He's a dirty rat! He kicked us little kids!"

Then the urchins began to chant in unison, "Arrest that man! Arrest that man! Arrest that man!"

The old cop bellowed "Shaddup!" at the urchins. "Back! Get back!" at the pressing onlookers. Hardin held his arms out at his sides. The cop's nightstick was back in his belt now. The meaty paw gripped the service gun. The cop said, "Okay, smart boy, reach. But don't pull nothing but a card unless you want a big hole in your pretty vest."

Bart took a wallet from the inside pocket of his jacket, flipped it open, extended a police press card in a glassine en-velope to the cop. The cop took the card in his left hand, examined it, said, "So you could've stole it. We'll just walk up to the *Broadway Times*."

Bart said, "Damn it, man, I'm in a hurry!"

The old cop chuckled, said, "What's the matter? You got a hot piece waiting for you somewhere? It'll keep."

A younger cop pushed through the crowd, asked, "What's the matter, Gargan? This guy's Hardin, editor of the *Broadway Times*. He's Romano's friend."

"Well, well," the old cop said. "That's just who he said he was."

"Thanks, Fitz," Bart said to the young cop.

The old cop said, "He's in a hurry. He's got a hot piece waiting for him. These newsboys do all right with dolls." He turned his wrath upon the crowd. "Ahright, ahright!" he bel-lowed. "Break it up! This guy ain't Waldo!"

The urchins continued to screech, "Arrest that man! Arrest that man!" until the old cop prodded their tails with his nightstick.

Hardin pushed through the crowd. He walked uptown fast. He crossed Forty-ninth against the light and the fender of a careening cab scraped against him. The heap jockey howled obscenities after him. On the north side of Forty-ninth he turned east into Jacobs Beach. Pops Taylor was standing outside the fleabag where he lived, talking to a small character in a green gabardine suit. The small character was saying, "If I'd of bird-caged them three goats, I'd of owned Moe Selig's goddam book."

Pops called out, "Hey! Hey, Bart! What's the hurry?"

"No time," Bart snapped.

No time. That was the trouble. Time had given out, Bart thought despairingly. He was in tune with the whole damned world, thinking just a little bit too slowly, doing things a little bit too late.

Outside the Church of the Theater a small group of men and women was standing, smoking and chatting. They did not belong on Jacobs Beach. They looked as if they were respectable suburbanites attending a Parent-Teachers' meeting. Bart passed hurriedly between the people, walked toward a door marked "Actors' Chapel and Auditorium." A glass-fronted notice board announced the topic of Sunday's sermon. Beneath that was a hand-lettered card reading, "Friday Night at 9:15—The Academy of Dramatic Arts Presents *Justice* by John Galsworthy." Helen Larsen's name appeared in the cast of characters.

It was bitter irony that the young people's group should be presenting this particular play on this particular night. The theme of *Justice* is that offenders against the law should be treated as patients rather than criminals.

Hardin mumbled apologies as he brushed past the persons outside the chapel and in the small lobby. In the auditorium he approached a black-eyed young girl who wore a frilly white dress. On her breast was a ribbon reading "Usher."

Bart said, "How do I get backstage, Miss? I'm from a newspaper. The *Broadway Times*."

The black-eyed girl seemed impressed. She said, "Oh! Your dramatic critic was at our dress rehearsal last evening. You can't go by way of the stage now, sir. You'll have to take one of the exits over on that aisle at the right and go through the little garden of the church to the rear door."

"Has the first act been over long?" Bart asked.

"Just about five minutes," the girl answered. "The curtain will be up again in a few minutes, sir."

The auditorium was lighted. It was half-filled with people

who had remained in their seats between the acts. Bart crossed the auditorium, pushed open a heavy side door. He was on a narrow walk between the church and an adjoining building. He walked rapidly to the rear, trying to move silently. There was no illumination in this little alleyway except the after-glare of Broadway's lights. He entered the garden at the rear of the church and it was even darker. The "garden" that bloomed on Broadway was a tiny plot. It was mostly paved, but plants and small treelike shrubs were set in great tubs. Marble statuary of saints gave the place a ghostly look in this weird, wan light. Light glowed from behind a partially low-ered blind at one of the windows in the rear. For a second Bart thought he saw a silhouette against the window, but he could not be sure. He stood stock-still, waiting, listening. The only door was at the far corner of the building, beyond the lighted window. The silhouette outside the window had dis-appeared—if it had ever been there.

Hardin sensed movement. He did not see or hear it. It was a still evening without wind. One of the potted shrubs that loomed like funeral fronds in the wan light shivered as if something had brushed against its foliage. The shrub was near the wall of the church. Hardin moved slowly, softly toward the trembling shrub, ducking down as he passed the lighted window. At the far corner, near the only rear door, was a blacker pool of darkness. The blind brick wall of the Bucking-ham Chambers loomed stark on this side of the church, cut-ting off even the reflected light. There were no windows in the blank wall to shed radiance, only a sign in yard-high spectrally white letters reading "Rooms—$1.50 Up."

Hardin froze against the building. There was a sound like a faint, insistent whispering, not far from him. The whispering sound formed words.

"Helen! Helen Larsen! Come here a minute, Helen!"

A young girl's voice, muffled by the narrowly opened door, called, "Did someone call me? Did someone call Helen? Who's out there? Is that you, Orville?"

The husky voice from the shadows said, "Yes, Helen. This is Orville. Come out here, Helen."

The door flew open wide and light spilled a golden fan · into the gloom. Bart moved hastily from the wall. For the briefest instant he thought he saw a dark-cloaked, crouching figure in the yellow radiance, but then the figure melted into the shadows again. The light gleamed on a white tulle dress and bright gold hair.

Bart shouted, "Get back, Helen! Watch out! It's Waldo!"

The white-clothed figure in the pool of light wavered un-certainly, retreated a step. Something black and shapeless hurled itself like a leaping animal from the blackness to the pool of light. Hardin was running, head down, over the six yards that separated him from the door of the church. The girl's thin scream quavered in the night. A male voice roared something unintelligible. The door slammed fully open, crashing loudly against the wall. Hardin's foot caught in a low wire that fenced off a small bed of trailing ivy. He crashed to the cement on his face, stunned. Something brushed past him. Something rubbery slapped against his face. The girl's screams still rang out. A big foot kicked his head. A weighty body fell heavily on him. Flailing fists sought his head, but landed on his shoulders. Hardin was dazed, but instinctively his knee thrust upward, hard. It sank into a yielding belly. The thing on top of him expelled its breath. Hardin's free arm threw a hard fist with a slashing motion.

The fist smashed into something soft and blubbery before it encountered teeth. The teeth broke, cutting Hardin's knuckles. The heavy thing gasped and rolled off Hardin.

The young actors were pouring out the stage door now. Somebody turned on outside lights in the garden. Hardin scrambled to his feet. Orville Cartwright was sprawled against the wall. Blood ran from his mouth. An hysterical group surrounded the screaming Helen Larsen. "He tried to cut my throat! He tried to cut my throat!" the girl repeated over and over again.

Orville Cartwright said with surprise, "It's you, Mr. Hardin, sir! But you're not Waldo!"

"No," Bart answered. "I'm not Waldo. Are you?"

"I'd just come backstage from shifting props for the next act," said the flabbergasted Orville. "The actors were all in the dressing rooms or getting ready to go on. The back door opened and Helen screamed. I ran to her. Somebody in a long black coat was slashing at her with a knife." Orville felt his mouth, said, "You broke my teeth. I'll have to have more bridgework now. He had a kind of scarf or something around his face and his hat brim was pulled down. Somebody was yelling about Waldo. This guy with the knife ran and I ran after him. Helen was still standing there yelling, so I guess she wasn't hurt. She's *still* screaming."

This last intelligence was unnecessary. Miss Larsen's screams were more than audible.

Orville said, "When I fell over you, I thought it was the guy. That's why I hit you. The guy ran this way."

Bart cursed. He raced to the little path that led to the front of the church. Several members of the audience had come out the side door attracted by the screams. They were looking toward the little garden curiously. Bart ran up the path. Two cops entered the path from the street. One grabbed hold of Hardin. It was the same old cop who had stopped him on Eighth Avenue, the one named Gargan.

Bart said, "You goddam stupid fool, let go of me. You're letting Waldo get away."

The old cop snarled. He said, "This time you really asked for it," and swung the nightstick at Hardin's head. Bart ducked. The nightstick slashed down on his shoulder. His reaction was mechanical. He kicked the old cop hard in the groin. The cop doubled up with pain, went to his knees. The young cop, Fitz, had hold of Hardin now. He said, "You can't get away with this, even if you are Romano's friend." He shoved Hardin against the church wall. A prowl car had stopped in front of the church. More cops ran into the narrow alleyway. One of them was Grierson.

Grierson said to Fitz, "What the hell is this? What you shoving him around for? He's a editor."

Fitz explained. Bart explained. Grierson said, "Come on, let's go back and see this girl."

Fitz still had hold of Hardin as they entered the little garden, brightly lighted now. The young actors had taken Helen Larsen back inside the church. Grierson leaned down, picked up a small object. He said, "It was Waldo. He dropped his little calling card." They entered the church. Miss Larsen, pale beneath her make-up, was sitting on a straight chair, the center of attention. Orville, blood still dripping from his mouth, was making futile patting gestures at her shoulders. A pansyish man who seemed to be director of the play was smearing a scratch below her jaw with mercurochrome and putting an adhesive bandage over it. Miss Larsen had regained some control of herself after the fit of hysterics but she could tell them very little. Someone outside had called to her and said that he was Orville. She had opened the door, stepped out, heard someone shouting "Waldo!" Just then a man in black, unrecognizable, had leaped at her with a knife and scratched her throat and might have killed her if it hadn't been for the heroic Orville hurtling out the door like the U.S. Cavalry to the rescue. After that, she supposed, she had just fainted standing on her feet. She could remember nothing more, really, until they'd sat her down and put smelling salts beneath her nose.

The pansyish director was wringing his well-kept hands. "What should we do?" he asked. "Should we call the whole thing off?"

Sixteen-year-old Miss Larsen rose, both from the chair and to the occasion. Her chin was held firm and high, her blue eyes flashed. She had the dedicated look of St. Joan approaching the pyre of Rouen.

"We mustn't disappoint the audience," she said. "The show must go on."

Bart said to Grierson, "Tell Fitz here to take his goddam paw off my arm. And let me get out of here. I've got things to do."

"I don't know," said Grierson. "Old Gargan's going to be kind of mad about getting kicked in the crotch. He might want us to put you in the pokey, even. Besides, you were out there in the garden. You might be Waldo."

"Tell Romano this for me," said Bart. "Tell him to come to the *Broadway Times* at midnight and I'll hand him Waldo, if I haven't killed him first."

Grierson said, "I guess we could let you go for now if we know where to find you." He looked at Orville's smashed and bleeding mouth and permitted himself a grin.

"But you shouldn't kick an officer of the law," Grierson said. "It ain't ethical."

24 Fifteen minutes later Hardin reached the Bellefonte Theater. The second act was still on and the lobby was deserted. The house man stood beside the door in a slightly rumpled dinner jacket, smoking a cigar. Bart had brushed himself off as best he could, but the black flannel jacket showed dust and grime and there was a small tear near the shoulder. The jacket was buttoned, but the ripped satin vest still showed beneath it. There was dirt and a little blood on Hardin's nose. He held a handkerchief to his bleeding knuckles that Orville's teeth had cut.

The house man said, "What's the matter, Mr. Hardin? Have an accident?"

"Fell down dodging a taxi," Hardin said. "How much longer does the second act run?"

The house man glanced at his watch, said, "Just a few minutes now."

Hardin nodded. He stood by the door, his pale eyes searching the street. Passers-by still milled on this main stem tributary, but none entered the theater. Hardin said to the house man, "Did anybody go into the house a long while after the second act had started?"

The house man shook his head. "No," he said. "But someone went out. The playwright. He didn't want Arlene Lash for the star but your boss wouldn't put up his money if she didn't get the role. The playwright said he couldn't stand it any longer. He said Waldo wasn't the only murderer on Broadway tonight. I don't guess you'll put *that* in your paper."

Hardin searched the street again. The face he sought did not appear. He wondered where Romano might be. Uniformed cops and a man he recognized as a detective were in the immediate vicinity, but he did not wish to speak to them. He had asked Grierson to keep the attack on Helen Larsen as quiet as possible until midnight at least, on the long chance that he could deliver Waldo to Romano as he had boasted he would. He didn't want the story of the events in the churchyard to be published in a tabloid extra before then. Faces surged and bobbed past him like the idiot masks of a mummers' parade, but the face of Waldo was not among them.

"Break, Mr. Hardin," the house man called, opening the door to the theater. Bart tried to watch the faces that poured out of the three doors, and realized it was impossible. They surged toward him in an enveloping wave, jostling, chattering. Only the faces in his immediate vicinity were visible. The others were hidden behind the heads and shoulders of the pressing throng. The crowd filled the lobby, swept out to the strip of sidewalk. Bart thought bitterly that there were two other exits into alleyways where the crowd might stand and smoke and that there were also lounges in the theater. From a distance, Bart saw Maddox Slade and a group of sycophants push their way out to the sidewalk. The crowd closed behind them, then a moment later it parted again briefly to reveal Slade in earnest conversation with Cole Denham. Bart had no desire to see Slade. He did not wish to explain his disheveled condition. People were regarding him curiously anyway. He pushed his way to the door, went inside the theater.

Old James Lennox was the only occupant of his row who had not gone out for the intermission. There was no one at all seated within his immediate vicinity. Bart took the seat next to Lennox, said, "Before you start exclaiming over my appearance, I fell down hard, dodging a cab. I'm not hurt. There's something important I've got to know. I want you to think as hard as you can before you answer."

The old man was wide-eyed, perplexed. He said, "Of course, Bart, of course. Anything at all that I can do."

"Who was on stage when the curtain went up for the second act?" Bart asked.

The old actor said, "Why, Bart, is that all you want me to remember? Arlene Lash was on stage all by herself for an incredible length of time. Minutes. It was very bad direction, because she wasn't even engaged in any interesting business, although she was on stage long enough to have recited Hamlet's whole soliloquy. I fancy she insisted on the scene to reveal her

obvious charms without distraction. She wore the most shock-
ing negligee I've ever seen. It beat anything they ever had in
the old Al Woods' bedroom farces, even. The garment was
thin, white stuff and it was quite transparent! Furthermore, it
was cut extremely low and Miss Lash has—well, an ample
bosom."

Bart nodded, said, "That's all I want to know. I'm going to
leave again as soon as the lights go down. Do you think you
can stand another act? Don't stay just to be polite."

The old man said, "I love the theater, Bart, even poor theater. The footlights, the audience, the actors moving and speaking—for me it's like coming to life again. Perhaps my criticism
of the play just reflects the fact that I'm old-fashioned. They've
a new style now. They mouth and mumble their lines as if
they wore false teeth that didn't fit quite right."

"Mouthing and mumbling's the fashion now," Bart said,
"just as bellowing was the fashion in the days of Edwin Booth."

"Between the two extremes, I'd be inclined to favor Booth's
histrionics," Lennox answered. "Bellowing is at least direct
and audible. Understatement can be refined to the point of
complete obscurity."

The curtain warning sounded and the audience streamed
back. The seats of several of the more important critics were
noticeably vacant. But Cole Denham was in his accustomed
place. This was one show the critic of the *Broadway Times*
could not walk out on. As the lights went down and the curtain rose, Bart squeezed Lennox's arm, rose and moved silently
up the aisle.

Outside the theater he encountered the detective in the pepper-and-salt suit. "Where's Romano?" Bart asked.

The detective said, "Who's asking?"

"Hardin of the *Broadway Times*."

The detective shrugged. "He's somewhere else," he said.
"He's got a lot of stake-outs to check tonight."

Bart said, "Tell him to drop around to the *Broadway Times*
at midnight. I want to see him. Tell him it's important."

The detective said, "He'll be back. I'll tell him."

Bart turned uptown on Eighth Avenue again. On Forty-ninth
he headed east to the Sligo Slasher's. Across the street, the
crowd was flowing out of the Garden like a dark, spreading
stain under the blazing marquee. The welter champ must have
knocked out the old stumbling block in an early round, Bart
thought.

A moment later he discovered it was a TKO. The Sligo
Slasher, who had watched the event on television said, *"Tech-
nical* knockout! There ain't no such a thing. When the Sligo
Slasher was champion of the Emerald Isle there wasn't any
knockout till the man said 'Ten.' Cream-puffs, that's what we

got today. When I knocked out Doomsday Danny Briscoe on St. Patrick's Day in 1916 all me ribs was broke like a old umbrella and me face was made of catsup."

"Men aren't really tough any more," Bart told the Slasher. "They're just vicious."

Bart drank at the bar until the clock showed a little after eleven. Then he walked up to the office of the *Broadway Times*. The old firehouse was deserted except for the grizzled night watchman, who was packing the remains of his evening lunch into a tin box. Bart tossed money to the watchman, said, "Go wash down your sandwich with some beer, Tim. I'll keep watch the next hour or so."

The watchman said, "Ye're an understanding man, like yer daddy usta be."

Bart went into his cubicle. I wonder what I understand? he asked himself. Maybe I carry money for the panhandlers in my pocket because I understand that everyone on this street is for sale. Gert, the whore, sells her sex in a cheap bedroom. Arlene Lash, the actress, sells the same thing on a lighted stage. Fritz Graham sells the last vestiges of a fine talent for the price of a little forgetfulness and old James Lennox sells his memories. I wonder what I sell. A character in a fancy vest. A tough guy with a heart of gold who's a sucker for a sob story. A Broadway "pal" who'll put your name in the paper or stake you to your pork chops when the dice are rolling wrong. It all adds up to "Phony."

A pile of photographs that he had not yet sent to Orville to file lay on the desk. One was a glossy print of Angelle Brann, scaled for the engraver with white crayon. Bart wet a handkerchief, erased the crayon marks. He found thumbtacks and hung the picture in the vacant space on the wall. He was staring moodily at the photograph when Cole Denham stuck his head through the door.

Denham said, "You in there, Hardin? Well, Waldo didn't make his boast good this time. At least there's no report of any murder and the shows are over now. He couldn't have killed between the acts."

Bart said, "I had it figured wrong. I thought he'd try to murder Arlene Lash."

Denham said, "In that case I would have regarded him as a public benefactor. Eliminating Miss Lash would have been the most constructive step in the drama since the invention of the revolving stage."

"I take it you won't say that in your notice," Bart answered.

"No," said Denham. "As I remarked earlier tonight, when you grow older you learn to compromise. I shan't even damn with faint praise. I shall be downright effulgent about Miss Lash's performance. That will please Mr. Slade. He spoke to me between the acts and assured me he wished an 'honest' expression of opinion. That means, of course, that I should say just what Mr. Slade thinks about the play. If I were a man, I'd hand you a withering blast and my resignation at the same time. I'm not a man. I'm a mouse who likes his little luxuries."

"I left right after the third act started," Bart said. "The thing had one redeeming feature for me. There was a belly laugh right at the beginning of Act Two, at curtain rise when Lash was on the stage so long all by herself."

"I'm afraid I was not amused," Denham answered.

"Maybe I've got a low sense of humor," Bart continued. "I mean it seemed funny to me having our Mr. Slade's glamor girl out there dressed in a man's red flannel nightshirt."

Denham said, "Oh, that. Dressing actresses in men's clothes was considered amusing some thirty years ago, I suppose. Perhaps it had its appeal as farce when the actress was petite, like Laurette Taylor. Such artifices hardly are effective in any era with a bovine specimen like La Lash, however."

Bart Hardin said, "Denham, you've made two mistakes."

Denham raised his eyebrows over the sleepy lids, said, "I don't think I quite understand."

"You pulled your first bad boner early Thursday morning in my apartment," Bart went on. "You were tired and your nerves were raw and when you met Romano in my place it, upset you more. So you made a slip. You said that the police could not believe that a man like you had killed *five* women. So far as anybody but the cops knew at the time, Angelle Brann was Waldo's fourth victim, not his fifth. Only the cops and some people down at the morgue knew Waldo had killed Geraldine McLennan. Only the cops and the ghouls—and *Waldo*, Denham."

Denham stared at Hardin in amazement. Finally he said, "But Bart, this is utterly ridiculous! The *Broadway Times* ran a story saying that Angelle was Waldo's fifth victim."

Bart shook his head. "Uh-uh," he said. "The *Times* ran that story on Thursday night. It hadn't been published on Thursday morning. The only ones besides myself who knew about it were under guard in a Turkish bath. They couldn't possibly have told you. And the story itself was in the bottom drawer of this old desk. You couldn't have seen it. The bottom drawer is always locked. I keep my Irish there and my Irish is one thing I'm stingy with."

The lizard lids drooped over Denham's eyes. He said, "My God, Hardin, are you charging me with being a psychopathic murderer? I don't know where I got the idea that Angelle was the fifth woman this Waldo killed. I don't read crime news much. Certainly I had no reason to keep a box score on Waldo's victims. It was a slip of the tongue, Hardin, or an error of

129

memory, that's all it could have been. The whole thing is insane."

"You just made another slip," Bart persisted, his voice completely unemotional, as if he were reciting a list of cold statistics. "I baited a pretty flimsy trap for you, but it worked better than I had ever hoped it would. If you'd been in the theater tonight you'd have known that when the curtain rose on the second act Lash was on stage alone and that all she wore was a white negligee so transparent she was naked, practically. No man sitting in the fifth row could have mistaken that for a red flannel nightshirt. I was afraid you wouldn't bite. I knew that you weren't there, but I was afraid Lash's costume might have been so startling that someone would have mentioned it between the acts when you were chatting out there on the sidewalk. They didn't, obviously. You swallowed the bait whole, Denham. And it's too late now to spit it out."

Denham's lizard lids had closed almost completely. He said, "Let's clear the air, Hardin. Are you accusing me of being Waldo?"

Bart spoke in a voice that was low and calm and almost casual. "Yes, Denham," he said. "That's what I'm doing, Denham."

"And you expect to convict me as a psychopathic murderer because I didn't happen to remember how many women some lunatic had killed and because I slipped out of that horrible play tonight and had a few drinks while the second act was in progress?" Denham asked.

Bart said, "No, not just because of the slips you made, but they're significant. It's pretty clear now what you did. You're crazy, Denham. You must have been for years. I don't know how many murders besides the Broadway kills you might have committed and got away with. There wasn't any motive for any of them until Angelle Brann came along. They were just the work of a maniac. But then Angelle started pressing you for money. It was blackmail, I suppose. As you say, you're a man who likes his little luxuries. You didn't want to have your rich wife cut you off without a cent, divorce you. And you didn't have money enough of your own to buy Angelle's silence. Maybe you could borrow from Moe Selig and buy it once, but you couldn't keep on buying. So you had to kill Angelle. You knew nobody suspected you of being Waldo. So you made a date to give the money to Angelle at her apartment and you killed her and blamed it on your alter ego. You even set the stage by writing that letter to the paper. Angelle had told you about Orville going a little nuts that time she teased him. So you chose him as the dupe, in case there had to be one. You knew that he was mentioned in her diary.

"You came here one night when no one was around and

you wrote the note on the typewriter you found in Orville's morgue. After the murder you lost your head. You came to my apartment the next morning to find out what I might know, and the presence of Romano there knocked you further off your balance. You could see he was suspicious. So you planned to implicate Orville further. You came to the office from my apartment to write the second note when no one was around the editorial department because it was early in the morning. You went to the morgue, but the typewriter you had used was gone. It was at the Turkish bath. So you used my typewriter. You chose Helen Larsen as your next victim because she was Orville's girl, would lead the police directly to him. You knew Orville would be on the scene at the church tonight, helping to shift props. You went to the rehearsal last night to plan your time-table.

"The Galsworthy play did not start until a quarter after nine, some twenty-five minutes after the scheduled curtain of *A Borrowed House*. Even allowing for the usual late curtain of a Broadway show, you had some ten minutes to spare, ten minutes to get from the Bellefonte on Forty-sixth to the church on Forty-ninth, if both shows had the standard forty-minute first acts.

"You must have noticed backstage at the dress rehearsal that Helen had a habit of going to the back door for a breath of air between the acts, and that the other actors did not. That was your chance. You called her out and you would have killed her if Orville hadn't happened along in the nick of time. When Orville charged you, you ran and got away and you waited somewhere until you saw the audience coming out of the Bellefonte for the second intermission, then you sidled up and mingled with them as if you'd just come out of the theater with the others. You made a point of talking to Maddox Slade. You almost murdered Helen because Romano and I were stupid. We figured you were after Arlene Lash. You hated her because you're a damned fine critic even if you are a maniac, and you knew she was a lousy actress. But you had to say nice things about her every time she got a role because she sleeps with Maddox Slade and Maddox Slade pays you your salary. I should have known you had a stronger motive. The second murder—or the sixth, if you prefer—was to be committed for an ironic reason. You planned a murder to prove you weren't a murderer."

Denham had moved toward the office door and was peering out. Bart said, "You can't run, Denham. Not now. I'm younger and bigger and stronger than you are."

Denham's face was white with rage and hatred. "I have no intention of running," he replied. "I'm looking for the watchman. I want you to repeat what you have said in front of him.

I intend to sue you, Hardin, to bring a criminal charge, even, if it's possible. These ridiculous theories of yours are pure moonshine. You're the one who needs the services of a psychiatrist."

Bart said, "The watchman isn't here. He won't be back for awhile, because I sent him out on purpose. You don't need a witness, Denham. You need a lawyer. There's more proof than I've mentioned."

Bart's pale eyes held Denham's. His face set in rigid lines. He was not good at lying, and he needed to be impressive now. He said, "You were recognized tonight, Denham. Two people recognized you. You thought the coat and the turned-down hat and the scarf around your face was enough disguise, but they weren't. A lot of light flooded into the garden when Orville Cartwright threw that door open wide. The scarf slipped just a little when you lunged at the girl. Orville and Helen both saw your face."

Denham laughed. "How ridiculous can we get? How far can you carry this?" he asked. "Romano, dozens of others knew where I was tonight. The lieutenant saw me at the theater. If I had been identified as Waldo, they'd have arrested me by now."

Bart shook his head. "No," he said. "Orville and Helen haven't told the cops yet. They told me. I asked them to wait, on the long chance that they could be mistaken. That's why I baited the trap with the red flannel nightshirt. You weren't at the Bellefonte when the curtain rose for the second act. You were in a churchyard on Forty-ninth. You dropped the little Waldo card in the churchyard. Those two kids will swear from the witness stand that yours was the face they saw in that sudden flood of light. They'll swear you were the one who attacked Helen Larsen and dropped the little card tonight. They'll swear you're Waldo."

Denham's small, trembling fingers moved slowly toward his pocket. The pale fingers fluttered like an insect's antennae as they sought the knife.

Hardin's eyes narrowed. He regarded the small man curiously. Denham seemed to have withdrawn entirely from the room, from any consciousness of the enormous charge Bart had just made. One hand crept into his pocket. The other pressed against his temple. His eyes were completely shielded by the heavy lids and his smooth face, which appeared hairless rather than shaven, had turned from the gray of dirty snow to the ghastly pallor of the dead.

"The headache," Denham said softly, as if he were speaking to someone far away. "The pain. The pain is sweet. It passes."

Bart sat in the swivel chair, staring hard at Denham, saying nothing. A muddy semblance of color returned to the small man's ashen face. Denham's jaw and lips jerked and quivered spastically. Still speaking to a distant presence, Denham said, "The fire. The fire is warm and red, like blood."

The lizard lids flew open. Denham's eyes were glazed, yet they shone with a light that Bart had never seen in them before.

"Hardin!" Denham said, as if he had made a surprising and not unpleasing discovery. He laughed. It was a schoolgirl's titter and it was horrible. "You know, you're quite right, Hardin. I am Waldo. I killed the women. They were evil, lewd and evil, and I killed them with the knife. There was no pain. There was only the blood, red and warm and bright, like fire."

The drooping lids fluttered. "I killed another," Denham said. "One they never knew about. It was so many years ago. I was just fifteen, I think, and afterward I was terrified. It was in a wood, back home, back in Ohio. She was young and her flesh was lewd and foul. She had thick thighs."

The eyelids closed again, completely, as if they shielded nightmare memories. "There were no others," Denham said. "Not for many years. Not until my wedding night. But always there were the headaches, the pain. And the sounds. The music and the voices." Denham shivered. "On my wedding night it almost happened. My bride awaited me and suddenly the knife was in my hand. Then I came to myself and I ran. I ran shrieking like a madman into the night. My wife could never understand that I had saved her life. She took refuge in nervous collapse. She has never been my wife. She never demanded that I be her husband."

The clouded eyes opened and regarded Hardin. "I could not have been her husband. You knew that, didn't you, Hardin?"

Bart spoke for the first time in minutes. He said, "I never thought about it."

Denham shook his head sagaciously, like a child who has convinced himself. "Yes," he declared. "You always knew, and you despised me. Angelle did not despise me. She was the only one who ever understood. She let me hold her sweetness close to me and she asked for nothing more. I gave her little presents. Money, small gifts. That's all she asked of me, all that she expected. She was not lewd and evil like the others. Not with me."

Denham's voice rose hysterically to a eunuch's pitch. "But she was with you!" he shrieked. "You made her lewd and evil! Look at your hands! You put them on her and bruised her flesh and made her lewd and evil!"

Denham shook his head sadly. "Then she asked too much,"

he said. "She asked more money than I could afford to give, and I knew I had to kill her. Besides, you had put your hands on her and bruised her and she was no longer sweet. She was lewd and the knife would purify."

Suddenly the madman stared at Bart. "I did not kill Angelle," he said. "I meant to kill her. I had it planned. She had a date with me, a date with death. But she did not show up and I could not find her. I killed all the others, but I did not kill Angelle!"

Hardin said, "Take some advice, Denham. Don't try to deny that murder. Just plead insanity. If you try to say you didn't kill Angelle they'll try you for that one murder, maybe, and if they do they can prove you had a motive and fry you in the electric chair."

Denham's hand moved so fast that Hardin had not seen it come out of the pocket. The scalpel-sharp blade was within an inch of Hardin's throat.

Denham spoke quite calmly. He said, "I have to kill you, Hardin. You know that, don't you?" His mad eyes held an expression of childish curiosity. He said, "I never killed a man before. I wonder what it's like to kill a man?"

The knife was closer now. The cutting edge was cold against Hardin's throat.

Denham said, as if debating with himself, "It will be easy." He nodded. "Easy enough. You were the one who put your big hands on Angelle and made her lewd and foul. When I strike, I will remember."

Denham did not hurry. He seemed calm and calculating. He pressed the knife forward the tiniest fraction of an inch as if to test the sharpness of the blade delicately against a strand of hair. His heavy-lidded eyes glinted with excitement but there was no anger in them. He mumbled words like "Blood" and "Fire" and licked his dry lips with his tongue.

Hardin's right hand was placed against the edge of the desk. He clutched the desk and shoved as hard as he could. The swivel chair lunged back on its rollers and crashed into the wall a yard away. The photograph of Angelle Brann was dislodged from the wall and fell to the floor.

Waldo's expression had hardly changed at all except that the flicker of a smile played at the corners of his mouth as if this were a game that he enjoyed. He extended the knife. He stepped a foot toward Hardin, pinned in the chair against the wall. Another foot.

Hardin sprang from the chair in a crouch. The knife slashed through the cloth of his coat, bit into the flesh of his shoulder. Hardin grasped the small man about the waist, plunged with him to the floor. As Waldo fell the knife slashed again and missed. The incredible strength of the insane had flowed into Waldo's small hand. The hand grasped Hardin's blond hair, sought to force his head back to expose his throat to the thin, poised knife.

Hardin disentangled his right arm from Waldo's waist, smashed his fist full into Waldo's face. Waldo's knife ripped through the flesh of Hardin's arm, but Bart hardly felt the bite of it. He was kneeling on Waldo now, his knees pressed hard into the soft belly. Fists smashed the flesh and bone and cartilage of Waldo's face, pounding straight down like heavy plummets. The hand that held the knife quivered briefly like a fish on sand and then was still. Hardin ceased his pounding, breathing heavily. Then his eye fell on the photograph of Angelle Brann there on the floor beside him, and his fists mangled the mad face again. And again. And again.

A heavy arm encircled Hardin's neck, forced him back. A spring-steel hand held Hardin's arm.

Romano said, "Ease up, honey boy. You'll kill him. If he's Waldo, he's crazy, and we don't kill crazy people any more."

25 The green-shaded desk lamp shone full on Romano's swarthy face in the dark cubicle he occupied at Manhattan West. The weird radiance gave the lieutenant an unearthly look. Romano's battered golden-oak desk was piled high with police journals and criminological pamphlets. The lieutenant looked up from one of the periodicals that was spread out on his desk as Bart Hardin entered the office.

"Hello, honey boy," he said. "You're up mighty early and you're way downtown for a Broadway rounder. It's only a quarter after nine and this is Twentieth Street. If you come down to square the beef about kicking that old cop in a certain place, it's already squared, so you can go back to bed. You might send Patrolman Gargan a case of beer, just to show there's no hard feelings, though. Patrolman Gargan is very fond of beer."

"I don't give a damn about Patrolman Gargan and his sore spot," Bart replied. "I came down about Denham and Angelle Brann."

Romano sighed and brushed away a necklace of sweat beads that gleamed like jade in the green light. "Well, now," he said, "we had this Denham about six days now, only the first two didn't count because he was in the hospital. The lumps you give him were pretty bad."

"Part of the beating I gave him was justifiable self-defense," Bart answered. "He had a knife and he was trying to cut my throat with it. I quit hitting him when he passed out and dropped the knife. Then I saw Angelle's picture down there on the floor beside me. I saw the funny little smile on her mouth and I thought how she looked that night when Waldo finished with her and I flipped my wig. I started breaking his face wide open with my fists all over again. I'd have beaten him to death if you hadn't come in just when you did."

Romano said, "Well, he won't die, but his face won't ever be the same again. He don't need to look pretty where he's going, anyway. They don't have beauty contests in the violent ward. The police bug doctors have examined him. They say he's entirely lucid most of the time, but when he comes down with the spells and thinks there's some kind of fire burning inside him he's buggy as a skid-row flophouse. He makes no bones about being Waldo. But he's still screaming he didn't kill Angelle Brann, though he admits he planned to on the very night she was murdered."

"The bug doctors think he's leveling?" Bart asked.

Romano shrugged. "They don't know. They just know he's Mr. Hyde when he's not being Dr. Jekyll. It don't make much difference, anyway, except to a dumb cop like me who likes things neat and orderly. Broderick, the D.A., isn't going to press for Murder One. He's satisfied to let him cop an insanity plea and catch butterflies in a padded cell from now on in. But Denham's hired Marty Land, the Broadway mouth, to defend him. Land'll take an insanity conviction, but he don't trust Broderick. Claims Broderick double-crossed him once when he agreed to Murder Two for some hood who was his client, then went to court with Murder One. Marty's afraid Broderick's pulling a fast one, that he'll try Denham for the Brann kill and attempt to prove motive and malice aforethought and that he'll claim Denham was sane and knew right from wrong when he chilled her. He thinks Broderick's got his eye on the next election and that the voters want Waldo in the hot squat even if he is crazy."

"You think Broderick will do that?"

Romano shook his head. "Uh-uh," he said. "He couldn't very well, because the state bug doctors wouldn't certify Denham sane and that would practically make 'em witnesses for the defense. But Land can't know that for sure. So yesterday he called in an expert and last night this expert gave Denham a lie-detector test. He called in the best lie-detector expert that there is, too. Doc Fred Remer, from up in Greenwich. I know the doc. He's a fine psychologist and an honest man. He looks too young for it, but he was associated once with William Moulton Marston, the granddaddy of the lie-detector business."

Bart said, "What does the test show?"

"I'll know any minute now," Romano answered. "Doc Remer wrote up his report last night. Marty Land is bringing the doc down here as soon as he gets in from Greenwich."

"Is lie-detector evidence admissible in court?" Bart inquired.

Romano said, "Not exactly. It's what you might call extralegal. They got two precedents here in the city where lie-detection men were qualified as expert witnesses and allowed to render their opinion on the stand, but their testimony was thrown out on appeal. New York cops use the lie-detector a lot, not as legal evidence but to guide them in examining suspects. With the defense, the effect is mainly moral. When a suspect demands a lie-detector test, the cops have got to let him take it or his mouthpiece hollers 'Foul' in the papers. If the test should show the defendant is telling the truth, the mouthpiece gets that in the papers, too, and it creates what you might call a favorable climate for his client. Land is plenty smart. He hasn't let the newsboys know yet there's any doubt that Waldo killed Brann along with all the others. He's holding that out as a threat over Broderick. He knows damn well the D.A. wants to wash up all these murders at the same time and clean the books. He won't bring up Denham's claim he didn't kill Brann if Broderick plays ball. If Broderick won't play ball, a lie-detector test favorable to his client is extra ammunition for Land. You can bet the test is favorable, or he wouldn't be bringing Remer here."

The intercom on the desk buzzed. Romano answered, said, "Send 'em right in." He turned to Bart, said, "You can stay if you don't print anything till I give the word."

Martin Land was a slender man who wore a pin-striped gray flannel suit, a light gray homburg and a tie from Sulka's. His eyes were jet black and piercing. His temples were iron-gray. So was his carefully trimmed and waxed mustache. He said, "Hello, Hardin. You damned near killed my client and lost me a fee. Bart Hardin, Dr. Remer."

Remer was exceptionally tall and slightly stooped, as if he were accustomed to bending down to address shorter men. The eyes behind his glasses were keen, intelligent and at the same time kindly.

Land said, "Give me that report, please, Doctor." Remer took a manila folder from a brief case. Land tossed the folder on Romano's cluttered desk, said, "Read 'em and weep, Lieutenant. Or maybe you'd rather have the doctor digest it for you."

Romano shrugged. "He's your expert, honey boy," he said. "If you want him to talk, I'll listen."

Land nodded to the tall doctor. Remer said, "I examined one Cole Denham with the Stoelting polygraph apparatus yesterday. My conclusions are largely favorable to the police case, Lieutenant, even though I have been engaged by defense counsel. The gist of the report there on your desk is this: The subject suffers from periodical fits of insanity during which he becomes a homicidal maniac. He killed his first victim, a young girl, when he was a youth of fifteen. He was terrified of what he had done and there was no recurrence until some fifteen years later on his wedding night, when he came very near to killing his wife, but fled from the house instead. His condition is complicated by certain physical aspects, most notable of which is that he is and always has been sexually impotent. After killing the young girl, he repressed his compulsions for many years, even though he suffered from terrible headaches, nausea, trembling and other symptoms, which, if borne long enough, finally become a kind of euphoria. Last year, at a critical age in a man's life, he gave in to his compulsions and went completely berserk killing four women. Last Friday night he attacked another young woman, Helen Larsen, and tried to kill her, but was unsuccessful. He also planned to kill the woman known as Angelle Brann for reasons that had nothing to do with his insanity. But he did not kill her. He did not even see her on the night that she was murdered."

Dr. Remer consulted his report, said, "To sum up, Cole Denham is without question the insane murderer known as Waldo. He killed an unnamed young woman in the state of Ohio many years ago. He killed Alice Kenyon, Bertha Del Rey, Margaret Stringer and Geraldine McLennan in New York City last year in fits of insanity. He attacked Helen Larsen outside a rear door of a church on Forty-ninth Street last Friday evening. For reasons of his own, he had planned to kill Angelle Brann, and he admits as much. But the record of the polygraph shows most emphatically that he did *not* kill her."

Marty Land grinned, said to Romano, "Any questions, sweetheart?"

Romano disregarded the lawyer. He picked up one of the police journals on his desk, said to Remer, "Cops don't get much time to read, they're on their feet too much. You got to sit down to read. But I been reading a lot of articles here on lie-detection. Some of 'em are by you, Doc."

Remer smiled pleasantly, said, "I've written quite a few, Lieutenant."

Romano said, "In this particular article here you say the lie-detector doesn't work sometimes with narcotics addicts and psychopaths. Do you consider this Cole Denham a psychopath, Doc?"

Remer nodded emphatically. "Cole Denham is insane," he answered. "It is a periodical condition. What I say in that article is absolutely true. Narcotics addicts and psychopaths often do not react at all to the lie-detector apparatus. Don't misinterpret that statement, though, Lieutenant. It doesn't mean that psychopaths can lie successfully. It merely means that sometimes they don't react at all. In that case the honest examiner simply says he doesn't know. If a psychopathic personality *does* react to the test, his patterns of truth and falsehood are just as plain as any other man's. Denham's insanity is periodical. He was entirely rational and lucid when I examined him. He reacted perfectly. He has an unusually strong distaste for lying, even. In his fashion, he is highly moral. He could never get away with a lie. His truth-patterns and lie-patterns are among the most pronounced I've ever seen. I'll stake my reputation that he's Waldo. And I'll also stake my reputation that he did not kill Angelle Brann."

Marty Land said, "I've got a buy, Lieutenant. You want to make a buy?"

Romano regarded the lawyer, said, "I don't make buys unless there's a bargain sale."

"It's a good buy," Land declared. "Good for you and good for Broderick. Reasonable."

"Name it."

"I don't want Waldo loose, any more than you do. I want him put away. But I won't stand for a D.A. making political capital by frying a crazy man in the electric chair for a murder he didn't commit. So here's the buy. If Broderick commits Denham to a state institution for the insane, the Waldo murders are solved, so far as I'm concerned, *including* the murder of Angelle Brann. I won't peep to the papers, and you'll get credit for closing out the case, lock, stock and barrel. That way everybody's happy. You try to hang the Brann squeal on Denham and get a Murder One, I'll fight, and I'll win, too, and you've got another murder to solve and Waldo loose on the town again, maybe. That's it."

"Why don't you take your buy down to the D.A.?" Romano asked.

Land shook his head vigorously. "No. I don't trust him. I trust you. You can deal with him. You give me your word and I'll take it."

"I'll tell you something out of school," said Romano. "The D.A. don't want a Murder One. He just wants Waldo put away. All he'll do is commit him if you don't fight that."

"Your word is good enough for me," said Land. He picked up the manila folder. *"Your* word. But I'll just take this report along in case Broderick might even double-cross a homicide lieutenant."

After the lawyer and the doctor left, Bart said, "Don't look so glum. Everything is solved, isn't it?"

Romano said, "I guess it is, but I don't like it. I like things tied up neat in ribbons. That's because I'm a cop. Being a cop is a curse, sometimes. I'd still kind of like to know who killed Angelle Brann if Waldo didn't."

"I know what you mean," said Bart, "but I guess this is the way it has to be. The doctor could be wrong. Waldo could have killed her. He left his card."

Romano said, "Yeah, maybe."

Bart got up. He said, "I'm shoving now. I'll send the beer to Gargan."

"Yeah," said Romano. "That'll be right nice of you. Gargan is very fond of beer."

Bart walked to Eighth Avenue, turned uptown, headed for the subway at Twenty-third. Usually he took cabs, but he'd lost a week's salary the day before on a three-to-one shot at Jamaica that couldn't lose, according to word Pops Taylor had received from the Broadway smarts. He was on another of his economy kicks, although the Chiselers' Bank and Trust Company in the pockets of his jacket was ready for business. At Twenty-third, Hardin saw a dime store across the street. He drew up short, stood undecidedly for a minute. Then he crossed the street and entered the store. He walked to the cosmetics counter. A plump and pimply girl behind the counter admired his lean frame and the lavender forget-me-nots that decorated his vest. Bart searched the articles on the cluttered counter for several moments, finally handed the girl a little card, said, "How much?"

"Twenty-nine cents with tax," said the girl.

Suddenly the girl realized what Bart was buying and she shook with laughter.

"Don't bust your girdle, sugar," Bart said, handing her a dollar. "Just wrap it up and give me change."

The girl said, "I—I'm sorry, sir. But a big man like you, buying a thing like that. . . ." Her voice rose in hysterical laughter again. Finally she handed Bart his package and his change. She said, "I hope that crummy little section manager didn't hear me laughing. He's a crumb."

"Tell him I told you the one about the traveling farmer and the salesman's daughter," Bart advised her, and hurried out.

Hardin had forgotten all about the subway and his economy kick. He hailed a cab. The driver was an old man with a weather-beaten face. When they reached the flea circus, Bart paid the heap jockey and overtipped him. The old man said, "Thanks. So you work in Bromberg's trap? I made you for a carnie when I saw that vest. Used to be a carnie myself. I was a talker for a kootch-pitch."

"I'm a talker for a kootch-pitch, too," Bart answered. "The biggest kootch-pitch in the world. They call it Broadway."

In his flat, Hardin took off his jacket and rolled up the sleeves of his shirt. He sat down and began at once to experiment with his purchase. Old Bones, snuggling affectionately beside his pal, Klaw, regarded his master's strange behavior with curious, old-dog eyes. When Bart finished, he sat still and silent for minutes. Then he began to scratch his bare arm reflectively. The more he reflected, the harder he scratched. At length he rose, went into the bathroom and washed his hands.

The experiment had been successful. Bart Hardin knew for certain now that Waldo had not murdered Angelle Brann.

26 The doorman in the marble corridor of the apartment house across from the Metropolitan Museum of Art looked askance at the forget-me-nots that twined over Bart Hardin's vest.

Hardin said, "Mrs. Belknap's apartment, please."

"Mrs. Belknap was taken to the hospital last evening," the doorman answered superciliously.

"I know that," Hardin bluffed, his voice harsh. "I'm from the hospital. She needs a few things and I want to see her companion, Miss Prudence Dean."

The doorman studied the forget-me-nots another moment before he reached for the phone. He said into the phone, "There's someone who *says* he's from the hospital wishes to speak to you, Miss Dean." He hung up, said to Hardin, "You're to go up. The tower elevator is to the left."

The door of the penthouse opened almost as soon as the bell chimed. When Prudence Dean saw Bart Hardin her eyes flew wide open behind the big, round glasses. The short-nailed fingers of one small hand smacked against her gaping mouth.

Bart said, "Hello, sugar. The black dye job's not too bad, but that Mother Hubbard you're wearing is strictly for the birds and those horn rims give you a kind of goony look."

"How'd you find me, Bart?" asked Angelle Brann.

"It wasn't too tough," Bart replied. "My old man came from Kentucky. He bred bloodhounds."

Angelle Brann motioned him into the penthouse, closed the door. She said, "Mrs. Belknap had a stroke. They took her to the hospital. The maid is out somewhere. You turn me in, Blond Beast? You holler copper?"

Bart said, "Why should I holler copper? There's no law against being alive instead of dead. Some folks even think it's nicer that way."

Bart started to seat himself on an inadequate love seat upholstered in pale pink satin. Angelle said, "Don't sit there. That's my pink cloud. I sit on it and pretend that I'm an angel."

"Angels don't have much fun, sugar," Bart told her, choosing another chair. "Their wings get in the way."

Angelle sat on the love seat, said, "I'm going to sit on my pink cloud again and pretend I'm an angel for just a little minute more." She tittered. "It's hard for a girl to be an angel around a guy like you." She looked at Bart searchingly, sunlight from the picture window glinting on the round lenses of her glasses. She said, "How'd you find me? I've hardly been out of here at all since I came a week ago today. Maybe you're a bloodhound, but you couldn't have sniffed my perfume out. I haven't worn any since I left Hymie Keppel's trap."

Bart said, "Mainly it was the falsies, I guess. The false fingernails. I didn't think you wore falsies. On your fingers or anywhere. But you might have, of course. You might have, until I thought of Orville Cartwright and his scratched-up face. You clawed him that time he made a pass at you because he thought it was expected of him. He had the marks for a week or more. Today I made an experiment. I bought false fingernails at a dime store, the biggest size they had. I went up to my flat and glued 'em on with that little tube of paste they give you."

Angelle tittered.

Bart continued, "I let them set, like it said to do in the directions. Then I tried to scratch my arm. I couldn't claw hard enough to break the skin. When I tried to, the fingernails flew off. It might have been just possible to draw blood with them if they were cut short. But your nails weren't cut short, I remembered." He glanced at her close-clipped fingernails. "At least they didn't used to be when you were Angelle. You had those bright red spikes like all the other Broadway hoofers. False fingernails as long as that would have come right off when you tried to scratch. I know, because I experimented.

"There were other little things. The body on the floor had a red indentation around the stomach, marks from the elastic of a girdle. You never wore a girdle. You bought one the day before the murder, but you never had it on. You took it out of a box and showed it to me that Tuesday night when you were up in my apartment, but you forgot to take it with you when you left. And there was that last entry in your diary. 'Help! Waldo is coming!' If you'd known it was Waldo coming up the stairs, you wouldn't have written an entry in your diary, you'd have picked up your phone and called the cops. And you'd never have opened the door to him. That entry in the little book meant somebody was trying to frame Waldo for a kill he didn't make. It was in your handwriting.

"I remembered the name of Prudence Dean, then, because it was the only woman's name connected with the case except the names of women who were dead. Romano told me Prudence Dean was a kind of prudish young woman who had studied social sciences and who took care of a nice old lady. Yet she'd read that she was wanted in the *Broadway Times*. She had to read it there, because that was the only place that it was printed. I couldn't dig a dame like Prudence Dean being interested in Broadway gossip or race-horse tips. So I came here."

Bart lit a cigarette, looked dubiously at a porcelain dish so fragile it was transparent. It seemed too valuable for an ash tray, but he dropped the match into it, anyway, said, "So finally I figured that the body on the floor wasn't yours, and I felt right relieved. I kind of like you, sugar."

Angelle lowered her eyes, said softly, "I like you, too, Bart. Next to being an angel on a pink cloud, I like you best of all, I think."

"It must have been your sister down there on the floor," Bart said. "Your sister Polly that you'd told me about. You'd said that she was dead, but when I thought back I remembered you'd always phrased it a little oddly. You'd tell me of some nasty thing she'd done to you or to your mother or that gentle fiancé of yours and then you'd say, 'But she's dead. For me she's been dead a long, long time.' For you she was dead, maybe, but she was still alive and she must have found out where you were and showed up to persecute you again. So you killed her and blamed it all on Waldo. There are a lot of angles that I haven't figured yet, of course."

Angelle said, "I'll tell you everything, Bart. It doesn't matter now. They took Mrs. Belknap to the hospital last night. They say she's going to die. She was like my mother used to be before she died, before my sister Polly killed her by not buying the medicine she needed. She was sweet and helpless and awfully sick. She depended on me. She was like my mother would have been if she'd ever had a chance in life. Kind and gentle. A real lady. I could have been so happy here, even if I am a murderess. It's nice knowing someone

143

loves you and depends on you. I only wanted to stay on here and take care of her and sit on my little pink cloud and pretend I was an angel and listen for her to call. It's the first time I've been really happy since the Gentle Boy made love to me. It was kind of soft and good and dreamlike. Most things are hard and nasty and real. Oh, well, it lasted for a week. I've learned you shouldn't ask too much."

Angelle ran her tongue over her full, unrouged lips. She said, "I don't know for sure how Polly found out where I was living. A few months ago I ran into a nice-looking boy from back home in Sparrows Point. I used to go to school with him." Angelle laughed. "I guess I just can't resist nice-looking boys. I asked him up to my apartment for a drink. I guess maybe he met Polly in Baltimore later and she wangled my address out of him. Monday of last week I got a letter from her. She'd been going under the name of Prudence Dean. I'd known that right along, of course. I'd even written sarcastic things about Prudence Dean in my diary. I'd forgotten that. In the years since I'd seen Polly, since she'd died as far as I was concerned, she'd been nurse-companion to three sick old ladies. All three died and left little sums of money. Not much. A few hundred dollars or a thousand, maybe. She gave it all to this crazy, crooked preacher, of course. He had some strange hold on her. I think Polly killed the three old ladies to get the money for him. In her letter, she almost hinted that she did. One was crippled and fell down a flight of stairs when nobody but Polly was around. Another died in bed with asthma. Polly could have smothered her with a pillow. The last one needed certain medicine every few hours to keep her going, and I think Polly held it out on her just like she did with Mother.

"Polly said in her letter she was arriving in New York on Wednesday night to take a position she'd obtained through correspondence with a rich old lady named Mrs. Belknap. She said she was coming to my apartment at ten on Wednesday to spend the night and start work the next day. I was desperate because I knew just what she'd do. She'd make scenes at the Salome Club and try to get me fired. She'd try to poison everybody that I knew against me. I suspected she planned to kill the old lady once she got herself into her will. She was good at getting herself into old ladies' wills. And I hated her. The thought of seeing her made me sick. She had killed my mother and the boy I loved.

"I thought if I could give her a big lump sum I could pay her off for good. I don't know just how I hit on two thousand dollars, but it was a nice, round number. I went to see Cole Denham on Monday and told him I had to have the money by eight o'clock on Wednesday evening. I—I threatened him

144

with blackmail but I never could have gone through with it. The poor little man was scared to death. He made a date to meet me at eight on Wednesday at some funny little restaurant near Ninth Avenue. He said he'd bring all the cash he could scrape up.

"I felt terrible, though, the way I felt that time I teased Orville for a laugh and drove him nuts. Denham had been pretty good to me in his own way. He'd got me the job, helped me out with money, given me little presents. It was a lousy thing to do. He'd got mighty little in return. He—well, he wasn't a man, Bart. He'd never really been with a girl. All he wanted to do was lay his head against my breast and whimper like a little boy and tell me all his troubles. I felt protective toward him, sorry for him. At the club that night I realized I couldn't go through with such a dirty deal. He was reviewing a new show and I knew he'd be back at the office late to write his notice. I skipped out between shows and went to the *Broadway Times* to tell him not to worry about the money. Nobody was there but that old watchman and he was sound asleep. I heard a typewriter clicking down a kind of hallway. I went toward it. Cole came out of that place you call the morgue. He didn't see me. He closed the door behind him and lit out for the little boys' room. I wondered why he wasn't using his own typewriter. I pushed the door open and went into the morgue. There was a letter beside the typewriter. It was addressed to the editor of the *Broadway Times* and it was signed 'Waldo.' I read it. It was the letter you published in the paper. It said Waldo was going to kill a girl between eight and midnight on Wednesday. Cole wrote that Waldo letter Monday night, but I read in the papers it wasn't mailed until the next night, Tuesday. I guess he didn't want to give the cops too much warning.

"Cole had a date with me at eight on Wednesday. I went out as fast and quiet as I could. I went back to the club and I was hysterical, I guess. I stole a knife from the kitchen with the idea of protecting myself, I suppose. Then I saw a way out. Waldo used a knife. If I killed Polly with the knife and left a little Waldo card beside her and you got that letter it would be blamed on Waldo. The best way to get away with that was to make it look like I'd been killed. There was a family resemblance between Polly and myself, only we looked a lot different because she never fixed herself up and she wore big glasses and these awful clothes and corsets. She was a few years older, of course, and a few pounds heavier. I had to figure some way of making her unrecognizable. I got so wrought up thinking about it, I couldn't stand to wait for the last show at the club. I took off and went to the Slasher's place and tried to plan it all over a few highballs. I got to talking

145

to this poor guy Clements. He knew about the Waldo murders because he'd been a cop and I thought I might milk him some, so I took him to the apartment and fed him and gave him a drink or two of gin. He thought I was going to kill myself with the knife and he took it with him when he left. I didn't really care. I knew I could never use the knife. I couldn't stand the blood. And I'd borrowed the janitor's hammer to hang your picture. I thought it would be easier with the hammer. Next day I borrowed the lye and pretended that I needed it for the drains in the bathroom.

"I was busy on Tuesday. I'd needed rest glasses a long time, so I went on to an oculist and told him I had to have them by the next day. I insisted on these big, black rims and I gave him the name of Prudence Dean. I bought black hair dye for myself. I already had bleach for Polly's hair. It was dark brown. I bought false fingernails because Polly bit her own. I planned to wear Polly's clothes, but I knew I couldn't stand those stiff corsets of hers and it would be out of character to let the bulges show, so I bought the girdle that I left at your flat. Oh, I was busy all day on Tuesday, all right." Angelle smiled. "And then you had to keep me busy most of the night, too, Blond Beast. I went down to the New York *Times* and I read the files about Waldo's murders and there was a photograph of one of his little cards. I memorized the words and how they were arranged. Then I bought a rubber stamp and some cards at the dime store and I printed the one I left on Polly. Wednesday night I cleaned my apartment from floor to ceiling, because I didn't want any fingerprints around to show the body they found wasn't mine. I dyed my hair black. It's naturally dark but I'd bleached it for a long time."

Bart grinned.

"I dyed my hair and cut my fingernails short and washed off the polish and paint. I got the hammer and the lye and I waited for Polly. I thought the way I mentioned Denham in my diary would lead the cops to him. When Polly was coming up the steps I got another idea and I scribbled down something about it being ten o'clock and Waldo was on his way. I thought that would lead the cops to Denham sure, because I'd written in the diary that I had a date with Cole that evening."

Angelle lowered her eyes. "I don't like remembering the rest," she said, "but I guess I've got to. Polly came in, carrying her bags. She was nastier than usual, even, and that made it easier. I killed her almost as soon as she arrived. It wasn't hard. I think the first blow killed her. But the rest was awful. Undressing her, dressing her, throwing the lye in her face and watching what it did. And dyeing her hair. Bleaching her hair and fixing it to look like mine, that was the worst of all. I pinned the card on the red and gold housecoat.

146

"It was over, finally, in half an hour or so, I think. I put her clothes on, picked up her bags and left. I got a cab on Sixth Avenue and went to that woman's hotel on East Twenty-ninth and registered as Prudence Dean. Next morning I reported to Mrs. Belknap. I knew she'd never seen Polly. I knew Polly had no friends, that no one was likely to try to get in touch with her. I loved Mrs. Belknap at first sight. She was pretty sick when I came, but she was sweet. She wanted a daughter and I wanted a mother, I guess that's the way it was. I sent out for the *Broadway Times* and I read about the police wanting to see Prudence Dean and I thought the best way was to brazen it out. I called them and this lieutenant came up. I told him a good story. Some of it was even true. I thought he swallowed it."

Angelle's mouth twisted into the funny little smile. "It was nice," she said. "It was wonderful just being here."

She looked at Bart, said, "Do you hate me, Blond Beast?"

Bart said, "I told you, sugar. I kind of like you."

"Like me enough to kiss me, maybe?"

Bart said, "Maybe. If you'll take those God-awful horn rims off."

Angelle took off her glasses. Bart walked toward her. She held up a small, restraining hand, said, "Not here, Bart. Not on my little pink cloud. On my little pink cloud I'm an angel." She rose.

Bart took her in his arms. The kiss was a long one. When it was finally over, Angelle said, "I liked that. Did you?"

Bart said, "I'd like the next one even better if you didn't have that damned Mother Hubbard on."

Angelle snickered. She said, "I took the glasses off. I could . . . "

Her hands fumbled with buttons. The door chime sounded.

Angelle buttoned the shapeless blouse again, put her glasses on. She said, "It's the maid. She always forgets her key."

She opened the door.

Three men stood at the door. Romano's hat was on the back of his head. Grierson appeared as stolid and immovable as usual. The third man was tall and middle-aged and dressed in the somber, three-button uniform that exclusive tailors invariably fashion for conservative customers. He did not look like a cop.

Romano motioned the other two into the room, said to Bart, "Hello, honey boy. It seems like everybody's calling on Miss Prudence Dean today." He nodded toward the tall man, said, "This is Mr. Heavenridge. Mr. Heavenridge comes from Baltimore."

Mr. Heavenridge disregarded the introduction. He was staring hard at Angelle Brann. He said, "Is this the young woman?"

147

Romano said, "Yeah. This is Miss Prudence Dean."

Mr. Heavenridge shook his head. "This is not Miss Prudence Dean," he declared. "Not the Prudence Dean who was companion to my mother in Baltimore. Not the Prudence Dean who *killed* my mother by pushing her down a flight of stairs, although we could not prove the charge."

"You sure now?" Romano asked.

Mr. Heavenridge said, "I could never forget that horrible young woman's face. This girl has a superficial resemblance to her, although she is younger. A sister or a cousin, perhaps. But not Prudence Dean. This is a pleasant-looking young woman. Prudence Dean looked positively evil. She *was* evil. When this horrible charlatan who forced his followers to handle live rattlesnakes went to jail, I discovered Miss Dean's connection with him and I gave her two weeks' notice. Later I found she had got around my mother and was left a thousand dollars in her will. The day before Miss Dean was to leave us, my mother fell down the steps. I am convinced that she was pushed."

"Thank you, Mr. Heavenridge," said Romano. "You can go back to your hotel. If we want you, we can call you there."

The tall man nodded, left the apartment. Romano sank into a chair, said, "We might as well sit down and rest our feet."

Angelle stared at Bart Hardin with glazed eyes. She said, "Did you double-cross me, Bart? Did you turn me in?"

Romano said, "He didn't turn you in, honey. I finally figured it all by myself. It wasn't brilliant, like the detectives in the books. Just routine police work. The plodding stuff that bores a cop to death and gives him fallen arches."

Romano finally took his hat off, wiped sweat from his brow. "The first thing was, you cleaned up too good. It's just not natural if there's not at least one fingerprint, even a smeared one, in an apartment. There wasn't one in yours. Waldo wouldn't have scrubbed the place like that. Waldo just wore gloves. We didn't have much identification of the body with the burned face. Just Mrs. Latti, the janitor's wife, and she could hardly stand to look at it.

"When we found out you'd been in the Hickory Knoll Reformatory, we tried to get your prints from the Maryland authorities. But they didn't fingerprint juvenile delinquents at the time you were there. We went to the Salome Club and the girls there showed us a cold-cream jar and a plastic comb they said you'd used. There were prints on them. They didn't match the prints of the body that we found. They didn't match the prints of any of the other girls at the Salome Club, either.

"When I talked to you here last week, you told me that you'd been a social worker in Baltimore and that Angelle's sister, Polly Branowski, was dead. We couldn't find a record in Maryland of any social worker named Prudence Dean and we couldn't find a death certificate in Maryland or Pennsy or Delaware or any neighboring state for a Polly Branowski. We couldn't find any trace of a Prudence Dean graduating in social sciences or any other subjects at the University of Maryland. The police lab was working, too. Those lab men can tell an awful lot from mighty little. Like hair, for instance. They said the hair of the body we found hadn't been bleached before, or not often, anyway. That kind of confirmed our doubts. We knew Angelle Brann had been a blonde for at least the year she'd lived in New York. And we did find out from Mrs. Belknap's attorneys that you came to work here the day after the murder. We found out from them that companion-nurses for old ladies are about the hardest employees there are to find nowadays and that they were delighted to hire a girl from Baltimore who'd answered their ad in the New York *Times*, sight unseen. We also found trace of a Prudence Dean in Baltimore. She hadn't been a social worker, though. She'd been an old ladies' companion, and all the old ladies she'd been with seemed to have died under what possibly might be suspicious circumstances. And finally we found Mr. Heavenridge and he came up here and took a look at you."

Romano sighed, said, "I'm kind of sorry I wrapped up this case. I like you, honey. You're a good kid. It won't go too hard with you. The jury will be sympathetic. Even Broderick will be sympathetic. They'll consider your sister's character, the emotional stress you were under because you thought both your sister and Cole Denham might be murderers. It won't be too tough. But I learned one thing a long, long time ago. You always got to pay. Maybe not too much. But you always got to pay at least a little bit."

He rose, said, "You take her down, Grierson. This is my day off. I just come in because Marty Land wanted to see me and this Mr. Heavenridge was arriving from Baltimore. I'm going back to my little igloo in the Bronx and take a nice, long nap."

Bart Hardin's jaw was tight and quivering. He said, "I'll get you the damned smartest lawyer that there is, sugar. I'll get you Marty Land."

Angelle said, "You know what Mrs. Belknap said to me when they were taking her to the hospital, Bart? She squeezed my hand and said, 'What will I ever do without you, Prudence? You're an angel. That's what you are, a real, live angel.' "

Romano nodded toward the door, said, "Come on, Hardin."

Bart walked toward the door like a man in a daze.

Angelle called, "Bart . . ."

Bart turned, said, "What, sugar?"

"Good-bye, Bart. Just good-bye, that's all."

27 On the sidewalk, Romano said, "I got to go back to the office a minute. I bought a new pair of arch supports and I left 'em there. I'm going to blow myself to a cab. Can I drop you off somewhere?"

Bart nodded dumbly. The doorman whistled up a cab. Inside, Romano said, "Where to? The *Broadway Times* or your flat?"

"The Sligo Slasher's," Bart replied. "I want a drink. I want the biggest drink in town."

Romano gave the address to the driver. He said to Bart, "I can use a drink, but I thought you never drank till four. It's not even noon."

Bart said, "A fat drunk named Fritz Graham called the turn. He said there'd come a day when I'd take a drink no matter what time it was."

"Don't take it too hard," Romano urged him. "With Marty Land on her side, she'll be back on Broadway before the traffic lights can change."

"She's got five years more at most on Fifty-second Street," said Bart. "After that maybe five years in the Village honkytonks. Then nothing."

"They taught her typing at the reform school," Romano reminded him. "She could be a stenographer. There's good pay in that."

Bart said, "She doesn't want to be a stenographer. Or a hoofer, either. She wants to be an angel. But nobody will let her."

They were silent until the cab drew up at the Sligo Slasher's. For once, Romano managed to outreach Bart and pay the fare.

Fritz Graham and Eddie O'Grady, the Old Top Sarge, were the only customers at the bar. Maclaren was exhibiting a right cross to the Old Sarge. The Sligo Slasher said, "That's the punch that knocked out Caveman O'Toole on St. Patrick's Day of 1915."

"Didn't you ever fight except on St. Patrick's Day?" asked Graham.

"All me best fights was on St. Patrick's Day," Maclaren answered. "I was the champion of the Emerald Isle." He discovered Bart, shouted, "Hello, ya Protestant bum! We're four hours and fourteen minutes early."

Bart said to Graham, "Start laughing, Reporter. I'm going to have a drink."

Graham said, "I'm not laughing, Editor. Things like that don't make me happy."

Bart said, "A double, Tony. Give everybody a drink. We're going to drink a toast."

"I just got time for one wee sarsaparilla before I report for work at Selig's book," the Old Sarge said.

"You're having whisky," Bart told him.

"You know I don't drink whisky, Captain! I made a promise to me dear old mother!"

"You sonuvabitch," Bart snapped, "you never had a mother. My old man did an obit on you when you came back from the first war as Pershing's greatest hero. He was afraid you might win a bet some day and die of shock. You were a foundling in an orphans' home and the sisters brought you up. You think you're a big, rough guy but you can't handle booze, so you invented yourself a story." He said to Maclaren, "Give O'Grady whisky. Give him Irish."

Maclaren, looking doubtful, filled a shot glass and set it down in front of the Old Sarge. The Old Sarge's mastiff jaw was trembling. He said, "I'm an old soldier, Captain. If that's an order . . ."

"That's an order," said Bart. He raised his glass.

"To an angel."

The Old Top Sarge raised his glass obediently. "To an angel," he repeated. He drank, coughed, sputtered. He held to the bar and gasped for breath.

Bart pushed money toward Maclaren. Romano pushed it back.

"Uh-uh, honey boy," Romano said. "This round's on the cops."

ABOUT THE AUTHOR

DAVID ALEXANDER is well qualified to write a mystery novel with Broadway as a background. For ten years he was an editor and columnist on the staff of the New York *Morning Telegraph,* America's oldest theatrical sports daily, and he was well acquainted with the leading figures in the worlds of entertainment and sports. He also knew the gamblers and mobsters who lead their precarious lives on the Great White Way and as a newspaperman he often wrote of them.

Alexander's books have been praised by Federal and city policemen for their accurate depiction of professional cops. This is partly due to the fact that a few years ago he enrolled for an intensive thirteen-week course at the New York Institute of Criminology, graduating with highest honors in a class that included professional policemen and practicing private investigators. Because of his record in this school, Alexander was offered two positions as a private operative with detective agencies and one as house detective with a large hotel chain.